THE RELEASE OF SECRETS

THE RELEASE OF SECRETS

LITTLEST SPARROW GONE

A NOVEL

MEGAN MAGUIRE

ISBN-13: 978-1723238635

The Release of Secrets

First trade paperback edition: July 2018

Published by Miranda & Maxwell Books. No part of this publication may be reproduced, distributed, or transmitted in any form or by any means, including photocopying, recording, or other electronic or mechanical methods, without the prior written consent of the author.

For questions and comments about this book, please contact us at **authormeganmaguire@gmail.com**

Cover design by Eliza Ann Ryder Marketing
Front cover photograph by LanaG/Shutterstock.com
Back cover photograph by Noam Armonn©123RF.com
Interior vector illustration by Дмитрий Самородинов©123RF.com
Interior sparrow silhouettes by Soonthorn Wongsaita©123RF.com

PRINTED IN THE UNITED STATES OF AMERICA

THE RELEASE OF SECRETS

Littlest Sparrow Gone

Melancholy and sadness are the start of doubt, doubt is the beginning of despair; despair is the cruel beginning of the differing degrees of wickedness.

~ Comte de Lautreamont

ONE

Five, four, three, two, one.

One.

The quiet afternoon reminds me that I'm the only Whitfield who remains at Sparrow Lodge. Five of us once called this our home—our wonderland nestled amongst the trees—but four of the sunny voices are gone, leaving me to carry on the family business alone. Days have become years. Years will become a lifetime.

I can't say the lodge is the bane of my existence. If anything, it's a comfort knowing I was born here and will likely die on these grounds. With no plans to leave, I'm not like most women in this small town, the ones who have dreams of marrying into wealth and raising a family in a stately mansion. Or the ones who have their hearts set on some fast-paced urban scene, swallowed by steel high-rises and congested city streets, bright lights and noise. Designer fashion and the bar scene just aren't my thing. Kids and I don't click. I'm happy living in a rural community under the majestic red pines with my dog, my hiking boots, and peaceful afternoons to myself.

"Ollie." I whistle. "Here, buddy."

I place my razor on the edge of the tub and lean back in a thick layer of suds, waving a mountain of bubbles over my growing belly fat. At twenty-seven, I'm not as slender as I was a decade ago. Soon my stomach will protrude beyond my average-sized breasts. And if, God forbid, my hips widen past my shoulders, I'll end up looking like a pear—a pear-shaped woman with ivory skin and a potbelly, aka Salem Whitfield, the *witchpig*.

Witch was the name my high school classmates pestered me with, for obvious reasons: hair the color of coal and the name Salem. I can't blame them. Every kid gets a nickname. Except in small towns they seem to stick forever, and gaining weight will only incite the locals to tack the word *pig* on the end of *witch*. It's time to tackle the extra padding before that happens. Time to exercise. Time to eat right. Time to be more ambitious.

"Hey, Ollie," I call. "Come hang out with me."

Paws thump against the hardwood floor in the hallway. The door opens a crack, and the snuffling nose of my eight-year-old Corgi, Ollie-Oops, pops in.

"Hi."

He sticks his entire head inside and flashes a dopey smile.

"Come on in, all the way."

His chubby chest nudges the door open enough to squeeze inside. He waddles over, tail wagging, cute as can be. He drops his rump on the bathmat and rests his chin on the edge of the tub.

"We should go for a jog before guests arrive." I pet his head. "It'd be nice to get out of the lodge today, doncha think?"

His ears perk up. He tilts his head toward the hallway, tail picking up speed. A noise. Footsteps. The vintage, bronze bell on the reception desk in the lobby *dings*. Ollie goes into greeter mode, heading for the sound as fast as his stumpy legs can carry him.

"Ollie, stay." He makes it just outside the bathroom door, turning to me, then to the lobby. "Check-in isn't until four!" I shout. He ignores my request and inches forward. "Stay put or no table scraps tonight."

Ding-ding.

"We don't open until four!" I shout again. "Ollie, wait." He darts for the dinging bell, always full of pep when guests arrive. The sound transforms him into a pup, convinced he's due for an excessive amount of pets.

Ding.

It's odd the front door didn't chime, only the bell on the desk.

Ding.

"All right already. I'm coming!"

Water splashes over the side of the tub as I step out and put on my black satin robe. It's unlike me to leave the lodge unlocked during the day. My only free time is from eleven to four. In fact, the door is always locked unless a guest requests it be left open. And that's rare. People don't come to Tilford Lake to sit inside the lodge.

I pat my bangs into place and gather my hair into a ponytail. Wet ends soak through the back of my robe. Good enough, out of time. Drumming fingernails on the reception desk are an impatient plea for me to get my ass in gear.

"Coming, I said!"

I hurry down the hall in bare feet, holding the neck of my robe tight, stopping short when I reach the doorway to the lobby.

My God are the first words that come to mind. *Tall, masculine, handsome,* are three more.

Windblown hair—the same color as the espresso-stained logs on the exterior of the lodge—curls over the tips of his ears. With a strong jawline, square chin, and a Greek nose, this guy is a rarity in these parts. All man, no boy. And he smells great, a warm mix of cinnamon and vanilla. It was worth getting out of the tub for *him.*

"H–hello." I breathe.

He looks up with sharp blue eyes. "Too early to check in?" His deep voice echoes through the two-story space, bouncing off the wooden beams and back down. So heavy, I feel like I can catch it.

"Uh…" I glance at the beads of bath water dripping down my legs, visibly vulnerable. "Sorry, can you come back? We don't open till four."

"Four?" He checks the time on his cell.

Behind him, a second man sits in one of the leather armchairs next to the fieldstone fireplace, his legs crossed, face hidden behind a newspaper. I stand straight when I notice there're two of them.

"This the only hotel in town?" asks the man at the desk.

"Yes. And it's a lodge, not a hotel."

Ollie growls. Either set off by the guy's deep voice or upset the men haven't made a fuss over him.

"Hotel, lodge, doesn't matter, just give me a room." His fingers drum the desk.

My stomach clenches with apprehension, but I can't growl at the guy like Ollie. For now, I hold the neck of my robe tighter.

Good looks no longer matter. He's much bigger than me. With his wool coat unbuttoned, I can see the definition of his chest muscles pressed against his black shirt. If he wants to rob the place, or worse, I don't stand a chance.

Not a chance.

"Nate, stop playing games with her and get down to business." The man in the chair sets the paper down and scratches his scraggly beard. He owns a rounder, more boyish face, burdened with chapped lips and pockmarked cheeks. "Forget Nate's behavior. He always acts like a brute around beautiful women." The man stands and unzips his Carhartt coat. He's a shorty, my height, about five-eight.

"Talking about yourself again?" Nate asks. He looks to the side and then back. "Can we check in early?"

"We've got reservations," the bearded one says.

I cross my arms. "I don't have reservations tonight for two men."

"And we could use some food," Nate says.

"I said this is a lodge, not a hotel. I don't serve food here. And I *don't* have reservations for two men."

The guy next to the chair narrows his eyes and walks over to the desk, leaving a trail of snow on my braided, pinecone print rug.

"Oh, um … there's a diner a mile west of here." I thumb toward the road, but they don't take the hint to leave. My stomach twists when I notice the front door is locked. "How'd you two get in here?" Ollie looks up, detecting a quiver in my voice.

"My reservation is under Jim Gaines. Jim. Gaines," he says, stroking his beard. "Nate forgot to make his."

"Sorry, I don't have any rooms available." My pounding heart drowns out the sound of my voice.

"You can't be booked in March, not in this small town. I'm sure you've got an extra bed." Jim casts an eye on my private quarters and scans the balcony. "If not, Nate can sleep on the floor by the fireplace."

"Screw that. You can sleep on the floor." Nate's fingers drum faster.

"I asked how you guys got in here." My voice is hot. I point at the deadbolt. "That's locked, and I didn't hear the chime."

"There's always a back door," Nate says.

Jim finger-combs his greasy black hair to the side, a faint sneer of satisfaction on his face. "Every business has a back door."

"Bullshit." I pick up the desk phone and dial 9-1-1. "Ollie, get in the back!"

"Hold up." Jim grabs the phone and twists it out of my hand. "There's no need for that."

Flight kicks in. I scoop Ollie into my arms and run to my private quarters, back to the bathroom, locking the door behind us. "Go away!" Hefty boots thud down the hall. "My husband will be home any minute. He'll shoot you!" I put Ollie down and look for my cell—*it's in the bedroom*. "I'm calling 9-1-1!" My hands shake as I shout lies.

"Don't be afraid. We brought you something."

A leather cord worms under the door.

"What the hell is that?" I step back. "What are you doing? Go away and leave me alone!" The cord and the creepiness of the two men have me in absolute panic. "Get out of here!" I bang the door. "Get out. Get out!"

The cord writhes closer. It's released and their shadows dissolve.

I hear the front door chime.

Then. Nothing.

My ears ring from the dead silence. No footsteps, no breathing, no words or movement. I stand perfectly still. Five minutes pass, listening, waiting, too scared to move. I finally realize they could've given the door a swift kick if they wanted to get me.

"I think we're safe, Olls." He pokes his head out from the side of the toilet and struts to my side, pretending he wasn't one bit frightened of the beastly men. "Nice try," I tell him, snagging the leather cord with my big toe. I slide it closer to discover a brass key attached to the other end. The head is in the shape of a heart with a sparrow soaring across the middle. The same image that's on the vintage '60s sign in the parking lot, the logo my grandparents used for their dream business: Sparrow Lodge.

My knees buckle. I know the key well. I have one just like it with my initials SW engraved on the sparrow's back. My brothers and I all had one when we were kids. It unlocks the back door to the lodge, the *escape hatch*. A hidden door that we used so the front door chime wouldn't carol each time we ran outside to play. This key is one of *ours*, one of three.

I pick it up and examine the sparrow. My breath stalls when I see the initials EW on its back. I slide my finger over the engraved letters, needing to feel that they're real.

"Eli," I whisper.

TWO

Like a brand new house, a marriage starts out in pristine condition, only to become worn over time. Mechanical systems break down and infestations cause damage, leading to unsightly appearances. Decades pass and upgrades are necessary. Once beyond repair, it crumbles and turns to dust.

At least that's what happened to my marriage. It deteriorated. Our infestation was infidelity, and it ate a hole through my heart. No restoration or overhaul was able to hide the deep blemishes. I couldn't brush a fresh coat of paint over my husband and say, "There ya go, good as new." So I did what any resentful wife would do in my situation. I packed his bags and told him to get the fuck out. We had reached the seven-year itch. At the age of twenty-five, after marrying my high school sweetheart, the man who was supposed to be my prince charming *forever*, I was single. The demolition of my life was complete.

Two years later, I'm still single. I told the men at the lodge that my husband would soon be home, but that was a lie. Salem Whitfield is just a small-town girl with a high school diploma, penniless, simple, with limited options. No, I have no husband who will save me from intruders. That type of security is something I relied on for far too long. But I'm working on a change, working on transforming my life to become that strong woman who can take charge of any situation.

And caring for Sparrow is the one place where I *am* in charge.

While my ex-husband took off to god-knows-where with his skinny eighteen-year-old slut, I stayed in my rural hometown of Tilford Lake to continue working at my family's lodge. My first job—my *only* job—Sparrow Lodge is all I've ever known. I've been too set in my ways and too loyal to my family to do anything else. Or maybe it's because of my younger brother, Eli, who vanished without a trace when he was four. EW. Maybe I stay for him.

Eli's disappearance is only one of many family tragedies. When my granddad was alive, he insisted the Whitfield family was cursed. I have to agree, that curse has continued throughout my life. My grandparents died when their home caught fire from faulty wiring. My dad and older brother, Connor, drowned in a boating accident a decade ago. And my mom recently passed after a heartbreaking two-year battle with cancer. I'm alone now, but still holding out hope that Eli will return. He's the only one left besides me, and I promised I'd be here when he comes back. My mom always said one Whitfield must stay at the lodge for him. I'm here. I'll stay.

I bite my fingernail as I stare out the front window at the birds dotting the snowy landscape, waiting impatiently for the cops to arrive, holding Eli's sparrow key, thinking about him, our childhood.

The lodge was paradise when I was a kid. A magical land with an inground pool and a colorful playground, now worn, overgrown, and no longer in use. Time hasn't been kind to the property, falling to pieces after my brother Connor and my dad died. People often pull in and pull right back out, wide-eyed like they accidentally turned into the driveway of a haunted house. I'm guessing it doesn't help that the heart on the modest front sign is burned out. And the wood it's attached to is cracked down the middle, giving the appearance of a broken heart, just the opposite of what my grandparents intended when they built the lodge back in the '60s.

I'd have it repaired, but I've been broke since business took a drastic hit when Tilford Lake's two main tourist attractions— the winery and the marina—shut down. I'm just happy the lit sparrow on the sign is adamant about sticking it out to help usher in guests.

Ugh. One of the sparrow's bulbs is out. I just jinxed myself by looking at it. *Don't look.*

I take out my cell and place a call, blowing my bangs off my forehead as I wait.

"Come on, Joss, pick up."

Ollie and my best friend, Josselyn, are my saviors through the pain and isolation of losing my family. Coming from the only Hispanic family in town, Joss understands what it feels like to be a misfit. I love her to death. The fact that she's a curvy extrovert who drives a rusted-out, sickly green, 1971 Chevy Nova, and can out-swear any man she works with at the grape juice processing plant, says it all. Remarkably beautiful, adventurous, loyal, and bold: Joss embraces womanhood and her roots. Who wouldn't want to be friends with a kick-ass woman with sass?

"Joss."

"What's up, babe?"

"It's Eli."

I can feel the dramatic eye-roll through the phone. Since becoming my best friend in grammar school, she's heard me say this at least a thousand times.

"Don't snub me, Joss. It's him."

A long pause, she smacks her gum.

A few years back, I thought Eli was a cashier at a grocery store an hour north of here. And I swear he was sitting in the church balcony at my wedding. I know he's out there, somewhere.

"Salem, it's kinda early to be drinking."

"Joss, I'm not drunk. Two guys were here. I got the feeling they were gonna rob the place, or worse. I had to hide from them in the bathroom."

"They have guns?"

"No."

"They ask for money?"

"No."

"Oh, let me guess. They were after your granddaddy's treasure. That legend has brought so many freaks out to your property. When are people gonna realize it was a marketing ploy?"

"No, listen. They wanted a room, but they were seriously spooky."

"I'm not following. Are you saying one was Eli?"

"I don't know. The guy with the beard had brown eyes, and the other one had gorgeous, bright blue ones. But Eli's eyes were an icy-gray color, like mine."

"Then they're not him."

"But the bearded guy, Jim, his hair was black like Eli's."

"And the other one?"

"Nate? He had thick, dark brown hair. I wanted to run my fingers through it."

"Still not following, were you afraid of these men or did you wanna fuck 'em?"

I tune her out. My voice is quick. "I suppose Eli's hair could've lightened over the years. But I don't think he'd be as tall as this Nate guy was. He was tiny."

"Because he was *four* the last time you saw him, Salem."

"True. And I doubt I'd think Eli was as attractive as Nate, you know, deep down, my heart would never allow me to think that way about my brother. It's just wrong, so wrong. Might've been him though. Okay, it wasn't him, but something bizarre just happened."

"Can you slow down and take a breath? You're manic."

"Let me finish. I'm excited because the men gave me a key."

"To what?"

"The back door of the lodge."

"Since when does the lodge have a back door?"

"Since forever. Since it was built, I'll explain more when you get here."

"Get there? Babe, I'm at work. I can't take off right now."

"Trust me. You have to come." Again, I'm sure she's rolling her eyes. "Please. The key has Eli's initials on it. It's the same one I have, the same one Connor had. Our granddad made them for us. *Please*, Joss," I beg. "I need your help figuring this out. It could finally lead to an answer."

She hesitates. "Did you call the cops?"

"Of course I did." I turn the deadbolt and open the door. The first note of the chime sounds as cold air courses inside. "Brad Brenner just pulled in."

"He'll take that key away from you as evidence. You'll never see it again if you show it to him."

"But"—I open my clenched hand, my palm branded with the heart and sparrow logo—"he can't have it."

"Then don't tell him about it."

"You're right. I'll keep it to myself for now."

"You should've called me first. What are you gonna tell Brad now, that two guys came in and wanted a room?"

"No." I think for a moment. "I'll say they wouldn't leave when I asked, and then they followed me to the bathroom."

She smacks her gum. "Good luck. He'll think you're losing your friggin' mind, spending all your time alone in that lodge. Are you sure they were real?"

"Not funny, Joss."

Brad Brenner—a cop from our three-officer department, one of Connor's best friends—walks in. Ollie welcomes him with tail swishes and gets a pet.

"Gotta go, see ya soon." I hang up and stuff the key in my front pocket, lowering my sweatshirt over the bulge.

"Salem." Brad wipes a dusting of snow off his shoulders and tips his hat. "You had a disturbance?"

"Hi, Brad."

"Officer Brenner."

"Yeah, okay, Officer Brenner. These two guys came in and—"

"Jim Gaines and Nate Harlow. I know. I just passed them on my way out of the diner. They introduced themselves, must've been the uniform." He takes off his hat and twirls it on one finger, looking up at the pine garlands hanging from the wooden beams. I've been too busy with a flood of housework and laundry to drag out the ladder and take down the Christmas decorations that are now three months defunct.

"Well?" I raise my hands for more information.

He walks over to the double doors that lead to the sitting room, a place where guests gather for morning coffee and to read the newspaper. He peers through the glass panes at the empty chairs, distracted as usual. Not the best quality for a cop.

"Brad?"

"Officer Brenner."

"Well?"

"Detectives from the city," he says.

"Syracuse?"

"No, New York." He turns back, fixated on my chest.

"Brad, don't be such a perv." I'd smack him if he were a foot closer. "Didn't you get a good look at me when we were kids?"

"I wasn't looking…" He shifts his weight from foot to foot, cheeks strawberry-tinted, hat accelerating to full speed on his finger. Up until I was eight, Connor, Brad, and I changed our swimsuits in the same room, not a care in the world that we were naked in front of one another.

"New York?" I pull the conversation back.

He nods. "They came to talk to you about a key to your place, but you took off running and screaming before they had the chance."

"That's not true. The lodge was closed, and those guys sneaked in while I was in the tub. Why wouldn't they knock?"

"Said they knocked."

"I would've heard. *Ollie* would've heard." Ollie sniffs Brad's pant leg. "And they never said they were detectives. Did you see their badges?"

Brad widens his stance and places a hand on his holster. A habit of his, overcompensating for being five foot six, two inches shorter than me, and on the pudgy side. Add his curtained, sandy blond hair to his height and weight, and the guy doesn't have the most ruthless of looks.

"Did you see their badges?" I repeat.

"Salem, no offense, but maybe you should hire someone to help you out around here. Running this place on your own must be wearing you down. You tired?"

"I'm *not* tired."

"Not to mention you'll have the grounds to take care of once the snow melts. The Weather Channel said there might be a change coming as early as tomorrow."

"I'm fine."

"Crocuses are budding through the snow along the drive, and it'll be time to mow soon. Seems like a lot for one person."

"I've done it before, and I can do it for at least another ten years, maybe twenty. And this isn't about being overworked. One of those men ripped the phone out of my hand when I was trying to call for help."

"Because they're detectives. They *are* the help. There wasn't any need to call."

"How was I supposed to know that?" His expression is like a neon sign flashing the words—*you're nuts*. I cross my arms and say, "Fine, *Brad*. Sorry I called," hoping he catches the twinge of frustration in my voice.

"No worries. And it's Officer Brenner."

His walkie clicks and a woman's high-pitched voice vaults through the lobby. "Bradley?"

"Go ahead, Doreen," he calls back.

"We got a call about some wild turkeys in the high school parking lot. The principal said the kids are circling them with their cars. He's afraid they'll get hurt."

"Who'll get hurt? The kids or the turkeys?"

"The turkeys, Bradley!"

"Kidding. Tell him I'm on my way." He turns to me with a smile. "You good?"

"I'm good."

"Okay then. I gotta take off."

"Good luck."

On his way out, he stops to admire a photomural above the front door, shot over twenty years ago from the far end of the long driveway, facing the lodge.

My grandparents are on the front porch with their arms locked in a majestic pose, like king and queen reigning over their land. I'm proud to be their granddaughter, proud to call myself a Whitfield. The name, this lodge, they're the only things that make me feel powerful in this small town.

In front of them, our black cat, Boo, is licking her paw, while my parents tend to flowers in a window box. I'm a blur, circling Connor with a toy lawnmower, a massive smile on his face as bubbles jet out the sides. We're too old to be playing with such toys, but having too much fun to care.

And Eli. Eli stands out the most in that photo. He's closest to the camera, riding his tricycle up the gravel drive in his favorite bear cub tee, the heart and sparrow key low on his chest. My baby brother, the picture of innocence—a Band-Aid on one knee and his chin stained with a thin line of grape juice—reaching to the camera, or to the future, or to whoever is looking up at the photograph. I wish I could take that hand and pull him to safety.

The summer he vanished is forever frozen in time. Connor was seven. I was six. Eli was only four.

"Scary how fast life can change," Brad says, inviting a blast of cold air to enter the lobby when he opens the door and steps outside. "Later, Salem."

"Later, Brad."

THREE

I light a fire in the lobby and put on a pot of coffee. Joss holds her ski goggles and white helmet under one arm, her left shoulder sugared in snow from the three-mile drive to the lodge. When she bought the Chevy Nova, the windows on both sides wouldn't roll up because of broken window cranks. It took her a week to realize the glass was missing altogether. She tried sealing the windows with plastic and duct tape, but the flapping noise was unbearable, and the plastic distorted her view. She decided the helmet and goggles were cheaper than the repairs. They've served as a barrier to weather, and as it turns out, have protected her from other hazards. Like the time a bird flew inside her car and struck the side of her head, a rare occurrence that could only happen to Joss.

"I'll take a latte, Salem. And when you pour the steamed milk, try to get the design on the surface to come out in the shape of a dick." She slicks her mouth with a tube of plum lipstick.

Driving to the lodge is a trek compared to her half-mile drive to work. I'm out on the edge of town, close to the vacant marina that no one wants to buy.

"My coffee comes black or with cream."

"Fine. Cream." Her bottom lip juts out in a playful pout. She sets her helmet and goggles on the reception desk and heads to the sitting room. "These guys were hot, huh? Better than the men down at Martin's Bar?"

"Um, hello? If you mean better than Kenny, who's never without a wad of chew in his mouth, or Rick, who takes pride in picking hamburger meat out of his beard, or Pete, who starts hog calling after one-too-many, or Brad—"

"Is that a yes?"

"Or Brad, who can't keep his eyes off women's boobs, then yes, no comparison."

"Cool."

She swipes her hand across a vintage map of Tilford Lake, preserved on one of the tabletops under a clear coat of epoxy resin. I have boxes of old maps and brochures collecting dust in a storage closet, dating back to when the town was a scenic hotspot for tourists. Besides boaters heading to the marina, the roads used to be alive with people traveling to Joe Clayton's Winery for tours and wine tasting. Or to have their wedding at the famous Clayton Barn, a place way out of my price range.

The barn was built on the highest hill in town, with tall windows overlooking the lake. Sounds picture-postcard perfect, and it was. At one time, guests at the winery and the marina could rent swan-shaped paddleboats to cool off on scorching summer days. After Joe Clayton died, his daughters decided to close the winery and pour their hearts and souls into weddings. Luckily, I still get some business from them. And the miles of cross-country ski trails along the lake can bring in a handful of families each night during the winter. The same is true in the summer when hikers and mountain bikers use the trails.

"Smells good in here." Joss sniffs.

"Probably the fireplace."

"Sugar cookie-scented logs?"

"Shut up." I laugh. "If you smell cookies, it must be the sachet packet in the Bissell. I just vacuumed before you got here."

"Ooh-la-la, *sachet*." She flaps her hands. "You getting all fancy on me?"

I pat her shoulder. "That's enough blabber for now. I want to show you something."

She follows me through a curtain patterned with pine trees and prancing deer.

"I had no idea this was here," she says. Her brown eyes double in size when she sees the tiny room and the back door.

"We called this our *escape hatch* when we were kids. My granddad painted the door to match the log walls so it wouldn't stand out. He didn't want guests using it to sneak extra people in late at night." She looks high and low, curious for once about one of my stories. "It was a laundry and storage room years back, and the door was a private exit." I open my hand and let her admire Eli's key.

"That's awesome. Looks like the one you showed me when we were kids. I thought it was for the main door."

"I let you think that because this room was off limits after Eli disappeared. My parents wouldn't let us go near it." I point at the back door, my finger hovering a bit too long. "It's hidden on the outside by bushes. I never showed this to anyone, not even Steven."

"Blech, I hate hearing that name. Your husband's such a dirtball."

"*Ex.* Ex-husband. Like I've been saying since the divorce, long on sleaze, short on substance."

She throws her head back, igniting the room with a cackling laugh. Her cheeks flare, and her long hair slides off her shoulders like thick molasses.

"Anyway, I never come back here. Being in this room makes me queasy." I feel a pinch in my throat when I swallow, close my eyes and slip my pinkie under my collar. "It was open the morning Eli went missing."

Joss senses my unease and hitches her arm to mine. "Let's get out of here then." Her voice is brisk. She takes control and pulls me out of the room.

I close the curtain to disguise the doorway, then block the entrance with a tea cart. Guests are left with the impression that it's a window.

"We wore the necklaces whenever we went out to play. My dad said we'd lose them like our heads if they weren't attached to our necks."

"And somehow these guys knew about the door?"

"Yeah, Brad said they're detectives, so I'm guessing they read Eli's case file. Still, it's weird they came in that way."

"Totally weird." She takes off her black puffer coat and slumps into the leather armchair next to the fire, her breasts spilling out of her low-cut shirt. "So your family never changed the locks because you thought he'd come back, right?"

"Is that even a question? He still might, Joss. What if the detectives know where he is? I haven't felt this close to him in such a long time."

"Salem."

"Don't say it." She knows I'm not the type to ever lose hope or complain about having a shit life. There's always a chance Eli will come home. *Always.*

"All right, I won't fight you on this one. So what do we do now?"

"We wait for the detectives. Then we find Eli."

"Salem."

"What?" I sit across from her, raising my feet to the fire.

"You're delusional."

"Maybe so." I shrug.

"But I love you anyway, babe."

FOUR

Seven o'clock fetches nightfall. Nine passes at the speed of a semi up a steep incline. By midnight, Joss and I are anxious from the long wait. We order a pizza and play rummy next to the fire, forcing our concentration on anything other than the detectives. An hour is all we can take until our butts are numb from the stiff leather chairs, and our necks ache from craning incessantly toward the door. We end up staring out the front window like a couple of kids waiting for Santa. And then take our irritation to the front porch in a huff.

But the men don't come. And maybe they won't. It could be I'll never see them again.

Joss twines her fingers through mine and gives my hand a firm squeeze. My disappointment couldn't be more apparent.

"Sorry," she comforts.

"It's okay."

"Is it?" She pulls me back inside.

"No. Not really." Unlike previous setbacks, the night doesn't want to rest. I expected more, got nothing. After hours of tense muscles, jiggling feet, and a cluttered mind, I should be ready to crash. Instead, my body ferreted out a hidden sugar reserve and I'm wired.

"Mind if I hit the sack?" Joss asks. "I'm beat."

"Go for it. I'm gonna hang out by the fire a little longer, brush my hair a hundred times or something."

She laughs. "Don't stay up all night doing that. You might go blind." Her silent feet climb the stairs to the second floor.

Guests are in three of my eight rooms. Joss got one of the remaining five, welcome here anytime.

When we were in high school, my mom let her stay whenever she wanted, aware that Joss and her dad were mixing like oil and water. He was a crabby man, religiously strict and abusive, and Joss had entered her rebellious years, curious and wild, not the best combination. One night, her dad stumbled home from the bar in a rage over the rumors that his *slut* daughter was spreading her legs for the locals. He didn't want the Arriaga family to stand out more than the color of their skin, so his daughter whoring around was a total embarrassment.

To me, it was a teenage cry for attention, a shout for love. That's all Joss ever wanted, what anyone ever wants. And she found it wherever she could. A measly fifteen minutes in the back seat of some random guy's car wasn't uncommon. Her legs would lock him in, hips in a steady thrust until she came. A way to bury her loneliness—something she never outgrew.

Her dad had hit her before, but he never left any marks for Tilford Lake eyes to gossip about. Not until one humid summer night when Joss showed up at the lodge with a bloody nose and a red handprint marking her cheek, her hair a tangled mess, eyes swollen red. She had walked two miles in bare feet and landed in my arms, sobbing, begging us not to call the cops, afraid she'd be taken away from her mom, her friends, from me. I agreed. My mom agreed. She was offered a room indefinitely, and she stayed in the private quarters when we were booked. She still does. Joss never gets turned away. Our friendship is tighter than Spanx, much sexier than Spanx, too.

Following a cup of tea and two games of solitaire, I recline in the leather chair with my legs over the armrest. Every fifteen minutes my body flips to find a more comfortable spot. Sleep reaches me in short waves.

I know staying in my feather bed isn't an option. Too many memories of my family are stirring because of the key. And the rooms in the private quarters seem to be occupied by spirits of my past.

When I was married, my husband and I rented a house close to the local grocery store where he was the produce manager. I worked at the lodge during the day, and my mom took over at night. She would say her home once was filled with a loving family, but now is just a house full of strangers and ghosts. I get that. I feel the same way she did. But I also can't imagine what life would be like without these strangers ... and the ghosts. My life, the lodge, these guests that pass through, it's a love-hate relationship.

Thankfully, more love than hate.

•   •   •

"Salem, wake up, Ollie's barking outside my window." Joss nudges my arm.

"What?" I'm groggy as she leads me out of sleep. "You sure?" I sit up. My legs are snarled in a fleece blanket.

"Yeah, it's his little yip."

"How'd he get out?"

"Beats me."

I escape the blanket, put on my boots, and grab a flashlight from behind the desk. We race out the front door, Joss in only a thin pair of socks.

"Get your boots," I tell her.

"There's no time. If he's barking at those men, I wanna see."

"Ollie! Come here, buddy."

We run to the side of the lodge and round the corner to the back. Lit by the moon, the landscape is cast in blue and crisscrossed with boot tracks. I see Ollie staring fixedly into the darkness of the pine forest. He growls when a branch snaps, then whines and paces along the edge of the trees.

"I hope that's not a bear," Joss says.

"Bears aren't out this time of the year. Ollie, get over here!"

She looks down. "Those are bootprints."

"I know. NOW, Ollie!" Free of his leash, he's having the time of his life. "Come here!" I start in his direction, and he immediately runs to my side. "How'd you get out?" He rolls on his back, his stumpers kicking up snow, head rocking back and forth with excitement. I shine the flashlight toward the forest, not a thing is out there but pines that rise to the moon and dead branches on the ground, flecked with snow.

"Is that blood?" Joss asks.

"Where?"

"On his leg."

I bend down and part his fur to check his skin. "There's no cut. It's not blood." I sniff my hand. "Smells like ketchup."

"Pizza sauce?"

"No. Ketchup."

I shine the light across the yard, over the fiberglass hippo that now rests on its side, past the drained pool, and to the back of the lodge, checking to see if footprints go to any of the windows.

"Son of a bitch."

The back door is slightly open. Two sets of tracks climbed the steps and went inside. I push through the bushes, pick up a dog-devoured fast food bag, then follow a trail of melting snow and burger wrappers, coming face to face with the two detectives in the lobby. Jim is warming his hands by the fire, while Nate leans alongside the reception desk. Both men drop black travel bags on the floor when they see me.

"Hey, beautiful. Think I can get a room now?" Nate asks.

Joss comes in with Ollie in tow. She hits the brakes, slapped with disbelief. A soft whisper, "Holy shit ... men," as she attempts to finger tame her curly black hair.

"Nice," Jim hisses. "Two of 'em." He takes off his knit hat, licks his palm, and slicks his hair to the side. "I get the short one with the luscious ass."

Joss flings her hair off her shoulder and sallies back. "I'll reject the short one who's oblivious and doesn't stand a chance."

The guys laugh too loud and for way too long. Nate steadies himself against the desk, the smell of alcohol thick in the air. They're wasted. And I'm livid.

I walk past them and stand behind the desk, using it as a barrier. "Give it." I hold out my hand. "Give me the key to that door right now."

Joss bends over and takes off her socks, a flirty way to flash her cleavage toward Jim. His eyelids turn heavy, thrilled with the show.

"Give it." I prod Nate's chest.

"The door was open from when we came in earlier," he says.

"No, it wasn't. You must've made a copy of Eli's key. Now give it to me, or I'm calling the cops."

"Who? Bradley Brenner?" He smirks.

"I'm serious. I'll have you arrested for breaking and entering, trespassing, driving drunk, and—"

"We didn't break in. We have a key."

"Good. Give it to me. And I want to see your badges. Then you're going to tell me everything you know about Eli."

Nate's head dips until it lands on the desk. He stays there, arms dangling low enough for Ollie to lick his fingers, probably salty from French fries.

"Where's your imaginary husband?" he asks. "Is he still going to shoot us?"

"Who told you I wasn't married?" A pause. No response. Must've been Brad.

His breathing slows and alters into a fake, subdued snore.

"Wake up." I dope slap the top of his head, getting a laugh in return.

"Get him a room before he passes out," Jim says.

"How the hell did you guys drive out here without ending up in a ditch?" Joss asks.

Nate straightens up. "I'm not drunk." His blue eyes sparkle and a handsome dimple in his left cheek flares to life. He tips to the right and grabs hold of the desk to steady himself. "What do you guys put in the liquor up this way?"

"I bet they went to Martin's Bar," Joss says.

"It's the elevation, you idiot," Jim tells Nate. "Said it would do you in, but you never listen to your big brother."

"Brother? Are you friends, brothers, detectives, which is it?" I ask.

"Maybe," Jim replies.

"What kind of answer is that?" My mouth stays open, encouraging him to speak. "Forget it. I've had enough. Front and center, both of you." I tap the desk. "First, give me whatever keys you have to the lodge. No more clowning around." I hold out my hand. They look at one another and nod in agreement, digging in their coat pockets, dropping two keys in my hand. "Now, show me your badges."

They laugh. Jim elbows Nate and looks down. Again, they nod in agreement, this time unbuttoning their jeans to strip.

"That's not what I meant by badges!"

Joss, tough-as-nails Joss, is always prepared to step in. She kicks Jim in the back of the knee, positions her feet—one behind his ankle and the other behind his knee—and pulls his body down. He lands on his back, wide-eyed in awe.

"When my friend asks you to do something, you better friggin' do it," she says.

That's one reason I wanted her here. She's great at defending me while flirting at the same time. "Thanks, Joss."

"You're welcome."

Jim gets off the floor, using Nate as a crutch. He glares at Joss. She beams back.

"What?" she says with attitude, putting a hand on her hip, throwing her weight to one side. "I said, *what?*"

He gets in her face, slicking his hair into place. "If you're like that in bed, I'll make you my wife."

"In your dreams."

"I can make all your dreams come true, brown eyes."

"Show her your badge, or you'll be flat on your ass again."

"What badge?" Nate asks. He puts his elbows on the desk and presses his temples. "I'm not a cop."

"You told Brad you were detectives," I say.

"*Private* detectives. We don't have badges."

"Private? Who hired you? Why are you here?"

He shuts his eyes. "Can I just get a room and go to bed? These log walls are closing in on me."

Joss gives me a slight headshake. I copy the action. It's obvious I'm not getting a word out of them tonight.

"Here's the deal. I can't kick you guys out because you'll end up killing someone or yourselves on the road. I *can* call a cop to pick you up to take you to the station to sleep this off. But then I don't know when I'll be able to talk to you about my brother … or if you'll even come back, so I'd prefer to keep you where I can see you. But I'm charging double for the rooms." Jim yawns and stares into space. "Pay attention." I smack the counter. "You guys let my dog out, you let him eat fast food, and you broke in here, twice."

"It's not breaking in when you have a key," Nate repeats, likely not remembering he tried that one on me already.

"Save it." My voice is stern. "Give me your IDs and your credit cards before I change my mind."

Jim elbows Nate. "We've got cash."

They slide their driver's licenses across the desk, and Nate drops a wad of money in front of me. "That's three grand for the week. Since this is your off-season, it should be plenty."

"A week?" My jaw hits the floor.

"Maybe longer."

I pick up their IDs, my fingers turning wobbly. "Jim Gaines, twenty-eight. Nathan Harlow, also twenty-eight." I hold up the cards and compare their faces to the photos. Both are from Vinland Falls, NY, but with different street addresses. Brad said they were from New York City. Either he's the worst cop ever, or these guys are lying through their teeth about every damn thing.

I type in their information and hand them their IDs, along with keys to their rooms.

"You're upstairs in the back, above the sitting area. Be quiet when you go up the stairs so you don't disturb my other guests. I'll have coffee and tea out in the morning from six to ten, along with two newspapers." Ollie waddles over and nudges my leg, warning me not to do this. "Check-in is from four to eleven each night, *not* three in the morning. If you're staying the week and are out past eleven, the door will be locked when you get here. You *won't* get in past that time. It's for the safety of my guests and so I can get some sleep." Jim cocks his head and fingers the inside of his ear, the earwax more important than what I'm saying. "*And just so you know, we have a lot to talk about in the morning.*" I point at Nate. "If you're not up by nine, I'll be pounding on your door until your ass is out of bed. Got it?"

Nate, puffy-eyed from booze, leans in and places his hand over mine. Our pale complexions are a perfect match, his touch comforting until his fingers clamp down on my wrist.

"Salem, keep cool. We have an entire week together. Don't ruin everything by rushing it." His hand slips away.

"How do you know my name?"

They stagger upstairs with their bags, Jim giving his finger a sniff, Nate mumbling about being drunk. Two doors open and close, a TV turns on in one room, water runs in the other.

Joss and I stare at the balcony and wait. What for, I don't know. We just wait. I didn't tell Nate my name, but if he had Eli's key, he must know something about my family.

After a long silence, and when our necks ache from gazing upward, Joss says, "OMG, they're so hot. Jim looks like Jake Gyllenhaal, except his hair is black, and his eyes are brown, and he's shorter."

"Then he doesn't look like him at all."

"He sort of does."

"Aren't you just a little bit afraid of them?"

"Pfft." She flaps a hand in dismissal. "I think we can take 'em."

"Okay, maybe *afraid* was the wrong word. Troubled? Bothered? Bothered is a better word. They keep dodging my questions. Besides, I'm not looking for a date. I wanna know how they got the key."

"But hooking up would be a bonus. And you know, you don't have to date a guy to fuck him."

"Duh. I know."

"But you won't do it."

I shrug.

She cups my cheeks, her hands lightly scented with a flowery lotion. "Get with it, babe. What Tilford Lake woman wouldn't jump at the chance of having one of those guys on top of her? It's time to get back in the game."

I bite my bottom lip to stop a smile. It *would* be nice, but I haven't had a one-night stand since high school, since before I got married. Joss is the expert at casual sex, not me. She still dates and sleeps around like she's seventeen. It's been years since I've done anything like that, and it was never as easy for me to kiss and let go.

Jim's door opens. He walks out and looks down at us from the balcony, bare-chested, torso teeming with vintage-style tats: roses, skulls, an anchor, and a pirate ship with a sea serpent coiled amid the hull.

"Just checking," he says, his voice smug. A smile curls as he walks back to his room.

"Hell," I whisper.

"Holy hell. Did you see his abs under all those tats?"

"Uh-huh."

"Salem, you got an extra bed for the week?"

"Always, Joss. Always."

FIVE

My alarm is set to go off at five-thirty every morning. That gives me enough time to freshen up and get the sitting room ready for six o'clock coffee and tea. I usually get plenty of sleep. Guests rarely check in after ten at night. But this morning I'm sluggish from the overnight madness.

I rub my eyes and wait for the two coffee pots to fill, badly needing a cup before I have to put on a cheery face for the next five hours. Jim said I *must* have empty rooms because it's March, the off-season. But I'm never on vacation. There's always something to do.

"Mornin'." Jim's gruff voice makes me jump. He leans alongside the doorjamb of the sitting room, still shirtless, still creepy.

"Can you *please* put on some clothes before my other guests wake up?"

"Why?" He raises his arms and holds the top of the doorframe, leaning forward to show off his tats and abs.

"Because I'm not running a brothel." I'm short with him, checking the clock to see that it's almost six.

He walks over and pours a cup of coffee, sniffing it before he takes a sip. "Sugar?"

"Cream and sugar are on the side table by the newspapers."

He puts two heaping spoonfuls in his cup and gives it a whirl. "Go easy on Nate," he says.

"What does that mean?" I pour myself a cup and follow him to the lobby. He heads upstairs without answering. "Wait. Where you going?"

He thumbs his chest. "Not a brothel, right? Gotta get a shirt." He continues up the steps.

"Tell me what you meant by that."

"About Nate?"

"Who do you think I'm talking about?"

He stops on the landing, turns, takes a sip of coffee, and licks his lips.

"Talk," I insist.

"Mellow out," he says. "Give me a chance to answer." He drinks again, and again.

"Come on."

He smiles. "All right. Nate's a good guy, but he's also turning into a drunk because of this case. Stop with the barrage of questions. He'll talk to you when he's ready."

"No, we're gonna talk as soon as you guys get down here."

"I said he'll talk to you when he's ready. Leave it at that."

"Well, why can't you talk to me?"

"I'm just here for mortal support."

"Moral?"

"Huh?"

"*Moral* support."

"That's what I said."

"Yeah, no," I retort. "Tell me how you got my brother's key. Do you know where he—"

Jim cuts me off, holds up a hand. "See, there you go again. Take it easy."

"Oh, for Chrissake." I blow my bangs off my forehead. "I won't take it easy."

"You'll learn." He retreats to his room.

I'll learn? That's what my ex-husband always said. *Salem, are you kidding me? A tasteless salad for dinner? You'll learn to eat what I eat. Now order us some pizza and wings.*

What did I ever see in Steven?

You'll learn to enjoy throwing money away on a rental house. You'll learn to like my TV shows, my immature friends, my new motorcycle, and taking care of my nephew every Friday night. You'll learn.

You know what, Steven? NO, I won't!

Like many women, I married a guy who I thought I loved, but later realized I settled out of fear of being alone. Ignorant and all too common a response, I'm surprised Joss never fell into that trap.

I knock the sitting room chairs against the tables as tiny rivulets of sweat form in my armpits. I'm trying to keep my cool, but that Jim guy really ticks me off.

"Foggy." The gentle voice of an older woman startles me.

"Hmm?" I turn.

Her yellow-gray hair is in a long, thick braid down her back. A wrinkled pinkie finger lifts as she sips her tea.

"It's foggy this morning," she says. "Typical, isn't it? Never have I buried a loved one without rain or fog."

Sympathetic, I tell her that I'm sorry.

My parents taught me not to ask people why they're in town, precisely for this reason. It's a giveaway when guests walk in with winter gear or get dressed up for a wedding. Other times, I don't know unless they offer more information. This woman, Virginia Pullman, has been here for two days. She's quiet, friendly, and polite, but I wouldn't have guessed she was here for a funeral.

"I haven't noticed the fog," I say. "It's still dark outside."

She stands in front of the oversized window and wipes away the condensation on the glass. "Look closely. It's a dense cover, suffocating the trees and strangling the life out of the light."

I put my hand on the window next to hers. Her manicured fingernails, painted light blue, are a clear juxtaposition to her wrinkly skin freckled with age spots.

"A warm front must be moving in over the cold water. We get a lot of fog in the spring with the lake being so close." I pause, seeing the first light of day. I can sense the weight of the humidity in the air, and the fresh scent of rain is pleasant after such a long winter. "It'll be pretty once the sun comes up."

She drinks her tea and makes an effort to smile, but a tear drops down her timeworn face. She removes a used tissue from her navy cardigan to dry her cheek.

"Dear. If the moonlight can't penetrate what crawled in while we slept, the daylight won't either. There'll be no sunshine today. I guarantee it."

She sounds educated, maybe a former college professor, frail in her old age, but sharp. This time she tries a broader smile, keeping her thin lips tight. It's hard to know what to say in these situations. I don't want to come across as heartless by changing the subject. And I can't apologize again for her loss. I remember how that constant apology felt coming from Joss after my mom had passed. The repetition of her words offered no comfort after the fifth, sixth, seventh time.

"I think you can feel the warmth of the sun even when it's not out," I reply. She laughs, and I can't help but laugh with her. "I'm just saying that you can put a positive spin on it. It's all up to you."

"I see." She sets her tea and tissue on the windowsill, then takes my hand, turning it palm up. "What's your name, dear?"

"Salem."

"How unique. After the city or the cigarette?"

That's a new one. No one's ever mentioned the cigarette before. "The city. My parents visited Massachusetts the year I was born." I take a second to think. "What about you? The city, the state, or the cigarette?"

She smiles. "Virginia is a family name." Her hands are freezing. It's like they've been in ice buckets. "Do you have any siblings, Salem?"

"Yes. Connor and Eli, but they're no longer here."

She frowns and looks away. I'm glad she doesn't ask where they are. For that and other motherly reasons, I genuinely dig her. But like all my guests, she'll come and go in a matter of days.

"You must've dealt with many heartbreaks to become such an optimist. Suffering either makes you emotionally stronger or turns you numb." She traces the lines on my palm then feels a deep line at the base of my ring finger. "You have a good friend?"

"Yes."

"For years?"

"My whole life."

"Good." She bends my fingers into a firm ball and squeezes my hand. "Don't lose her."

"Lose her ... to anything specific?" I ask since she's shrewdly observant.

She releases my hand to drink her tea, having no response. At least not in words, but her eyes move like she's following something outside, directing me to an answer.

I squint through the window, catching a glimpse of a dark figure on the rusted remains of the playground.

Nate Harlow.

Damn, these men.

SIX

Under the shade of sky-high pines is the old playground where I spent most of my childhood. Connor and I wasted entire days here, racing up and down the metal slide and in competition over who had the longest jump off the swings. He'd try to distract me with a hardy laugh, but when I released my grip and rocketed through the air, my feet sank into the sun-warmed sand a safe foot or two past his leap. He said he let me win because I was younger than him … and a girl. I remember. It was when *bullshit* became the trending word in my vocabulary. *Bullshit, Connor. That's bullshit.*

But this time it's not Connor taunting me on the old swing set—it's Nate.

He's using the top bar to do pull-ups.

"Working out?" I ask.

My hands ball inside the front pocket of my hoodie. The cuffs of my jeans soak up the spring earth. I wait, but he gives me the cold shoulder. Either he's still drunk, or he's out of his mind. It's too early and too dark to be outside exercising on an old metal bar that could easily break from his weight. On top of that, he stole one of my Sparrow Lodge hoodies. I keep a stack of them on the built-in shelves behind the lobby desk, along with a pile of Sparrow sweaters, T-shirts, baseball caps, and a bunch of other stuff I rarely sell. Nate, the shifty thief, took the most expensive item.

"You have to pay for that."

He stops. The rusted bar is stressed by his weight. A smile leaks as his eyes rake across my outfit, his teeth straight and white, dimple wide-awake. *We match.*

Sparrow Lodge clothing makes up the majority of my wardrobe. Every top I own has the heart and sparrow logo over the left breast, always over my own heart. Yesterday I wore my favorite black sweatshirt. Today it's my black hoodie. Did Nate see what I had on before he took one for himself?

He continues exercising. Between short breaths, he counts, "Ninety-seven ... ninety-eight ... ninety-nine."

"Hey, I'm talking to you."

He tucks his legs into his chest then brings them over the bar, hanging upside down by the backs of his knees. With his arms crossed, he begins a set of sit-ups. "One ... two ... three." He has bedhead and stubble. "Four ... five ... six." Gray boxers inch out of his sweatpants. "Seven ... eight."

The top bar creaks and starts to bend like a string of taffy. Rust flakes off as he repositions his legs. He shimmies out of the middle and over to the side to steady the equipment. "Nine ... ten ... eleven."

"You sleepwalking?" I kick a clump of slushy snow in his direction, but the wet pieces merely roll along the ground. Doubt he even noticed. What a pain. It's too damn early for this. "Stop ignoring me!"

He does a flip off the bar and uses the hoodie to mop sweat off his forehead. His toothy smile is short-lived, replaced by a brief headshake as he crosses to where I stand.

I step back. "Don't come any closer." But he does anyway. The guy doesn't listen.

I bump the teeter-totter and lose my balance, my arms circling like a windmill. On instinct, I arch my back and lower my hands to meet the ground, forming a bridge pose. With the playground upside down, pines replacing the sky, I find myself suspended in midair. Nate has a solid grip on the waist of my jeans to keep me from landing on my head.

"Women are so impatient," he says, his voice flat.

"And men are so self-centered." I spin my arms. "Pull me up."

He brings me to his chest, smelling of stale beer, day-old cologne, and after an extended breath, peppermint toothpaste. His embrace feels familiar as if he's held me for years. I try to picture him as a child, possibly with a crew cut and less muscle, a scrawny preteen, but nothing clicks.

"Have we met?" I ask.

I wouldn't remember if we had. Kids came and went through the lodge so often they became a blur. Two hundred or more a year, some stayed a few days, others for just a night. John and Randy. Emily and Kate. Tom, Kevin, Anna, Laura, and Bethany. Tara, Ashley, and Noah. Then another John and another Emily. I didn't always ask for a name. Why bother? My dad called them *revolving-door friends*, in and out of the lodge without ever leaving an impression. Like me, my dad grew up at the lodge. He knew what it was like.

"Have we?" I ask again.

"No. But you might remember my granddad, Grady Murphy."

The taste of death penetrates my mouth. I twist to the left, but he has a firm hold. "Madman Murphy?" I whisper.

The insulting nickname causes him to wince. "I heard that people called him that. Were you one of the kids who threw rocks at his head?"

Panicked, I drive my fist into his chest and break free. I sprint to the front porch, fly inside and up the stairs to Joss's room. After two mountainous lungsful of air to calm my nerves, I look to see if he's coming and utter a yelp when the chime announces that he is.

"Joss, wake up," I whisper, not wanting to disturb the other guests. "Get up. Get up." I knock.

We had numerous nicknames for Grady Murphy, the old man with bad teeth and bulging, misaligned eyes. Beast, mutant, ghoul, ogre, and monster were some. Gruesome Grady and Goblin Grady were others. But Connor—after seeing him prowling on our property with a knife taped to a stick in one hand, lugging a dead raccoon in the other—started calling him Madman Murphy. "Don't go in the forest, Salem," Connor would say. "Madman Murphy is gonna getcha."

I listened to Connor. I was terrified. Grady's house was on the north side of our five acres of pines, and although he's gone, the thought of him so close still gives me the creeps.

"Joss, wake up." I fumble in my pocket for my keys.

Grady was the head janitor at Tilford Lake High School, but because he lived behind us, I knew about him long before most of my friends. My parents said he had a genetic disorder called Crouzon syndrome. That explained his features. I shouldn't have been afraid of him, and at times, I felt for the guy. Later I was disappointed in my lack of compassion. My *witch* nickname was nothing compared to the assault and harsh words Grady endured. Even *I* called him names to fit in with the kids at school.

Joss swings the door open just as I turn the key.

"Huh?" Her hair looks like she stuck her finger in a light socket. I push my way inside and lock us in.

"That Nate guy is Madman Murphy's grandson," I spit out.

The name is like putting smelling salts under her nose. Her eyes pop wide open. She grabs her clothes off the floor and dresses like she's missing an all-you-can-eat pancake special at the diner.

"Don't go out there," I tell her.

"Why? This is way cool."

"What is?"

"Grady. He was legendary. We can finally find out if the rumors were true. Like if he ate opossum, or if his giant eyes were made out of glass."

She bops my nose, not one bit serious. Joss is good at mocking my irrational behavior to keep me from slipping over the edge.

"I can't help it if I lose it sometimes. You'd understand better if someone in your family disappeared."

"Salem, Eli disappeared years before Grady took off. He wasn't a suspect. The two aren't related."

"But Nate and Jim had Eli's key. Why? We've only had two big crimes in this town, Joss. *Two.* Eli and Grady. What's going on?"

She sighs. "Madman Murphy moving away wasn't a crime."

"He vanished one night and no one knows what happened to him, same as Eli. That's a crime. And now these guys show up with Eli's key. And one of them just happens to be Grady Murphy's grandson?"

"Okay, that *is* a bit fishy." She crosses her arms, stares at the door.

"For all we know, Grady could've been murdered. His body might be at the bottom of Tilford Lake."

She sighs again. "Salem, that didn't happen to Eli."

"I know it didn't. I'm just saying it's *not* a coincidence."

"No one thought it was a big deal when Grady left, at least not that I remember. Did anyone look for him?"

"No one looked because everyone was glad he was gone."

"Babe"—she comes closer—"we were teenagers, everything we heard was gossip. We don't know what happened." Her hand squeezes my shoulder. "Maybe the cops searched for him."

"We would've heard about that in this small town."

"And you remember his wife died, right?"

"So what?"

"So, I know this is hard for you to believe, but some people move out of their homes when someone dies. People even move to a new town to escape the past. I bet Grady was like that. Why would he stay?"

"His wife wasn't real. No one ever saw her."

"Oh my God." She raises her hands at my craziness. "We never saw her. *We* didn't, Salem. *We*. That doesn't mean a thing. She was real. Your dad went to school with their daughter."

I pinch the bridge of my nose, sucking in a shuddering breath. Everything's coming at me so fast that I've forgotten the facts, the conversations with my parents, and how confusing life was after Grady disappeared. My family thought there was a connection, that another missing person might lead to more clues, more answers. But hope dried up quickly. The fact is: Grady was born with a defect. He was married, and he and his wife adopted a daughter. She moved away after high school. Grady's wife died. Then Grady probably left to live with his daughter. There's nothing more to it than that.

"You can't hide out in this room all day. Or all week," Joss says.

Our heads turn toward the door. There's a faint noise coming from the other side. Nate's out there, sneaking.

Joss pads over, listens.

"You think I'm embarrassing myself, don't you?" I ask.

She makes a teensy space between her thumb and forefinger. "Tiny bit." She smiles. "It is freaky that Grady's grandson had Eli's key, but you're not going to find out a damn thing by camping out in this room."

"Always my faithful voice of reason." I check my cell. It's seven. I have to get back to work. I think for a second, touching Eli's key in my pocket. "I should call Brad."

"Brad?" Her voice is hard. "For what?"

I find the number for the station in my contacts and place the call. "For *everything*."

"Tilford Lake Police Department."

"Doreen, it's Salem Whitfield over at Sparrow Lodge. Can you connect me with Brad, please?"

"Bradley?"

"Yes, *Brad*."

"Just a minute."

The floor outside the room creaks. That has to be him. He's out there. Just like when I was hiding from him in the bathroom, his shadow is lurking under the door.

"Salem?"

"Brad."

"Call me Officer Brenner."

"No."

"And if this is an emergency, you should be calling 9-1-1, not me. I'm still at home."

"Oh, I guess I should've called your cell."

"This early? No, don't. What do you want?"

I take Eli's key out of my pocket and thumb his initials. "It's Jim Gaines and Nate Harlow, those *private* detectives that you met."

"What about 'em?"

"Did you know Nate is Grady Murphy's grandson?"

"So?" He chews something crunchy. Toast. Maybe cereal.

"They had a key to the lodge, and like I said, Nate's Madman Murphy's grandson."

"So?" More crunching. "It's not a crime to be related to someone."

"Yeah, but—"

"Salem, give it a fucking rest and let me eat my breakfast."

"Don't talk to me that way." I put my hand on my hip as if he can see me.

"Why? I'm not on duty." He mumbles something about Doreen contacting him at home.

There're reasons why Brad is short with me. I called the station a zillion times when I first started running the lodge without my mom. Calls about creaky doors, windows found open, scratching atop the roof, which thankfully turned out to be a tree branch and not an intruder. I can't remember hearing any noises when the private quarters were buzzing with my family, or later when it was just my mom. It's unsettling that there's never silence when I'm here alone. It seems like that's when the lodge groans the loudest.

"Just hang up on that prick," Joss says, ear pressed to the door. She waves me over to listen.

Screw this. I toss my cell on the bed and stride to the door, unlock it, and pull it open.

The hallway is empty.

"I swear I heard breathing a second ago." Her voice lowers to a stage whisper. "Someone was just here."

Nate and Jim's doors are closed.

I look at the other end of the hall and hear a click as a door lock latches. It's the room above my bedroom, Virginia Pullman's room.

"Did you see someone?" Joss asks.

"No one."

"I don't see the guys. Who was out here?"

"I don't know, Joss. No one?"

"Then what was that?"

I shake my head. "Nothing."

"Nothing?"

"Just the wind … nothing but the wind, I guess."

SEVEN

Nate and Jim deactivated the chime on the front door. I'm blaming them because no one else staying here would do such a thing. But why they did it is another mystery. I noticed it wasn't working when Virginia Pullman walked out like an apparition, the door mute, not a sound as she wandered away.

The other guests have checked out, leaving the four of us. *Us*, as if it's fine to group Nate and Jim with Joss and me, that somehow we're all good friends. Although, Joss did decide to shower at the same time as Jim, which is *so* her. She believes she has the magical power to place herself inside a man's head by copying his routine. And after dealing with her countless boyfriends over the years, the longest lasting eight months, I know her flirting ways will get her what she wants. When Jim leaves his room, she'll follow him to the lobby and point out that they both have damp hair, then she'll twirl a strand around her finger. Sometimes I'm jealous of how easy it is for her to seduce men, except for now, since I have no desire to seduce Nathan Harlow. In truth, I want to smack the guy. I might just do so before he travels deep into the forest, which is my best guess as to where he's headed.

From this distance, he looks like he's waiting for something, back turned, feet apart, hands in his pockets. I move from the side of the lodge and proceed carefully through the slippery yard. The fog has thinned and lifted high into the trees, the boot prints from last night now icy oval blemishes amid tiny Ollie prints, a reminder that I had to lock my poor Ollie in the private quarters after his late-night escape. He's an unhappy pooch that he didn't get to say good morning to everyone, but a safe pooch, nonetheless.

I stop next to the overturned fiberglass hippo, given the name Annabelle by my dad. It's an excellent spot to watch Nate from new ground, the same spot I'd scan the yard for Connor when we played hide-and-seek. As I observe Nate standing as still as the pines, I can't help but fantasize that it's him, Connor. He'd wait for me in plain sight alongside a tree trunk and hold his breath, his face painted with green and brown camouflage paint, black hair merging with the dark forest. I'd pass right by him as a kid but would notice him today. He wouldn't be able to disappear on me like he once did. And now Nate standing in that same spot makes it hard to shake my memories of him.

Connor lived outdoors, more animal than human. The type of kid who nursed wounded animals back to health and knew every plant and animal species in our area. He slept under the stars with a pocketknife in one hand and a book about constellations in the other.

During his senior year of high school, he earned his way to Eagle Scout and then applied to college, wanting a degree in Forestry. Two weeks after he died out on the icy lake while fishing with my dad, we received his acceptance letter to an exceptional school in the Adirondack Mountains. My mom had it framed, and it still hangs in the small living room of the private quarters. I knew he'd get in, we all knew it.

I was so proud of him. Siblings fight, but Connor and I were best buds. I think losing Eli when we were young led to a stronger bond between us, different from what other brothers and sisters have.

Nate lifts his head and scratches his chin, the motion cutting into my memory. I stare at him for another minute before moving closer. There's no reason to be tiptoeing other than I'm not sure how else to approach the guy. I'm confused by his personality. He was threatening when he first got here, called me beautiful when he came back drunk, then was standoffish early this morning. Some people are assholes in the morning, but how about now? What should I expect from Jekyll-and-Hyde Harlow now?

He tilts his head as I approach, hearing the sucking noise of my hiking boots in the muck. With his back still turned, he reaches for me. Is that an offer? He's barely spoken to me and now he wants to hold hands?

He wiggles his fingers after I stop a few feet behind him. "Take my hand, Salem."

"Why?"

"We're going for a walk."

"I'm *not* going in the forest with you."

"After all these years, you're still afraid of Grady?" He lowers his hand. "He's not even here."

I look down and make a circle in the melting snow with my boot. "N-no, it's not that," I say. "I want answers first, that's all. Besides, I don't even know you."

"Trust me." He puts his hand back up.

"Why?"

"Because I might have answers."

"Right." I snicker. "Girl goes into the forest with a gorgeous stranger, never to be heard from again."

"I'll tell you what you want to know, but you have to come with me." He doesn't mention that I said he was gorgeous. "And Grady's not around. I promise."

"Don't you call him granddad?"

"No, Grady." He turns and flashes a warm smile, one that slows the heart. Is Nathan Harlow good-natured, or is he a wicked trickster?

"What've you got to lose?" he asks, taking a step closer.

I shrug. "I don't know, my life? What if you chop me to bits?"

Nate's amused, his eyes dancing. "Good sense of humor."

"I wasn't trying to be funny."

"I think you were." He bumps into me on purpose. "Salem, I'm a detective, not a killer."

"*Private* detective." I back up. "You guys make the best killers. Who hired you anyway?"

"No one. I hired myself."

"Why?"

He takes my hand and waits for a struggle, a smack, or a scream, but I only gaze at his touch in disbelief. My ex never held my hand. He didn't like to show affection in public. And there was no need to hold hands in our home. He touched me when he wanted sex, but he wasn't a cuddler. Neither were my fleeting relationships before him.

My eyes close when his thumb grazes my palm. Butterflies stir in my belly. Nate can jump-start something inside me with a single touch. His breath is like a feather on my cheek, his hand warm from being in his pocket. I want to say *more, more please,* but his gravel-deep voice snaps me out of my daze.

"Two steps forward and no steps back." He leads me into the pines.

I catch sight of the lodge one last time before the forest eats us alive. If we were closer, I'd see Ollie watching me from the bay window of my living room, one paw up on the glass, signaling not to go.

"Sorry to be such a dick yesterday," Nate says.

"And this morning," I add.

"Yeah, and this morning. I get testy when I don't eat, low blood sugar or something. Even after drinking, I couldn't sleep. That's not like me."

"Is being a dick like you?" From the corner of my eye, I see a smile. Or was that a smirk? A smile would be better. I hope he smiled.

"Is having clammy hands like you?" he retorts.

"I'm nervous."

"Don't be."

"I have to be back by four to reopen the lodge. No, before four."

"You will."

"And you have to fix my front door chime when we get back."

"It's broken?"

"Don't play dumb."

"I'm not."

He keeps a straight face, focused on where he's walking. I can tell he knows his way through the forest. We head east toward the lake, then north, choosing not to go west where the ground is rocky. He guides me along a stream but doesn't attempt to cross it. There's a reason. He knows about the felled tree that Connor and I once used as a bridge. The one my granddad cut down for us. It's still here, and still as massive as I remember it. This tree was our boundary when we were kids, never to explore past it because of Eli. And somehow, Nate's aware of it.

He knows too much.

"You've been here," I say, invaded with a jolt of confusion.

"Yep, years ago before my grams died."

He tests the trunk then waves to cross once he's safely on the other side. I raise my arms for balance and inch over the length of the old tree, remembering how I'd pretend I was crossing Niagara Falls on a tightrope when I played here as a kid.

That was before Connor warned me of Madman Murphy carrying the dead raccoon. I didn't wander this far from the lodge after that, but I know Connor did. He went everywhere. The creepy-crawlies, lack of light, and the eerie feeling that someone was always watching didn't bother him.

I slip when getting down from the trunk, but catch the sleeve of Nate's hoodie to help regain my footing on solid ground. He insists on taking my hand as we continue.

The ambient stir of wildlife in the brush and trees are oddly missing. No birds, or squirrels, or even a slight breeze. Sometimes the fog can deaden the sounds, other times the eeriness comes from human movement temporarily paralyzing nature.

I stay a step behind him to study his features. Eli could be this tall. He'll be twenty-five this year. Maybe he has the same manly jawline, broad shoulders, dark stubble, and thick eyebrows. Whitfield's all have thick brows, handsome on the men, a burden for the women.

"What are you thinking about?" he asks. The tips of his eyelashes are in wet clumps from the weather.

A pause. "Faces. Eyes. Eyebrows."

"Really?" He turns. "Not where we're going, but eyebrows?"

"You have a Whitfield face." I move right up to him, my eyes inches from his to examine their color. "Do you wear colored contacts?"

"No."

"Your eyes are blue then, not gray?"

"Blue as the sky above us."

I look up. The tops of the pines lost in a gray mist. There's not a spot of blue. "Are you joshing me?"

He pulls me forward to keep moving. "I'm not Eli, Salem. My eyes are blue, my name is Nate, and I grew up in Vinland Falls."

"Okay. It's just ... when things are about Eli, I'm allowed to act desperate."

"We're not related," he adds. "You wouldn't have that look in your eyes if we were."

"What look?" I try to stop him, but he tightens his grip.

"*That* look. The look women get when they're drawn to me."

"Wow. Smug much?"

"Experienced."

"Lucky you."

"Not really. Women who lust after me just to get laid become boring after a while."

"Hey." I tug my hand to get away. No luck. "I'm not out here to lust after you or to screw. I'm here for other reasons."

"I know."

My body stings. "Your friend Jim told me not to push you, that I should wait for you to talk. But I'm getting tired of having no control over this situation."

"I'm sure."

"And I have no interest in making out in the forest like a couple of horny teens."

He smirks, indeed a smirk this time. "I know you're not interested. That lipstick you put on is just to impress the deer."

I draw my lips into a thin line, embarrassed, hiding my raisin-colored lipstick. *He noticed.* Most men are oblivious to the small amount of makeup that I wear, but Nathan Harlow noticed.

"You're a distraction, Salem, but a good one. Those lips are a cruel tease, like a ripe grape I'd love to roll my tongue over."

My cheeks flush with heat. "So lust is a double standard? It's okay for you, but women like that are boring. How fascinating." I hope he picks up on the sarcasm in my voice.

"Having a healthy appetite for beautiful women isn't lust."

My cheeks are now on fire.

"Salem, here's my guess. We both have obsessive personalities. That along with the fact that you like me and I like me is another plus."

"Seriously?"

"And as far as I can tell, this will be a good week if we work together. I just need to ease off the booze for a bit, and you need to serve a meal or two at the lodge." He holds a straight face. Then, a grin expands. His unexpected playfulness puts me at ease.

"Well then, tell me what you're obsessed with."

"Same thing as you. Eli Whitfield."

"You *do* know something. Have you seen him?"

"We're here."

"Where?" My stomach climbs to my throat. I try to get my bearings on where *here* is, and if Grady's house is nearby.

"I like to call it my former summer home." He points to a run-down fort sandwiched between four pines. Boards nailed to the trees form the sides, and tied bundles of long branches lay over the top for a makeshift roof, half of them missing or on the ground. A sign nailed to the front with the words *Girls Keep Out* is etched in a child's handwriting.

"Yours?" I ask.

"Mine and Connor's."

My throat constricts. It's hard to swallow and even harder to speak, but somehow I manage to say, "You knew Connor?"

"For a few years, I did."

"When? Did you also know Eli? How come I don't remember you?" I grab his sleeve. "Why did you say we haven't met? We must've if you knew my brother."

He crosses his arms and looks at a clearing at the bottom of the hill. Below us is Madman Murphy's neglected log cabin, the roof marbled with moss, windows shattered, just a shell of how I remember it from when I was a kid.

"I met Connor when we were about ten. He was out looking for snakes in the forest. He showed me where they hid under the rocks. When I came back the following year, we built this fort and spent the summer playing in the pines. Just him and me, no girls allowed."

I spy over the top. Two wooden chairs rest on their sides, cocooned with sticks and pine needles. There's an empty shelf, and a metal cot with the stuffing of the mattress ripped to shreds by mice.

"He was a fun brother."

"Definitely a cool kid. But he didn't talk about Eli. A few times he said his little brother was missing, that was it."

"We weren't supposed to talk about him to any of the kids in town. My parents said our words would get twisted and stories would spread."

He walks closer to me. "I watched you, Salem. But we never met."

I wheel to face him. "You watched me?"

He nods. "I stood in the pines at the back of your property, even though Grady said not to pass the stream." He points in the direction we just came.

"We weren't allowed to pass it either."

"I know, but Grady was stricter about that boundary than your parents were. If he caught me, I'd get his belt." He lowers his voice. Our eyes meet and then skitter away. "I didn't listen. I wanted to see the pool and the playground that Connor always talked about. And the hippo, I didn't believe you guys had all that stuff. It sounded like an amusement park."

"What was I doing?" I ask.

"Running and dancing in bare feet through the yard." His face lights up. "Sometimes doing cartwheels, or swimming in a bright orange bikini. It was a sight."

"The suit with the white polka dots. I loved it. My grandma bought it for me."

"I loved it, too." He looks down and rubs the back of his neck. "You played the same song over and over while you danced."

"What song?"

"I didn't recognize it, but Connor told me it was 'MMMBop.'"

I laugh. "Gawd, Hanson was my favorite band for years when I was a little kid. He must've also told you how much I hated it."

"Yep. Me too, after hearing it so many times."

"Oh. How many times did you watch me?"

"Only a few."

"So ... three?"

"Five or ten. Maybe twenty."

"Twenty?" I scrunch my nose. "Why didn't you just say hello?"

"Because ... you ... because you were a pretty girl in a bikini, that's why."

"Oh, come on. I was *nine*."

He shakes his head like I'd never understand.

Twenty times, he watched me. *Twenty times!* I bet it was more. And I bet he touched himself while he snooped. How could a boy that age not? Innocent, though, we were only kids, but still. I must've been his first crush.

"It's no different from you watching me from the side of the lodge earlier," he says.

"Yeah, it is. You know it is, or you wouldn't be blushing."

He cradles his cheeks, rubbing them up and down. "I don't blush. It must be the warm weather." He pulls off the hoodie and ties it around his waist.

"Poor excuse. It's not even fifty outside." I turn back to the fort and trace the Girls Keep Out sign. "Connor made sure I was afraid to come out this way. He said Grady killed a raccoon with a knife, and I'd be his next victim if I ever wandered the forest alone."

"That raccoon probably had rabies. He killed quite a few of them over the years to keep us safe."

I look up. "Connor didn't tell me that."

"Yeah, well Connor could've had other reasons he wanted you to stay away. Maybe this was his only spot for privacy. That's why I came out here, to get away from my family. It's like being in another world when you're that age. I'm sure he felt the same."

"It's still like another world," I whisper.

He rubs my lower back, his skin scented with the juniper berry soap stocked in the lodge.

Nate has known me forever, but he knows nothing of me. I'm beginning to hope that will change, my initial scare over him was just a misunderstanding.

I wipe my sweaty palms on my jeans in case he wants to hold hands again.

"I didn't think Connor had any secrets," I say.

"*Everyone* has secrets."

"I don't."

"You must."

I shrug. "I can't think of any. At least none that Joss doesn't know about, which means they're not secrets if she knows. It's not like I've hijacked cars or dealt drugs or anything."

"I'm sure there's something, Salem." He takes my hand, and we start down the steep hill toward Grady's house. We use the trunks of the pines for support until we reach the edge of the unkempt yard.

"Grady left me this property."

"Really? Wait, Grady's dead?"

"Yeah, he died last year. I own the land from the fort, to an acre north of his house, to another acre down the long, dirt driveway. I tried to come up here yesterday, but a tree is down over the drive." He looks at the abandoned cabin. "It seems worthless, doesn't it?"

"It's not. The land is beautiful."

"Maybe the view, but not what's in here." He taps his head. "Not the memories. This place is a nightmare. It reminds me of when my grams got sick and came to live with us. Grady wouldn't come because he said he couldn't bear to watch her die. It was selfish. I realized then that my mom and I spent the summers here to see my grams, *not* to see him. And we never came back once she was with us. We never heard from him again until we got notice he was dead."

"He was a cold man."

"Bitter. He was distant because people hurt him. Angry at life is my guess."

"Where was he all those years?"

Nate looks inside one of the broken windows and up at the leaky ceiling. "No one knows. This cabin is his last known address. He was still paying taxes on this place and had a bank account. But his body was found close to my mom's house in Vinland Falls."

"Was he murdered?"

"No, it was a suicide. My mom thinks he became a hermit. More of a hermit than he already was. She said he lived off the land on this property, just not in the house."

My heart misses a beat considering the possibility. "Here? No way. Someone would've seen him. He wasn't here all that time."

"He was somewhere. In a tent, a cave, or on a boat on the lake."

"It's way too cold in the winter. He wasn't outdoors in Tilford Lake." My mouth feels like it's packed with peanut butter, my speech is bumbling and cumbersome. "I just can't see a person being out here for that long."

"Grady could do it. He never had anyone besides my grams. She was the only one who ever loved him. I bet he got rid of every trace of her after she died, which would've been everything. Then he spent his time roaming the land."

I swallow hard and look inside the remnants of the log cabin. It's just a carcass, stripped of all furniture and belongings. I place my hand over Nate's on the windowsill. He doesn't acknowledge the touch, possibly too distraught by what he sees.

"There's a secret inside this cabin," he whispers. "But I'm not going inside today."

"What secret?"

"This room can speak." He squints at one of the walls.

"What?"

"We need to go." He yanks me away.

"Why?" I stare over my shoulder at the empty cabin, allowing myself to be pulled up the hill and into the pines. "Nate, what's wrong?"

"I don't know where Eli is."

"What?" I sense deep creases in my forehead from another false hope. "What's the secret in the cabin? Was it the key?" I force him to stop by leaning back with all my weight. "Look at me." I swing his arm. "Tell me."

He stops and lowers his head, reluctant.

"Nate. Please," I beg, "please."

"All right." He cranes his neck, stares at the treetops. No eye contact. "Connor told me about the back door of the lodge. He showed me his key, said you each had one."

"But Eli's. Where'd you get it?"

"It was given to me."

"By who?"

His lip twitches.

"By. Who?" My voice changes from sweet to ruthless.

"It was in Grady's safe-deposit box at the bank, part of my inheritance."

I wrench free of his hand and take a step back, then two more steps. "Grady hurt him? He did, didn't he?"

"No. I don't know. Grady could've found the key somewhere, but ..." He stops and runs his hand down his face.

"But what?"

"The key. It was inside a metal box that wasn't his."

"What are you talking about?"

"A metal box was inside Grady's safe-deposit box. I remember it from when I was a kid. From out there." He looks at the fort. "We kept stuff in it, Connor and me."

"Excuse me?"

"It was ours. We called it our stash. Eli's key was in that."

My jaw drops. Did I hear him right? Connor had the key? No. Grady did. Not Connor.

"Either Connor put the key in the stash at some point, or Grady did years later. Then he put it in the bank. He must've saved it for me." He walks forward and I step back. "After I got the key, I searched for your family online." My ears buzz. I only catch traces of his words. *"I found Eli's case ... an article ... your dad and Connor died ... hypothermia ..."*

The towering pines begin to twirl overhead. I suddenly feel ill. I try to steady myself alongside a tree, but my head spins faster as I fight for breath. Connor? No, Grady knew something, not Connor.

"You okay?"

Daylight turns to black.

"Salem?"

A sharp pain shoots through my temple. I sway and lose my balance. Nate catches me before I hit the ground, but then I become nothing.

EIGHT

"Maybe you should sit down and relax for a couple of minutes before you do all this," Nate says. He crosses his arms and leans against the doorjamb of my living room, his eyes wandering to the keepsakes scattered about, reminders that my family once lived here.

"I'm perfectly fine. I could've made it to the lodge on my own."

Nate didn't need to carry me over the wet leaves and rocks, through snowy spots and mud patches, dodging low hanging branches and thorny brush. He didn't need to hold me so close to his heady scents of cinnamon and vanilla cologne, juniper berry soap, and peppermint toothpaste, fueling my growing crush on him. But I didn't fight or insist on being put down. Not when his low voice whispered that I'd be fine, not when he said he never meant to upset me. It was soothing. I gave in. I let him take control.

I haven't felt the comforts of being cared for in years, and not just by a man, by anyone.

"You passed out."

"No, I didn't."

I slide open the built-in drawers under the bay window seat, full of photographs, report cards, and family remnants that have accumulated since Connor, Eli, and I were born.

"I caught you, Salem. You were about to hit the ground."

"I was just overwhelmed."

I puff my bangs away from my eyes while rummaging through the items. I've torn the room apart in less than five minutes. Board games, books, magazines, and various papers have been pulled from bookshelves. The sofa cushions are on the floor, and Ollie's helping out by inspecting the open coffee table drawer.

"What are you looking for?"

"I don't know. Anything. Something. You tell me."

I've combed through the lodge before, believing evidence was missed. I'm wrong. Always wrong. There was no ransom note, no motive, only a missing boy who people thought wandered off and met an unfortunate fate with a bear. Thankfully, no sign of that ever was found. It was one of the many horrifying stories I'd heard from Tilford Lake locals with nothing better to do than gossip about my baby brother. People did the same with Connor, saying a kid with such remarkable survival skills was either drunk or on drugs to have died in the water. They said he would've lived if he were sober, and that he must've been horsing around and turned the boat too quickly.

"Salem, you're face is turning red."

But I know better. Accidents can happen quickly on a small fishing boat, and not from horsing around or drinking. Once in the water, Connor would've tried to help my dad, but it would've been difficult with heavy, waterlogged clothing and nothing to grab hold of. He knew not to swim to shore in the freezing water. He would've done the right thing by huddling close to my dad. It pains my heart to think that Connor knew they were going to die, and I have to stop myself from wondering what their final words to one another might've been.

Nate sits on the floor next to me. "Stop thinking about whatever it is you're thinking about." He takes a crumpled sheet of paper from my hand and flattens it back into shape. "I'm sure you've done this enough to know there aren't any answers here." He puts his hand on my leg to chill, but I just can't.

"It was Grady. I'm positive." I take Eli's key from my pocket and touch his initials. "He did something to him."

"That's what you think?"

"What do you think? You're here for some reason. What is it?"

He massages his forehead. "I don't know yet. I thought of Grady right away when I found the key in the box. It was instinct. Connor never crossed my mind. But there's nothing else to go on. Other than the key, I haven't found any evidence that he knew what happened to Eli. Like I said, Grady must've found his key on the property."

"Then he should've called the cops."

I push his hand away. Nate should've called the cops, too. And me. But I'll do it now. I'll call. Grady and Nate didn't, but I will.

"Doreen. It's Salem Whitfield over at—"

"Sparrow Lodge. Yes, sweetie, I know. You lookin' for Bradley again?"

"Anyone. I don't care. Someone competent."

"Hmm. I'll see if I can find somebody."

The front door chimes. I noticed it was magically functioning again when Nate and I came in. Jim must've fixed it.

Ollie barks at the sound of Joss's friendly voice. He bolts to the lobby. "Hi, Olls. Where's your mama? Show me where your mama is," she says.

"Back here, Joss." She's the only person I trust to have a key to the lodge.

"Salem," Brad answers.

"Hey. Do you have the number of the detectives from the city who were working Eli's case? I need it. Is it the same guys as before?"

"Salem."

"What?"

"What year are you living in? For real, do you call just to fuck with me, or what?"

I stand and look out the window. My hand tucked under my armpit, head angled to the same side. "Nate Harlow had Eli's key to the lodge. I need to talk to someone."

"No one's worked that case in years. It went cold over a decade ago."

"Are you deaf?"

"I heard you. Are you deaf?" His loud chewing is unbearable, done on purpose because I'm disturbing another one of his meals.

"I'm asking for the detectives because this is bigger than anything that's turned up in the past. I need to talk to someone who's *not* a Tilford Lake cop."

"I'll call you back, okay?"

"You're not sending anyone over?"

He slurps his drink and releases a quiet burp. "I gotta check on something first. I'll get back to you when I can."

"Brad? Don't you dare ... Uh, he hung up on me." I turn as Jim and Joss walk in carrying plastic bags filled with snacks and beer. "This isn't a sorority house."

"Or a brothel," Jim adds. "Looks like a bomb went off in here." He looks at Nate. "Take it you told her where you got the key. I told Joss everything when we were out getting some grub." He lifts a bag. "You want a pizza pocket?"

"Pizza pockets?" I step forward. "You're not moving in. This isn't your home *or* your kitchen."

"Salem, do you think Connor—"

"No!" I shout at Joss. Then feel horrible for doing so. "No. No, Joss. Connor would've told someone if he found the key. Look at this. Look." I point to the open room at the end of the hall where we slept. "He slept on the top bunk with Eli on the bottom, and I had the bed on the other side of the room, only a curtain between us. My parents were right across from us in the private bedroom next to the bathroom. This is everything." I hold up my hands. "This is us. This is it. We were close, like gypsies. No privacy and *no* secrets."

"Gypsies, Salem?" Joss questions. "That's the wrong word, babe. Hippies?"

"Yes, hippies, okay? I'm too frazzled to think straight." I walk up to Nate. "What else was in that metal box at the bank? Anything you didn't recognize?"

"No, everything else was the same as I remember it. A pile of baseball cards and letters to our parents if we ever decided to hit the open road."

"Really?"

He shrugs. "What kid hasn't thought about that?"

"What else?"

He stares at the mess on the floor, rolls a pencil back and forth under his toes.

"Tell her," Jim says.

"I'm getting to it." He looks up. "There were some nudes and five bucks."

Joss laughs. "Like, *Playboy* nudes? Did you charge kids to look at them?" She laughs even harder.

"No. And they weren't Connor's, but he thought they were a good addition to the stash."

"And?" I ask, my arms crossed, foot tapping.

"And kids' stuff. You know? Things we found."

"And the flyer," Jim says.

Nate rubs the back of his neck.

"Flyer for what?" I ask but already have a suspicion.

"To find the Whitfield treasure," Nate says.

I close my eyes. "Come again?"

"The Whitfield treasure. Grady told me about it. He said to keep my eyes peeled whenever I was out in the pines. How much was it anyway? Did anyone ever find it?"

"Shut up." My finger stabs his chest. "Now it all makes sense. You're not here about the key or my brother. You still want to find the treasure. You're here for that!"

"It doesn't exist," Joss says. "It was to attract business."

"Not true."

"It is true." I point at his face.

"Doesn't matter, the answer is no. I didn't come here for that. It was only a game when I was a kid, completely meaningless."

"Do you have it? The flyer?"

"Yeah. I brought the entire stash with me."

"Go get it. I wanna see."

A shadow cast from the lobby into the hallway catches my eye. "Hold on." I peek out of the private quarters and see Virginia Pullman walking up the stairs. She reaches the second-floor balcony, heading to her room with a beautiful white crocus in her hand.

I look at the front door and back upstairs. Did the chime not go off?

"What is it?" Joss asks.

"I'm losing my mind."

"That happened a long time ago. Why else would we be friends?" She smiles. "Crazy people need to stick together."

"You didn't lock the door when you came in."

"So what? We're all here. You're safe." She elbows me and places the bags in the galley kitchen that's across from my living room. Jim comes over to help her unload.

"Get the stash," I repeat to Nate. "I wanna see the flyer. Do it now."

"It's in my room." He waits to see if I'm going to follow him before leaving the private quarters on his own.

It's been a while since a guest walked in with a flyer. My parents didn't have them at the lodge. My granddad was the one who created the legend and did the marketing. He placed ads in city papers and put flyers at area tourist attractions. Like Clayton Winery and down at the marina. My parents said luring people to Sparrow to search for the unsearchable was false advertising. They felt terrible for treasure hunters who arrived just to scout our land.

However, there was some truth to the hunt. Connor and I knew what our granddad meant by the Whitfield treasure. I found it every day. Guests who looked closely enough found it, too. The scenery, the wildlife, the beautiful grounds, too bad most people took the hunt literally. They expected gold coins to appear under their feet, missing the real treasure of the forest.

"Here." Nate walks in and sets the rusty metal box on the coffee table. He kneels next to it and opens the top. "I swear I didn't come here because of an old treasure tale. I came to see my property and to figure out some stuff about Grady. Maybe I'll uncover other secrets he had besides the key." A hesitation. "It's been on my mind for months. I'm on edge by what I might find."

"That's putting it mildly," Jim calls from the kitchen. "He's been a total dick and a drunk."

"Not so," Nate calls back.

"How many times did you call me for a ride home from the bar?" Jim comes into the room with one of my grandma's cooking aprons around his waist. "He dropped our other cases to come here. Now I'm not getting paid."

"Take that off," I tell him.

"I'm paying you. We've got money," Nate says.

"*You,* you've got money. I need to get back to work."

"Hey, I'm paying for your room, so just shut up and enjoy your weeklong vacation."

Jim looks down at the apron. "Can I keep it? It will be a blast to wear in bed." He flips the bottom up like he's flashing us.

"Absolutely not, it belonged to my grandma."

"Jim, take it off," Nate demands.

"Fine. You guys do your thing, and I'll look for the treasure. How's that?"

"There is no treasure!" Joss and I say in harmony.

"We'll see," he says.

Nate points for him to leave. Bickering men crack me up. Connor and my dad were like that. I always thought it was a sign of unspoken love disguised behind a power struggle.

"So," he says, "I took the five bucks and the nudes out but kept the other items in here. Everything but the keys."

I kneel next to him and look inside. "*Keys*? There were other ones besides Eli's?"

"Yep, the copies you took from us last night were in here."

"Why? That doesn't make sense."

"No idea. Did your family have extras made?"

"No, just the three with the lodge's logo. They weren't everyday nickel-plated keys, not like the one I have for the front or those extras you had. Why do you think Grady put them in the stash?"

"I don't have any answers, Salem."

"How come? What the hell's wrong with you, Nate?"

He smiles at my playful nag, which I'm glad he could hear in my voice. I'm more relaxed knowing he wasn't the one who made copies of the key. At least it's a start to trusting him.

I put Eli's brass key on the table next to the box. It was part of the stash but looks out of place with the bits and pieces of Connor's life.

My brothers have been walled off from one another in my mind since I can remember. The separate tragedies split my memories of them, and now I have a hard time picturing them together. That includes their belongings. Eli's key doesn't fit with Connor's collection. The key is unique to Eli and meaningful to our family. But Connor's items in the stash look like they could belong to anyone.

Nate removes a small turtle shell from the box and taps a folded sheet of paper hidden underneath. Scribbled in Connor's pointy handwriting are the words, *Mom & Dad.* My hands tremble as I pick it up. I fan my face and take a mighty breath before I unfold it and start to read.

Mom & Dad,

Are you mad I am in the forest? Don't be. Nate is here. He is my new friend. He is fun. His mom makes good cookies. I ate two. They were peanut butter.

We are going to hike to the Grand Canyon. Do not worry. I have my pocketknife and a map. We will not hitchhike. We will walk and run all the way there. I want to live with the lizards and eat berries. I can make tea from leaves. Nate can build a fire with flint and my knife. We will be good. We have two pairs of underwear. Each. Can you feed Fred?

Tell Salem to get my homework when school starts. Tell her to do my math. She is good at it. I will pay her.

We will be home for Christmas. I want a new fishing pole and a Half Dome tent. Do not buy me socks. I have some. I will wear Salem's if I run out. Get good presents. She has enough Bratz dolls. Buy her a razor scooter. I can use it.

I love you,
Connor

PS – I might be back for Halloween. Can I be Harry Potter? Nate said I look like him. I need glasses. I can make the wand and Mom can make the cape. FEED FRED!

My lip quivers as I wipe a tear. "That kid," I whisper. "He was so witty and bright. And I remember Fred the frog. My dad accidentally killed him with the lawnmower. We buried pieces of the poor guy next to Annabelle the hippo."

"He talked about you a lot. Hard to tell from that letter, but he loved you."

"I can tell, and I always knew. I wish my mom could've read this." I set it on the coffee table then place Eli's key on top. I was wrong. These two items belong together.

I finger through the rest of the stash, finding three orange beaver teeth, a Pokémon card, and a short stack of baseball cards. The ragged edges stink of mold. I remember the cards were in this condition when Connor had them as a kid. All of his store-bought toys were well worn—treated as invaluable material objects—but whatever he picked up in the forest was prized.

"He didn't talk much about sports," Nate says.

"No, he wasn't a big baseball fan. My dad bought him a couple of packs to try to get him interested in something besides scouting. He kept only a few because he thought most of the men on the cards looked at him funny."

"That sounds like Connor."

I set three cardinal feathers next to the turtle shell and take out three rocks crammed with trilobite fossils. In our old bedroom closet, buried under piles of boots and sneakers, are three shoeboxes that Connor once kept under his bunk. They contain what he called *nature's pickings*. Leaves, bark, rocks, bird nests, an owl skull, and a few unidentifiable tiny bones, likely from mice or other rodents that he'd pretend were spider monkeys. There's also a four-leaf clover sandwiched between wax paper. I promised him I'd never to touch it. Still haven't. We learned early on to respect people's property, a necessity because of the business we were in.

But the groups of three in the stash ... in the past I hadn't noticed he collected a specific number.

"It's a coincidence, right?" I ask Nate.

"What?"

"That there were three keys in the box, and Connor collected in threes."

He tugs on his ear and looks at the floor. "I don't know."

"But you noticed?"

"I noticed. Not when I was a kid, but when I sifted through this stuff again."

"But it was Grady, right? Tell me he put the keys in here and not Connor."

"I don't know."

My shoulders droop like tomato plants in a heat wave. Grady could've caught on to the number of objects Connor collected. If we did, he did, too. He could've made the extra keys to make it look like Connor put them in the box. Or he had them made to represent Connor and me to go along with Eli's. The three keys together like they once were. But why? And I won't even try to think of reasons why Connor would've done it, because he didn't.

"Dammit."

"You okay, babe?" Joss looks out from the kitchen.

"No, I'm frustrated."

I pick up a small magnifying glass—one of the last items in the box—and twirl it between my thumb and forefinger. Three beaver teeth, three feathers, three rocks, and three keys, plus three boxes in the closet. Despite the peculiarity of the collection, Connor wasn't a loner or deranged. He wasn't a psychopath. He had plenty of close friends. Only once did I ever hear a negative comment about him from two boys who came over and said he was boring. Go figure. We didn't have a TV or video games, and my parents preferred books to movies, homemade meals to fast food, a land line to cell phones, and staying active to living like sloths. They said we'd thank them later for living in a wonderland.

I use the magnifier to study the items, moving back and forth over each one. No markings, nothing unusual. There's no hint or trace of any meaning. Nothing. I lean in and look closer. "Do you think the lodge is a wonderland?" I ask Nate.

"Depends."

I sit up and look at him through the magnifier. My eye must be triple its size. "Depends on what?"

"On what your needs are."

"I don't have many needs."

"That's too bad." His hand rests on my leg. "Being with people is one of the secrets to happiness. At the very least, you need that."

"You mean sex."

"Ah. Yeah, that would be nice. Sure."

"I wasn't asking."

"You will."

"I won't."

"You should!" Joss calls out.

I shake with silent laughter.

"You know, I used to burn ants with that magnifier." He tactfully changes the subject.

"Ugh." I set it down. "That's so typical for a boy."

He shows off a wide grin, his fingers raking through his hair.

"This also belongs to you." I put the Pokémon card in front of him.

"Yep. Porn and Pokémon were my top priorities when I was a kid. Is it that obvious?"

I nod. "You look good in that hoodie, by the way."

"Thanks." He pats the logo over his chest. "I'll pay for it."

"You overpaid for the rooms, so it's not so much the money as the principle." I twirl the magnifier again. "I hate dishonest men."

He listens with a straight expression, gently sliding his fingers up and down my leg. An apology? Another come-on?

Or both.

I'd love to touch him back, hold his hand again, kiss him. I can't remember the last time...

"You blush easily," he says. "Thinking about anything in particular?"

"Nope. And I don't blush."

"Right. Just like me. We must've caught a bug when we were outside."

The hell with it, I should kiss him. There haven't been any hot guys in Tilford Lake since forever. Why be shy? Nerves, I suppose. I'd probably do something nerdy, like lean in and knock his teeth, or worse, "he'll back away from my kiss and I'll feel like an ass."

"Try it."

I look up. "What?"

"Huh?" He acts innocent.

Please tell me I did NOT say that aloud. I couldn't have. Dummy. I did! My face is on fire. I did. I said it!

"I wasn't talking about you." I try to cover.

"Sure."

After clearly embarrassing myself, all I can think to do is plunge back into the stash.

The final item is a water-stained, tri-fold flyer. On the front is an ink drawing of the lodge, the heart and sparrow logo at the top rising high like the sun. The inside has a coupon for ten percent off our weekend rate, and a hand-drawn map of the property. I've seen flyers similar to this one with the same tagline at the top: *Come one, come all, to find the greatest treasure of them all!* The description under it is also like the ones I've seen:

> *It may be below or may be above. You might need a shovel or to sift with a glove. Riches and gems, good fortune and loot, have a good look around, I promise I won't shoot! If you find the hidden booty, or even just moss, bring it into the lodge where I can admire my loss. I swear you can keep it, all that you find, everything but my wife's delicious cheese rind. Gosh darn it, that's mine!*

I giggle. "This is priceless. Granddad Felix had me in stitches up until the day he died. He was so much fun."

"I can tell. I laughed the first time I read it, too. Grady tried to convince me the flyer was new, but it looked like it was from the sixties." He points to the vintage drawings and handwritten text. "Whoever made it didn't use a computer. It's all done by hand."

"He made these when I was eight or nine. Not in the sixties. It was an attempt to help us out following a bad year of business. Families were afraid to stay here with their kids after Eli went missing. This fake treasure hunt was his big idea." I wave the flyer in the air.

Nate looks about and tips his head toward the hallway. "You all lived here, even your grandparents?"

"No, they passed the lodge down to my dad after Connor was born. They lived in a small mobile home out by the lake, but still got a share of the income from the business. Financially, it was a tough time. We had to take care of this property and theirs. But we survived."

"Ollie!" Joss squeals from the kitchen.

"That's your fault for giving him beef jerky," Jim says.

"Salem, Ollie barfed on the floor. Should I clean it up?"

"No, Joss. Leave it so we can step in it."

Nate laughs and leans back on his elbows.

"Fine. Go 'head and hang out with your new boyfriend and ignore poor little Ollie. I'll take care of him," she says.

"Ollie would be fine if you didn't feed him jerky. Olls, come here." He waddles in with his head hanging low. "You're fine, don't be sad. It's not your fault people keep feeding you junk." He offers an apology by placing his head in my lap. "Good boy." I scratch his favorite spot behind his ear. "Next time she feeds you garbage, vomit on her foot."

Joss doesn't respond. I glance over my shoulder and groan at the sight of Jim's hand under her shirt. It won't be long now.

Nate looks up. A floorboard creaks above us. I throw my head back and stare at the ceiling.

"The bogeyman," he jokes.

"The bogeyman would be better than mice. Rodents are hard to get rid of."

A second board creaks on the other side of the room.

"Sounds like the mice in Tilford Lake weigh as much as a human. Should I run up and check?"

"No, that's okay. Someone is in the room over mine." I point toward the back. "Above my parents' old room at the end of the hall, the sound must be traveling from there."

A third creak.

Nate looks up again. "Nope, for sure that's above us."

"Impossible, that room is locked and I'm the only one with a key."

"As far as you know you are." He looks at Eli's key, and I think of the other two that I didn't know about.

"True, anything's possible." I get up to have a look, but the front door chime distracts me, still unlocked from when Joss came in. This time, for sure, it sang.

"Joss, watch Ollie for me."

"No problem."

I walk to the lobby and catch Brad sniffing the air like a dog.

"Cooking something?" He licks his lips, hoping for an invitation.

"Pizza rolls."

"Splendid."

"Did you call the detectives? Are they coming?"

"Chief told me to come see what you've got first."

"Why?"

"You know why, Salem. We go through this shit with you every year. Like that time you found a little sneaker on the property and swore it was Eli's, but it was only this big." He makes a two-inch space between his thumb and finger.

"It was bigger than that."

"No." He shakes his head. "No, it wasn't. We found a doll later that day sticking out of the sand in the playground out back. Remember?"

"Yes, I remember." I exhale loudly in protest.

"Ollie dug it up, buried for years. But your memory of Eli and the doll got jumbled."

"I said I remember."

"Okay, so show me this key."

I march to my bedroom, muttering *schmuck* under my breath. My memories of Eli aren't as vivid as the ones I have of Connor. I was so young when it happened, but that doesn't mean people shouldn't take me seriously. "Tilford Lake cops are totally inept."

"I can hear you," Brad calls down the hall.

"Is there a problem?" Nate says to him.

I picture Brad putting a hand on his holster, widening his stance to look intimidating, all five feet, six inches of him.

"Harlow," he says.

"Brenner." Nate's voice overpowers the lobby.

I forgot Eli's key is in the living room and not the bedroom. Or more likely, I didn't forget and walked past it on purpose. I stare for a long time at the two nickel-plated keys on my dresser, harking back to what Joss said about never seeing Eli's key again once it leaves the lodge. I wanted the detectives to have it. I planned to file a report with them, not Brad. And knowing Tilford Lake cops, there's a good chance they'll lose it.

"Nice weather," Brad says.

"Perfect weather," Nate responds.

I make fists as I stride back to the lobby. I'll do the detective work, not Bradley Brenner.

"You got it?" he asks.

"What are you gonna do with it?"

"For fuck's sake, Salem."

"Ease up." Nate steps forward in my defense.

Jim comes out and leans alongside the desk, crossing his arms and legs. He doesn't speak, but the expression on his face would unnerve a king cobra.

"Hey, she called me, all right?" Brad turns to me. "Thought you were afraid of these guys."

"I changed my mind. Here, take it." I give him one of the newer keys.

"What's this?"

"The key I told you about. That's it."

He looks at the one Eli's wearing in the photomural above the door. "Stop messing with me. It's insulting. *This* isn't *that* key. And it doesn't fit the description of the one we have on file."

"Then I guess it's like the sneaker I found."

"As predicted. Chief was right not to call the guys from the city." He tosses the key on the floor and plods to the door. "I'm not coming back if you call again. Not till you get some professional help, Salem. I'm serious."

"You can't say that to me. I'm part of this community just like everyone else. It's your job to—"

"Look, I've got a Slurpee bandit at the 7-Eleven, he's been stealing for weeks, and someone keeps dressing Mrs. Thompson's garden gnomes in thongs. There're more important things than…"

He drops the argument, and I can tell by how fast he turns away that he regrets what he was about to say. But it's too late.

"More important things than what? My brother?"

"Than your wild imagination."

"Whatever. Good luck with the thongs." I hold the door open and lock it once he's outside.

Jim nods to Nate, a signal that he has his back. He gives us a quick wave before heading back to the kitchen.

Nate steps closer to the door to study the photomural, shoulders back, chest out, stroking his chin. A minute passes before he picks the spare key off the floor and flips it in the air, catching it with the same hand.

"I made the right decision," he says.

"For what?"

"The key. You." He bites his bottom lip for a few seconds. "I found your mom's obituary when I researched your family. It listed you and her parents as the only surviving relatives."

"Yeah, her mom and dad live in Florida. They're too old to travel, and I'm too busy. I never get to see them … and I have an aunt who lives in Colorado, but she and my mom weren't close. I don't know her or my cousins. It's just me here."

"That was my impression." He raises a closed hand. "I had a key in my possession that was meaningful, and I knew I had to bring it to you, not the cops. It didn't feel right to make that decision for you. It was your choice what to do with it."

"Thank you," I whisper.

He flips the key in the air before placing it in my hand. "So how come you gave Brad one of these? Why'd you change your mind and keep Eli's?"

A flash of color on the mantel diverts my attention. Three purple crocuses lay next to a vase filled with red dogwood branches. With my hands clasped behind my back, and feeling Nate's eyes on me, I walk over to sniff the crocuses. Their scent is warm and faint, a little sweet, like hay. I gather them up, take another whiff, and look to the balcony for any sign of life. Virginia, she must've put them here.

"Salem, what about the key?"

The answer that finally comes is based more on intuition and emotions than facts.

"Because"—I turn to Nate—"a corner of my heart tells me not to let go of what's already lost. Eli's key belongs here with me."

NINE

Guests have settled in for the night. I check my cell. Ten-thirty. It's quiet now. Jim and Joss promised to be back from Martin's Bar by eleven, and Nate regrettably disappeared on foot two hours ago. No need to guess where. Brave guy to walk the forest alone, wouldn't catch me out there this late without an army of friends.

I look out my living room window, ice pellets tapping the glass, the yard curtained by a black night. Nate could be checking me out from four feet away and I wouldn't know it. I'd like to think he's not a creeper. Although, I did leave the door to my private quarters wide open as an invitation for him to wander in, hoping that he is. Is that absurd? Should I care if it is? With those blue eyes, his charming dimple, rumbling voice, fit body, and wow, and the size of his feet, I'm okay if he decides to slink in here. Nothing's wrong with getting a little lost in him. Yesterday wasn't a terrific start, but he made up for it today. And even at ten, Connor was a good judge of character. He liked Nate. Nate gets bonus points for that.

I turn to see if he's standing behind me, but the room is dark and empty.

Ollie is asleep at the foot of my bed, full of cute, musical snores that I can hear all the way into this room. I'll join him after

Joss and Jim get in, after Nate comes back, and after I stop thinking about the metal box on the coffee table.

Rummaging through the contents of the three shoeboxes in the closet didn't provide any new clues to Connor's rationale for collecting in threes. It's baffling. I take out my cell and Google search "collecting in threes" and "the number three in nature." *The Power of Three, The Spiritual Meaning Behind Three,* Christianity this and science that sites pop up, the use of three in art and architecture, and loads of astrology sites. I browse a few of them, mindful that Connor wouldn't have known any of this at that age.

Three is a sacred number. It's the number of the Trinity. Vikings used three triangles intertwined as a symbol for the dead. Past, present, future. Birth, life, death. Death comes in threes.

Ugh, so much about death.

Three is the number of riddles to be solved or the presence of three characters in fairy tales and nursery rhymes. "Three Blind Mice," "The Three Little Pigs," "Goldilocks and the Three Bears." The explanations go on and on, but nothing relevant to my brother.

A lightning flash draws me away from my cell. I count the number of seconds until a roar of thunder vibrates the windows. Ten seconds. Divide by five. It's two miles away. A trick Connor taught me. After a second flash, the pattering of ice pellets changes to a downpour. Typical weather for Tilford Lake this time of the year: morning fog, afternoon sun, evening snow, sleet, or rain, warm winds, and cool breezes.

The temperature fluctuations mark that human mating season is just around the corner. When the women in Tilford shave their legs and the men trim their beards. Or vice versa.

The weather also brings to mind an anniversary song my parents played every spring. Connor and I would giggle at their clumsy dance steps—no grace—like a couple of drunken penguins. But more so, I recall the love that radiated in their faces. I flip through my music and find their song, "With or Without You."

U2, or at least this song by them, is like a soft breath against the ear. I press my hand to the window, disappearing into the music as water streams down the glass.

Three teeth, three feathers, three fossils, and our three keys: work, life, death, and family. Good things come in threes? That's what my granddad used to say. It could be as simple as that.

Ollie continues to snore through the thunder, not even waking for the front door chime. I listen. The melodic jingle is similar to a wind chime. Can't be Joss and Jim, they'd be talking, must be Nate.

The lodge is still for a few seconds. Then footsteps grow in intensity until his reflection is upon me in the glass. I pretend not to notice, fixated on the outdoors, not wanting to seem overly excited.

"Hi," he whispers.

I turn, one hand kept on the glass, not sure if it's him or the thunder that's making me shudder. Our eyes meet and two smiles dawn.

Nate—devastatingly beautiful Nate—with wet hair and water dripping down his face, slips off his waterlogged boots and pulls off his hoodie and T-shirt, dropping them in a pile on the floor. He saunters over and places a cold hand over mine. I close my eyes to keep from staring at his abs. It's unreal to fall for to a man I barely know, but considering the solitude of being on the outskirts of Tilford Lake, it's likely I'd fall for anyone who knows I exist. Men in these parts don't give women like me a second glance, or even a first. No tats, no enormous boobs, no high heels or flirty ways.

"Look at me." The backs of his fingers graze my cheek, his breath smelling of rum.

I open my eyes. "Did you go back there?"

He nods. "To the hill above the cabin."

"It's too dark to see anything."

"I wasn't looking. I was listening."

I don't ask what he was listening for. I know he won't answer. His wanting expression tells me so. He's here for *me*, not to talk.

I lean into his hand, my heart jack-rabbiting against my ribs. He presses his body to mine, stiff, proud, lips hovering closer, provoking my mouth to take the bait.

"I want you," he whispers. He tilts his head and traces my lips with his tongue, sharing the earthy taste of liquor. My lips part with his. Flashes of light streak under my eyelids, but diminish like the death of a sparkler when the kiss fades.

I want more. More kisses, a touch, his hands under my shirt cupping my breasts. Anything. *More Nate.*

His finger touches my lips, liquored eyes matching a secretive moon behind a low-hanging shroud of haze. He drops his hand and steps back to gather his clothes and boots.

"Night, Salem. Maybe I'll turn up in your dreams."

I can't formulate a response. His kiss erased everything from my mind. I'm lost in a racing pulse and a shiver crawling up and down my spine.

He closes the door to my private quarters. But even after he's gone, I can still feel him slick between my legs. It's at this moment that I know we're going to fuck.

TEN

"Salem, get up. Mom and Dad are yelling out back." Connor tugs at my mermaid sleeping bag then pries one of my eyelids open. "Get up."

"Connor, stop it." I swat his hand away. "I'm still asleep."

"You can't be asleep if you're talking to me."

"Yes, I can."

He climbs over my legs and jumps on the bed. "Get up. Get up."

"Tom, I'm calling the police," Mom shouts.

"Give him another five minutes to come out. He just wandered into the forest is all," Dad calls to her.

I sit up and listen.

"No," Mom says, "something's wrong. Something's definitely wrong."

Connor looks toward the door. "Told you."

"Where's Eli?"

"Haven't seen him."

Eli is always the last to wake up, sometimes in bed till ten. And Mom and Dad never yell. Never-ever.

I scramble out of my sleeping bag and swing my legs out of bed. My belly tosses and turns like the time a spider crawled under my pillow, scaring me so much that I couldn't sleep in my bed for a week.

"Salem, guests are up. Put on a shirt!"

I pick up one of Dad's dingy T-shirts from the laundry pile in the hallway—the one with Fred Flintstone and the slogan "Say No To Drugs"—and slip it over my head. It fits like an oversized nightshirt, a handicap when I try to sprint. Connor races past. He holds open the door to the lobby as I catch up.

I'm disoriented. Have I slept for an hour or through the night? "Is it still bedtime?"

"No, the sun is in the front window. It's morning."

We hurry to the escape hatch. I touch my chest to feel for the key, remembering it's still hanging on my bedpost. Connor's wearing his, but the door is already open when we reach the back.

"Who left it open?"

"I didn't," he says.

"Eli Thomas Whitfield, get your bottom out here right this minute. I'm not amused by this game," Mom pleads, her eyes darting back and forth through the dewy yard. Footprints are everywhere, but none small enough to be Eli's.

Dad steps out of the forest. "Eli," he shouts, "you win. I give up finding you. You can come out now."

Guests are gathering, searching the grounds, comforting Mom.

"What happened?" I ask her.

"When was the last time you saw your brother? Did you hear him get up this morning?"

I shake my head.

"Connor, did you go out the hatch this morning?"

"I just got up."

"Salem?"

I shake my head again.

"He's not anywhere," she cries. "He's not here."

"I'll check inside again," Dad says.

"No, he's not here, Tom. It's time to call. What are we waiting for?"

"Okay." He grabs a chunk of his spiky hair. "Okay."

Mom cries much harder. I hug her waist and nuzzle her side, taking in her warmth to ease my sick belly. The wobbly emotion in my parents' voices startles me even more.

Eli will come home when he's hungry. He will. He has to eat grape jelly on toast every morning, or he's a grump until his afternoon nap. He'll come home to eat. I look up to tell her this, finding it hard to make out her features. She looks more like Grandma than Mom.

"Connor, you stay right here," she says.

Despite her warning, he heads into the forest without looking back. I can't picture his face or Dad's. Everyone is blurry.

"Connor!" she persists.

I slip away and run to catch him.

"Salem, don't you dare leave me!"

"Connor, wait for me. Wait!" I could blame the oversized tee and my bare feet for slowing me down, but I know he runs faster than the rabbits, much faster than any of us. "Wait up!"

I've lost sight of him.

I hear the *cheep-cheep* of tiny birds, buzzing bees, and croaking frogs, the rustling brush—all familiar sounds—but not a whisper from my brothers.

Avoiding pine needles and sharp rocks, stopping every so often to rub the bottom of my feet, I make it to the top of the hill overlooking the back part of the property. Fragmented sunbeams cascade through the branches of the tall pines, blinding me like a strobe. I have to raise my hand to shield my eyes from the harsh light.

"Connor?"

Eli's teddy bear, Hank, is propped alongside a tree at the bottom of the hill. His head hangs low, his tubby, tan legs spread wide, set in that position after years of Eli's crushing hugs. I step clumsily toward the bear, over moss and gooey slugs, eyeing a cardinal tracking my every move.

"Shoo," I tell it. "Stop following me."

It swoops down and lands on Hank's shoulder, presenting a head tilt as if to ask what I'm doing in its territory. Its head tips to the other side and a flurry of flaps erupts into an urgent warning to stay back.

"Eli," I holler.

"What?"

"Eli?" I turn.

"Over here." The response comes from the opposite direction. The voice is deep, familiar, but not his. I can't quite place it ... Dad's maybe? It's hard to get my bearings with sounds ricocheting off the trees, crisscrossing from every direction.

"Where are you?"

A teenager wearing Connor's Boy Scout cap steps out from behind a tree. The key to the lodge dangles on his chest. My eyes are tricked to see an older Connor, my gut tells me it's Eli, but my heart knows it's neither. His clothes are wet, hair slick, lips the color of a blackberry, swollen and trembly. It's summer. The morning heat is already making my throat dry. He can't be wet and cold.

"Mom and Dad are looking for you," I tell him.

He shakes his head. The action seems like a burden. "It rained."

I look up. Branches divide the sunlight. "No, it didn't. Follow me home, would you? Everyone's waiting."

His eyes protrude, wrought with fright when my hand reaches out to him. His mouth drops open in a soundless scream.

"Eli?" I step forward. He makes a quick turn and bounds between the trees. I take chase, hurdling over fallen branches, but lag behind due to thistly bushes. The dry pine needles that blanket the ground prick my legs and feet. "Stop!" He looks over his shoulder, defiant as a teen full of angst. His face softens, sharp only when I focus on specific parts—eyes, lips, nose—but never completely intact. "Please stop!"

He finally listens, taking an easy jog before ending his flight. I stop a few feet away, bending forward with my hands on my knees to catch my breath.

"Salem."

I lift my head to meet hollow cheeks and raven-black pupils that have leaked through gray irises like an oil spill. My words knot between mind and mouth. Not even a grunt will form in my throat.

Please, please, let me talk to him!

He senses I'm troubled and comes closer, raising three fingers inches from my eyes. They change into cardinal feathers, a brilliant red, slowly molting to the ground. I ask if he's alive and when he's coming home. But every question is repressed.

I kneel in the grass, no longer in the forest, but on the side of Grady Murphy's house, in tears that he can't hear me.

"Salem." He knocks on the cabin window, his nose against the glass to see if anyone's home. "Salem?"

I'm here. I'm behind you.

"Salem?"

Eli, I'm here!

He opens the window, pulling himself up and over the windowsill.

Don't go in. Don't go!

He looks out from the inside, young again, with cute baby cheeks and icy-gray eyes identical to mine.

"Salem"—but that voice, that deep voice isn't his—"you're dead."

•   •   •

I wake with a gasp for air, drenched in sweat.

3:33

The only light in the room comes from the glowing red numbers on my bedside clock.

3:33

I pull my comforter to my neck and stare at the ceiling, hearing a creaky floorboard overhead.

3:33

The voice in the dream wasn't Eli's—it was Nate's.

ELEVEN

Low clouds smother the property. The day is cold and drizzly. Ollie runs free, sniffing every tree in the forest. He needs a bath when we get back to the lodge. Maybe two since his tan fur is painted dark brown from rolling in syrupy mud. And after cleaning Olls, I have an endless list of housework to face before the next train of guests arrives. I can't stay out with Nate for long. It will be a full house with Virginia staying an extra day, and four rooms reserved for people I believe are in town for the Tilford Lake Quilt Festival. I can't think of much else that would bring in a group of older women for two nights. It's not like Tilford Lake is a draw for seniors.

"Dregs of the day, that's all it was. I have dreams like that all the time." Nate assures me that my nightmare isn't a sign of impending doom. "The fog, keys, feathers, my voice, and being at the cabin … your mind sorts through what you saw during the day. Then it discards all the junk it doesn't want to store. Dreams are like cleaning up a desktop or trashing photos on your cell. You know?"

"No, not really." Hard to tell if I missed something in my high school classes, or I'm lost because I didn't go to college. Most of what I know I learned from Connor. "How do you know?" I ask.

"Dream Interpretation 101," he says, matter-of-fact. "One of those easy A's, like my art and communication classes. GenEd requirements. Boring as shit."

Nate's the ultimate tonic for the below average men I've dealt with. The guys my ex-husband brought to our house were proof that evolution *can* go in reverse. Their silos were lacking grain. Conversations centered on wrestling and reality TV, beer and breasts, never anything of substance, never dreams or family.

"How about the Fred Flintstone shirt? My dad didn't own anything like that or have spiky hair. And why were the faces blurry?"

"I don't know about the shirt. Years back you could've seen someone wearing one. Vague faces are common though. Aggravating, isn't it? Hard to focus on a face in a dream." He uses his flannel shirt sleeve to wipe raindrops off his forehead. "My dad died when I was a kid, and I can't see his face when I'm dreaming *or* awake, doesn't matter which. But I remember we have the same eyes and nose when I look at photos. Same chin." He stops and puts his hand on my shoulder. "Can you picture your family now?"

I think for a moment. "No." A frown. "Details, a mouth, a nose, but not an entire face all at once."

"Good thing we have photos then." He keeps walking.

"Yeah, good thing." I keep walking.

I lower the umbrella closer to my head as a gust of wind puts a significant slant on the rain. I regret wearing chunky-heeled rain boots. It's hard enough to walk through the muck in hiking boots, but far worse in boots without a treaded sole. The mud glues to my heel with each step, making me second-guess my outfit.

On the other hand, Joss gave the black dress and boots two thumbs up before she left for work, asking if I was going to a fancy brunch or I had finally gotten laid. "It was only a kiss," I said. A kiss that lingered on my lips for hours, meaningful enough to awaken something that's been dormant for years. One of those kisses that kept me licking my lips throughout the night, clinging to his taste. But still, "Just a kiss," I told her.

Joss knows better. She saw the spring in my step, the glow on my cheeks, the fire in my eyes—all the romantic after-the-first-kiss clichés that happen to me. She knows what it means when I dress up. This outfit screams *come and get me*. Not a bad thing, just stupid when it's in the low fifties. Tights, pants, even a pair of sweats would've been better than letting the rain run down my pale legs. My Sparrow hoodie over the dress helps to shake off the chill in the air. Without it, I'd feel naked. But I could've done better. Skintight jeans or leggings would've been fine. Just as sexy. Except, I thought my short cotton dress … well, easy access.

I step over Nate's empty rum bottle from last night, never asking why we're heading to the cabin. No need. It was a given we'd be out here today, even if neither of us knows what for. Any clues are likely gone, buried in mold and mouse droppings, washed away, or lifted by the gusty Tilford Lake winds. But even with all the rot, maybe there's something only I might recognize, something everyone else missed.

Years back, my dad said the only witnesses to Eli's disappearance must have been the pines. But Grady was out here. He was in these pines. There's always a slight chance we'll find something. It's not necessarily a waste of time. And Nate. Nate's kiss convinced me that spending the afternoon with him isn't a waste of time. Daydreaming about slipping my hand under his gray flannel to unbutton his jeans and reach my fingers down low isn't a waste of time, surely.

"Not talking much today?" He squeezes my hand.

"Sorry. I've got a lot on my mind."

"No kidding." His piercing blue eyes look down at me, causing my stomach to flip-flop like a shored fish.

"I'm worried about leaving Jim alone at the lodge." True. It's another thing to fret over, even if it wasn't what I was thinking a second ago.

"Don't be. Joss was walking crooked this morning. No question what they were up to all night."

"And?"

"And when Jim takes a woman to bed, he spends the next day sound asleep."

"Oh."

"Don't sound so disappointed. I can call Jim's cell and wake him up if you want."

"No."

"You sure?"

I nod.

I'm jealous, not disappointed. Jealous that the two of them spent the night together when Nate and I didn't.

"It's fine. Let him sleep." I raise my umbrella, looking ahead.

Keeping an eye on Ollie roaming the somber landscape is a challenge. A glut of earth tones masks him from sight. His wagging tail is the only blip on the terrain that gives away his whereabouts.

"Does Jim do that a lot?" I ask, starting down the hill toward the cabin.

"Fuck, or sleep?" Nate jokes.

"Fuck," I say, my voice direct.

"More than me." He takes the umbrella from my hand and holds it over us, his other hand on my back. His hair is drippy, ends curling over his ears.

"Meaning?"

"More than me."

"Thought you wanted to talk?"

"Not about Jim's sex life."

"Okay, agreed. Tell me how you guys met."

"He's my cousin."

"Really?" I move closer to his side, fingering the cord to Eli's key on my neck to make sure the knot is still tight.

"Yep."

"You don't look alike."

"Do we have to?"

"I guess not. Doubt I look like my cousins."

He smiles and slips his hand under my hoodie, rubbing my back. "My aunt had Jim a couple of months after I was born. We grew up together, best friends in Vinland Falls. But he's going through a rough patch right now."

"What happened?"

"Lost his job, his woman, *and* his dog."

"Ouch."

"I know. I've been trying to help him out, at least on the job front. I'm worried that his tat addiction and obsession with buying crap online will put him in debt. I never met a man who likes to spend money as much as Jim."

"What did he do?"

"He was a mechanic."

"I meant to lose his job."

We stop a few feet from the cabin. Nate surveys a dead oak tree and a large branch that has punctured the roof. There's a sizable hole in the door, the windows are broken, and the front steps are uneven.

"He got in an argument and pushed a guy to give him a scare. But the guy fell into an open tool chest. Now Jim's having a hard time finding another garage that will take him in. Word spreads fast in Vinland Falls, probably like it does here."

"So he's *not* a private detective."

"A tagalong for now. Good at paperwork and making calls. I give him the boring jobs that I hate."

"But you're one, right?"

"Yep, certified and licensed. I went to school for police science. Then shadowed a guy for a year before I set off on my own."

"You like it?"

"Love it. But not legal or financial work, I only take on personal cases, like tracking down long-lost family members and chasing husbands."

I look up at him. "Only husbands, not wives?"

"It's mostly women who think their husbands are cheating, not the other way around."

"Guess men just don't care."

"Or they're oblivious. Women pay more attention to things than men do." He sets his lips firm, winning brownie points with me.

"Huh, I could've used you a few years back," I say, not going into details. Even when he casts a sideways glance, my lips stay sealed about my ex-husband and his bimbo.

"What the hell am I gonna do with this place?" Nate asks.

I take a hard look at Grady's cabin. It's simple, boxy, something that a child might draw: front door square in the middle with a window on each side, stone chimney, an addition on the back that could've been a bedroom. The primitive home seems small for Grady, his wife, *and* their adopted daughter. Then again, the private quarters at the lodge are no bigger, and five of us lived there.

"We going in?" I ask.

"In a sec."

A sec is good, but minutes would be better since my feet won't move. Yesterday I was the daring woman, put my hand on the windowsill and peered inside, got close enough to get a whiff of the wet wood. Then. Eli's nightmare. Judging from the fact that my nail-biting habit is rearing its ugly head in front of Nate, the dream hit a raw nerve. And even if it makes me look mousy, I can't stop biting.

The fight to suppress *Candy-ass Salem* has been an ongoing battle. I'm the girl who was kept submissive by her husband, who was a victim of verbal abuse and easily deceived, who felt like a failure for becoming another twenty-something divorcee. A statistic. Like Connor said, "I let you win because you're a girl." *Girl* meant I was handicapped. *Girl* meant my husband was in charge. *Girl* is a conditioning word in a small town to be a shrinking violet, a cycle hard to break. So I continuously debate, weak or tough? Then wonder if a girl has to be one or the other. Can't she be both, depending on the situation? And why can't she just BE without having to worry about it? My daily struggle, maybe something I'll figure out by the time I'm thirty ... or forty.

"Nate, let's go in." Confident Salem crops up.

"Stay here." He passes the umbrella, a hand up to keep back. But I don't. I follow right on his heels.

He stops short of the porch, hesitant.

"What are you doing?" I ask.

"Listening."

I wait. Twist my lips. Lift a leg to scratch the back of my calf with my boot. "I don't hear anything."

"Good."

"This is what you did last night? Stood out here and listened?"

"Shh." Nate's face is drawn in, an ashen color.

"Are you afraid?" I whisper.

"Yes." He climbs the steps, black work boots thick with mud.

"Why?" I chase after him.

"Forget it. Not important."

"Of course it is."

"It's foolish."

"Try me."

I figure he's about to shut me down, tell me to drop it. Instead, he cups my chin firm and waits for our eyes to meet.

"Salem, I'm afraid of the past, not the present. Dumb, right?"

"No, I was just thinking the same thing."

He offers a half-grin. "Ever been inside?"

"No." I turn to the cabin.

A hint of mold and the faint tang of skunk linger from under the porch. The wooden door shows years of damage with dimples and scratches, waterlines along the bottom, and a softball-sized hole next to the handle. It's unlocked and open a crack.

My thought of the lodge resembling a haunted house is way off. This is more like it.

Nate puts his hand on the door and gets ready to push it open. "Salem ..." My name breaks apart.

"What?"

"The bones ..."

"What bones?"

"If you see bones ... they're not Eli's."

• • •

"Animal bones. They were Grady's fetish," Nate says, opening closet doors, kitchen cabinets, sliding out drawers. "He'd remove the flesh in front of me at the strangest times, like when I was eating dinner or in the tub."

"In the tub?" I smile with unease. "He was in there with you?"

"In the room. Someone always watched me when I took a bath. And when it was his turn to babysit, he'd bring the bones, sit on the toilet, and clean 'em."

"That's morbid. How old were you?"

"Young. From the time I was born until I was about six, seven maybe. And he cleaned them for years after that. I hated it."

"I bet."

"It was easier to watch when I ate. But seeing him remove the flesh when I was naked, it was like I could feel it, feel my flesh tugging off. Something to do with the way he looked at me, studying my face for way too long." Nate spreads his thumb and forefinger across his jawline and fingers his bones. "He'd look in the mirror at his deformity, then down at me. Sometimes I'd turn my back and pretend he wasn't there. He'd say, 'Boy, turn around and be a man. Look at your granddaddy.' "

As much as I want to comfort him, I hold still for now, hanging on his words.

"He'd put the bones in a pot of water and leave it in the living room, near where I slept." He points to the corner of the room. "The cabin had a stench after a few days that made my eyes water. Maybe it's why my grams got ill." His voice comes out pained. He's upfront about all this, an openness I haven't found outside my family and Joss.

"Then what?" I whisper.

"He'd dump the water outside in the garden and fill the pot up again, over and over until the water stopped getting rank. After that, he'd scrub the bones in the sink, then soak them in hydrogen peroxide to make them white."

I make a noise in the back of my throat. He meets it with a cold blink, waiting to see if I'm going to speak before he continues.

"After drying them outside for a few days, he'd spread them out on the porch on a leather cloth."

"Like a ritual?"

He nods. "My mom said they were for healing."

"For your grandma?"

"No, for him. I'm pretty sure for his face."

"Oh … that's sad."

He walks a circle in the middle of the room, kicking empty beer cans. "I don't see any now. All his stuff is gone. Looks like people are using the cabin as a party house."

"High school kids." With the cans, condom wrappers, cigarette butts, and smashed windows, I'm surprised the kids haven't burned the cabin down for fun. "Have any good memories of him?"

"No."

"That was quick. Don't you even want to think about it?"

I know Grady was cruel. I can hear the twinge in Nate's voice when he says his name, heard it when he mentioned he hit him with a belt. It's obvious Grady's tunneling into him, working his way under his skin now that we're here.

"I never gave him a 'World's Best Granddad' shirt, if that's what you mean. He was a lonely, distant drunk. I told myself I wasn't going to be like him. Guess that's not working out so well."

"You're not like him."

"In a way I am. He drank at night, said it helped him sleep."

"Yeah, but … did he hit your mom or grandma?"

"No, not women. I think just me because I didn't listen."

"You were just a little boy."

"I was a bratty kid. And I understand why he did it."

"Don't make excuses for him."

He shrugs, staring straight ahead at the living room wall. "If you got spit at, called a monster, had dog shit thrown at you, wouldn't you be livid? I know it's why he drank. And I know when he saw me, a boy with a normal face, he wanted to hurt me."

His words choke me. *A boy with a normal face, he wanted to hurt me.*

"And what about Eli?" I whisper.

"Grady wouldn't kill a kid."

"Why not? He killed animals. He hit you."

"A lot of people are hunters and smack their kids around, that doesn't make them murderers." He steps closer to the wall, his hand chest-high on one of the logs. "I came back to prove it so I can sleep again."

"That's what I thought. What you say and think are two different things."

He holds up a finger, quieting me the way Connor always did when he read. My dad did the same. He'd stand at the edge of the forest at nightfall, his eyes closed, ears pinned back, hushing us so he could listen. That's Nate right now. He's like a Whitfield.

"I'd sleep on the couch each night, but this wall kept me awake. It used to whisper." My silent feet come up behind him. "It spoke every night. A bunch of incoherent nonsense from a drunken old man."

"Grady was out here with you during the night?"

"No."

"Then where?"

"In here." He taps the wall.

I put my hand next to his. The cold wood is pitted like it was struck several times with a hammer. He follows the length of the log with his fingertips, moving across mine, stepping behind me to get past. I duck to let him through, my fingers tracking his from living room, to kitchen, to hall, where he stops and stares at the bedroom.

"Nate, he was there. Not *in* the wall, but back in the bedroom. That's what you heard. I bet he was talking to your grandma."

"No, he was closer."

"Noises are amplified when the rest of the world is asleep."

"I'm not crazy, Salem."

"I didn't say—"

He heads to the bedroom with his fingertips still on the wall like a kid running a stick along a fence. He stops in front of the bedroom closet, the bi-fold doors leaning inward and off their tracks. I help move them out of the way, and behind, a sheet of black mold covers the interior drywall of the closet.

Nate feels the back wall. He points out a dark line of mold in a distinct outline of a door. He sets his palms against the wall and pushes inward. My heart holds its beats in expectation. I hear a click, and a section lowers an inch. He tries to slide the section to the left, then right, with no luck.

I feel the top of the door. There's a bolt in the middle, attached to the ceiling.

"It doesn't slide. It spins," I say, forcing one side until it shifts a little. The bottom gets jammed on the sloping floor where the foundation has settled. He helps me push it, the door scraping floorboards as it revolves. I take a step back, waving a cloud of dust and the stench of dead animal away. "Nasty." I cough.

"Yep." He puts his shirt sleeve over his nose and mouth. We use our phone screens to light the space. There's just enough room inside for two people to stand. "This must be his safe," Nate says. "There're notches added to the wall for his shotguns."

"And vile filth I wouldn't want anyone to come across." I flip through a musty stack of decades-old porno mags and pick up a few ancient VHS tapes. *Riding Rita, Patty Down Under, Stacy's Big Surprise,* setting them down as quickly as I picked them up. "These are awful, Nate."

He shines his cell onto the pile. "I don't know about that. *Patty Down Under* might have a decent plot." He laughs.

"Riiight. I'm sure it's full of hot action, complete with a killer soundtrack. *Bow-chicka-bow.*"

He laughs harder, moving the light up and down each wall. "You shouldn't be touching those if you don't know where ... they've..." His voice drags, eyes set hard above the door.

Looking up, I see a tissue box on a ceiling joist. I stand on my tiptoes to reach for it, but Nate grabs my hand.

"Let me. Might be bones," he whispers.

I study his expression to see if he's worried. He stands tall before me with watery eyes and a twitchy nose from the pungent odors in the tiny space.

"But not bones of a boy," I whisper back, clutching Eli's key.

He exhales a long breath, resting his hand on my shoulder. "Go check on Ollie. I'll make sure it's not more of Grady's porn collection, or lube, or any trash like that."

I shake my head, not about to walk away from my brother.

"It's not him, Salem. The box is too small."

"Then I'll stay."

TWELVE

I slump against the living room wall in my private quarters, the tissue box tight against my chest. When I was a kid, I wasn't aware of much happening within the family other than the event with Eli. Broken bones, arguments, lack of money, or a missing cat. These significant events to some kids were meaningless to me. Nothing outweighed that one experience. Is it any wonder why I never knew my granddad was close to Grady Murphy? At least, close enough to exchange an ample amount of letters, enough to fill a tissue box.

And now the only written words I have of my granddad, besides a few birthday and holiday cards, are these letters. Everything else was lost in the fire.

A timid knock, I swing my head to the door, knowing it's Nate. Hard to believe he and Jim are pitching in, vacuuming and doing a mound of laundry, while I'm standing here in a daze. For the first time in years I'm suffering from Sparrow Lodge fatigue, still needing to bathe Ollie, make the beds, order more packages of coffee and tea. I wish it could all wait. I want to take a breather to read these letters, and *not* while I'm working this evening. I need a block of time without any interruptions. Time to myself. Time to cry, if necessary. But it seems improbable tonight with the daylight sky turning purple and four o'clock approaching.

A second knock, louder this time. "Salem?"

Ollie prances to the door, leaving a trail of dried mud balls on the floor. His tail wags, one paw up on the wood as a greeting to his new pal on the other side. I should let Nate in. I'm acting selfish, insisting I get to read the letters first.

"Yeah?" I say, cemented to the wall.

"Open the door so we can talk."

"Ollie needs a bath. I'm running out of time."

"Just open it for a sec. I wanna ask you something."

He wants the letters. We discussed this walking back to the lodge. They're his property, found at his place, sent to his granddad. However, my granddad wrote them. They came from my family. These letters will remain snug to my chest forever, just like the logo I wear over my heart each day. They're that special.

"What if there's a dark family secret I don't want anyone to know about?" I ask, walking toward the door.

"Like what? You think Grady and your granddad were lovers?" Nate shushes Jim when he laughs at the comment. "That's not what's on my mind, beautiful. I wanna ask you a question. Face to face."

Ollie steps back to give me his spot. I lay my hand on the door, Nate's energy surging through it.

"Salem." He breathes.

His scent seeps into me. The second I unlock the deadbolt, he rushes in and backs me up against the wall.

"Hi," he whispers. A thirst slips from his mocha lips as he digs his fingertips into the back of my thighs. I close my eyes in anticipation of a kiss. "You look hot today." His hand drifts under my dress, fingers traveling up and into the bottom of my silk undies. "Sexier than when you wore that orange bikini as a kid."

"That so?" I smile.

"Yep." His breath heats my neck. He presses forward, the tissue box a barrier between our chests. "I should've told you that earlier, out there in the rain under the trees ... maybe slipped my tongue into your mouth ... slipped it other places."

"Nate..."

"But the time wasn't right." He strokes my cheek.

This touch is what I want. This closeness. This was my plan all along: an easy access outfit served up with a dash of patience.

"Have dinner with me tonight."

"I can't. I have to be here from four to eleven for check-in."

"You can do both."

"You're whipped," Jim calls from the laundry room.

Nate, his eyes set on me, kicks the door closed to shut Jim out.

"How?" I ask.

"Dinner. Upstairs. I'll leave my door open so you can hear if someone's in the lobby."

"So you're saying *I'm* dinner. Is that the plan?"

He grins. "Promise, a *real* dinner. Come upstairs at six."

I'm skeptical, but I love the way his eyes smile when he looks at me. "Is lobster on the menu?"

"I'll do my best." He guides my hand over his erection.

"Takeout?" I tease.

He steps back and gives me a seductive look. "If you want to take it out, I'm game."

He opens the door and walks out, closing it between us. Footfalls leave me behind.

"Quick Ollie, to the bathroom buddy. I've got a lot to do." I set the box down. "Bath, then letters, then Nate." I lock the door. "Bath, letters, Nate." Ollie jogs alongside me to the tub. "Hurry, Olls. Bath, then letters, then Nate."

My cell rings as I'm warming the water. I pull it from my hoodie pocket, scrunching my nose at the name.

"We'll let that one go to voicemail."

I ignore the second call. The third gets on my nerves. By the fourth, I give in, answering in a huff.

"What do you want, Brad?"

"Officer Brenner."

"Stop it. I've called you Brad since we were kids."

"Salem…"

"Hold on."

I set my cell on the floor and lift Ollie into the tub. He holds his tail down low. Poor guy.

He suffers through a few cups of water poured over his back without a whimper.

"Salem, you there?" Brad shouts.

"Wait," I say down to the phone. I put a dab of almond-scented doggy shampoo in my palm and massage it into Ollie's back, down his legs, and under his belly.

"Salem!"

"Okay." I pick up my cell with a sudsy hand, sedately rubbing Ollie with the other. "What?"

"Can I get you to listen for a minute?"

"Yeah, go 'head."

He's suddenly quiet. For as long as I've known Brad, this is the first phone conversation we've had without him crunching, gulping, swallowing, or burping.

"I'm listening."

He clears his throat. "I'm sorry about yesterday."

"You should be." I grin.

"Hey, it's not easy."

"What, being a cop?"

"No, being called out to the lodge all the time."

"Like I said, being a cop. It's your job to help—"

"Salem … Connor was my best friend."

I stop washing Ollie. My head lowers to the edge of the tub.

A bottle cap twists, a fizz, a swig, followed by a lengthy sigh.

"Connor was my *only* friend. We were dorks back in high school. Or at least I was … a fat kid with pimples and bad hair. Remember the bowl cut my mom always gave me? I didn't win over any girls with that look. It sucked. Guys gave me wedgies and titty twisters. Connor was the only one who took the time to talk to me. He let me come over and be his friend."

"He didn't *let* you, Brad. He wanted you here. He liked you."

"Exactly. He liked me, and I miss the hell outta him. So it's hard to turn down the driveway to the lodge every week."

I know all of this. And I admit, sometimes I've overreacted and called in a needless complaint to Brad so I could see a familiar face. Maybe some part of me thought Brad needed the same. To be here, to see me, but I guess I was wrong.

"You're not the only one who lost him," he says.

"I know."

"Then stop torturing me. Stop calling me out for pointless shit, all right?"

His voice splits like the heart sign out front, a break straight down the middle. He's more upset than I thought.

"I didn't realize it was such a big deal."

He takes a long pull on his drink. "It is."

"But we were friends, too. I'd like to stay in touch."

"Oh."

"Oh? What does that mean?"

"Salem … look, there's something I should've asked … uh … a long time ago." He gets the words out between swallows. "Do you … you wanna go out sometime?"

"Excuse me?" I cover my mouth, a mix of surprise and disgust.

"To Martin's for a beer."

"W-wow. Where did that come from?"

"What?"

"Bradley Brenner, you *can't* be serious. Is this what's going on? You're jealous, aren't you? Jealous that two hot guys are here."

He hangs up.

"Damn him. Damn you, Brad!"

Ollie looks back, shivering. I rinse him off and bundle him in a fleecy towel. His sodden fur is dirt-free and back to its pretty tan and cream colors. "Looking good, Olls. A kiss on the head and you're all set." I unwrap the towel and he trots to my bedroom. He climbs his doggy stairs to the bed and shakes out his fur. Water droplets land on my comforter, matching the rain spattering against the old window.

I pick up the tissue box from the hall and join him on the bed. "Here we go, Olls," I say, a bit frazzled, but wholly excited that I have a few minutes to read some of the letters. I rub my palms together and take a shallow breath. "Here we go."

• • •

Grady,

Checking in, my friend. Haven't heard hide nor hair from you or Gert since I dropped off the treasure hunt flyers. Come across anything? Sure you'd tell me. I know my grandson's all I talk about now. Must be tiring for the two of you, but you're good to let me share. It won't be long until he's home. Then we'll have a beer and kick back like the good ol' days, maybe argue about the Paula Jones case, or gripe over skyrocketing gas prices. Can you believe it? $1.20? Outrageous! We're doomed when a cup of Joe hits the dollar mark. When that happens, the four of us should leave civilization behind and live a laid-back life in the mountains. Have we done that yet? Perhaps not. Not as far as we were once hoping to go. Remember when we were kids and we ran away from home, spent a week hiking along the lake? We said we'd never return to the hubbub of town. What happened to those adventurous lads from the fifties? Sure, we're out here, but are we roughing it? Tell me what you think, Grady. Gert and Carol get our food from that big chain grocery, and we can't live without our TVs or our cars. Carol was even talking about buying a computer. She has some cockamamie idea that we need something called dial-up Internet to talk to people. Do you know what that is? Talk to who? Why can't we pick up the telephone to talk to our friends? What's the world coming to? Do people no longer write letters? How impersonal have we become? It's a ruse. Do you feel the same? I want to know.

I'm laughing about it and crying at the same time.

Crying, Grady, always crying.

Felix

•   •   •

A shimmer passes through me as I straighten my shoulders and pick up the next letter.

•   •   •

Grady,

Haven't heard back. Should I stop by? I know you hate surprise visits, but Carol and I are worried. At least return my calls when you get a chance. What are you doing out there? Is Gert okay? Hope she's still making that delicious borscht.

Sorry to always be the bearer of bad news, but did you hear about Annie Merchant? Went down to Florida to visit her kids and was dragged to the bottom of a pond by a gator. Egads, what a horrible way to go. Carol hasn't been in the lake since she got the news, won't even go in the backyard, convinced someone's pet gator may have escaped and is living in the water. She's phobic of *everything since we lost Eli. And I suppose I've been looking over my shoulder a bit more myself.*

I have some good news, though. The flyers I made are working. My son said they've had a few guests search the forest for the 'Whitfield Treasure.' A man found a child's T-shirt, but it was too big to be Eli's. Maybe it's your grandson's. Is he still out there with you? Keep an eye on him. Next year, when our bones aren't so rattled, I'll tell Connor about Nate, send him out that way to have a playmate. They're the same age. Good boy, our Connor, doubt he'll make your hair turn gray. He'll keep his visits a secret so you don't get other people on your property. But in time, not this year, it's still too soon for our grandkids to be in the forest alone. Another year or two.

Well then, if I don't hear from you, I'm going to drop by on Friday. Fair warning, I'm bringing a 6-pack and a couple of cans of sardines. I'll catch you up on what the Tilford Lake gossipmongers are saying down at the marina. Big news about John Engle and another knee surgery.

Felix

• • •

I place the letter over my heart, my granddad's presence in the room, nudging me to keep reading. His past is weaving into the present to speak to me, to help guide Nate and me, to release the lost stories of his life. How many people get this chance?

I'm closer than I was yesterday. Closer to where I want to be tomorrow. I'm closer to deciphering secrets and unraveling haunting dreams, closer to Granddad Felix, to Connor, and to Eli.

THIRTEEN

Nate and Jim are eavesdropping on my conversation with Joss. I lean alongside the lobby desk, eyes up to the balcony, smiling at Nate as he looks over the wooden railing.

"He asked you out?" Joss freaks. "Brad Brenner asked you out for a drink? Does he not remember asking me out a year ago? Do guys not understand they can't prey on best friends like that?"

"I feel kind of bad for him."

"He's a creep."

"I know. He tries too hard." I slide my hand down my dress to smooth out the wrinkles.

"Nail polish?" Joss whispers. "Super sexy, babe." She slicks her lips with her favorite plum lipstick and puckers them at Jim, an invitation to come down to the lobby. It's a call he can't resist.

My nail polish is still tacky. I place my hands on the desk, splaying my fingers to admire the deep burgundy paint job, the color of fall maple trees. "The last time I wore nail polish must've been before my mom died. We always tried to match." I blow on my fingernails, thinking back to the first time she painted them— a crisp October morning when my grandma took Connor and me to Clayton Winery for an open house. We wore our sexless Sparrow Lodge sweatshirts and wool pants, walking advertisements for the lodge. My mom wanted my nails to look pretty so I'd stand out from my brother, to call attention to the fact that I'm a girl. She brushed on a golden-yellow color, and said that with the black sweatshirt I could pretend to be a bumblebee. I was thrilled, thrilled because, without it, my brother and I looked like twins.

Of course, my mom was mostly a wreck, no one ever needed to ask why, but those small gestures were always comforting. They're what made her a cool mom.

"He's keyed up," Jim says. "Haven't seen him this nervous about a woman since … well, never. Women usually chase after him, not the other way around."

Embarrassed, I turn to Joss. "Call up if you need anything."

"Girl, please. I can check people in and watch this place with my eyes closed." She smiles, and I signal to wipe a spot of lipstick off her teeth. "Thanks," she says.

I gather my granddad's letters and head upstairs. Nate's no longer on the balcony, but his door is open. I spy the downturned bed inside. On the small table next to the window, three lit candles flicker onto peanut butter and jelly sandwiches and a bottle of rum. He *did* make dinner.

"Salem." My name, soft whispered, comes from the direction of Virginia's room. Her bony fingers prowl into the hallway and wave me closer. I head through the dark hallway of the navy night, leaving behind the warm glow of Nate's room.

"Hi," I greet her from the doorway.

"Don't be shy. Come in." She's securing the delicate stems of crocus flowers to twigs, piecing them into a wreath with the help of twist ties. "What do you think?" She places it on her head, gesturing to the work of art like she's showing off the grand prize on a game show—a new car, a trip to Hawaii, a speedboat—only better, a gem, *her* gem. It's not a wreath; it's a crown.

After a shaky turn on her spindly legs, she takes it off and places it on my head. "Crocuses repel strong liquor odors. Take a whiff. Can you smell rum?"

I sniff. "No."

"Good, it works."

I remove the crown and set it on the bed. The soft mound of white reminds me of fresh snowfall in the forest.

"My first husband was an alcoholic. The stench bites into my stomach, but this should help me sleep," she says.

"You smell liquor in the lodge?"

"I have a nose for it." She points toward Nate's room. "He's handsome, but certainly looks don't make the man. That poor soul has a weak aura from all the liquor seeping out of his pores. And that weight he carries must come from his family's buried secrets. As does my weight and yours." She takes my hands and studies my palms like she did the other morning, tracing the lines, grimacing like something's wrong. "You've been married?"

"Yes."

"Divorced or are you cheating?"

"Divorced." I smile. "I hate cheaters."

She nods. "Good. And he was handsome?"

"I thought so."

"Anything else?"

"Meaning what?" I love her insatiable curiosity.

"Besides his looks, was he special? Did he offer you anything for a fulfilling life?"

I think about Steven and his constant need to be right. How I had no power. How he had to be the center of attention and the top dog amongst his friends. All because he had some worry or insecurity, when in reality, I'm the one who should've been worried. But lack of experience due to age is a handicap, blinding at times. It took me years to see the light.

"No need to answer, Salem. I'm not the one who needs to know, you do."

"I've figured it out, that's why I'm divorced."

A quiet laugh parts her thin, wrinkled lips. After a gentle pat on my forearm, she picks up the crocus crown and examines the ties with a satisfied smile. "These little flowers are also known to awaken love. Was lining your driveway with them planned?"

"Yes, by my grandparents." I return to the important subject. "So you think Nate has secrets?"

"Nate?" she asks.

I thumb toward his room.

"That name doesn't suit him. You can start there. Ask him who he is."

"It's Nathan Harlow. I saw his ID."

Joss giggles then bursts into laughter, as if Jim's tickling her. I look down the hallway and back at Virginia, making eye contact to apologize for my boisterous friend.

"It's fine," she says, "I made this for her. She needs love. Honest-to-goodness love and romance in her life, not just a bedmate."

Virginia is either a snoop or a psychic.

She steps into the hallway with the crocus crown and waits for me to follow. I close her door on my way out, and we walk together toward the balcony.

"Are you clairvoyant? Or were you like, a medium or something?" I ask, half-joking, half-serious.

"No, a live mannequin." Her voice warbles from age. She leers down to the lobby at Joss.

"Is that what it sounds like?" I ask.

"Yes, a live mannequin for window displays in New York City. I started in the sixties and retired twenty years ago."

"I never heard of such a thing."

"Most people haven't."

I picture her as a young woman standing in a store window, modeling clothing, her face caked in makeup, taking leaden breaths while listening to the world go by.

"I don't have the patience to sit still for long," I say.

Joss breaks free from Jim's greedy hold when she sees us. She mouths *sorry,* and I wave a hand for her not to worry.

"My friend would also suck at it."

"No, she fits the part. The outgoing ones mingled with the customers. I was one of the few who chose to be a statue."

"Sounds lonely."

She rests her hand over mine on the balcony railing. "Not so much. We had regulars who I watched for years. People I knew everything about—when their children married or a grandchild was born—but I never existed to them. Never seen nor heard. Just a fly on the wall." A pause. She looks at Nate's room for a second, then returns to me. "Not lonely, Salem. I was lucky. I knew people's deepest secrets without having to get involved. I saw men shopping for their wives. Then they'd come back another day to shop for their mistresses. I watched some of the wealthiest women in the city shoplift piddly items for no reason, other than for excitement. That's how they spruced up their dull lives. I'd say they were the lonely ones, not me."

"Fascinating."

Nate appears in his doorway, hands behind his back, leaning against the doorjamb. I meet his gaze and offer a coy smile, holding up a finger that I'll be a minute.

Virginia hooks her arm in mine and ushers me closer to the railing for privacy. "That man you like is afraid of what the truth might bring," she whispers, holding the crown like it's a newborn baby. I mimic her pose with my granddad's letters, keeping them close to my chest.

"Do you think he's dangerous?" I whisper back, looking over my shoulder at him.

"No, dear. He thinks you are."

"Me? Why me?"

"That, you'll have to figure out yourself." She pinches my cheek and heads down the stairs.

Joss smacks her gum as Virginia approaches, but the two pass without exchanging words. Joss sits across from Jim by the fire, and Virginia retreats to the sitting room.

"Psst," Nate prods. "You ready?"

I nod with a smile, running my hand across his waist as I step past him and inside. Without pause, the door closes and locks. "I thought you were gonna leave it open?" I tease, facing the bed, hearing him approach from behind. "Eager?"

"That's putting it mildly."

His breath emerges in gasps, fast and hard like when he was working out on the swings. He steps closer, moving the hair off the nape of my neck. "What are—"

"Shh." His teeth nip at the sensitive skin of my earlobe, conquering me without any effort. "I want you, Salem. I can't wait any longer," he whispers. "Let me take you to bed." It's too damn easy to lose myself in his tender touch. "You're so beautiful." His hands wander down my hips and under my dress, my undies hooked and slipped to my ankles. "So, so beautiful." His long fingers move smoothly up my legs.

"Nate"—I swallow hard—"we shouldn't."

"We should." He takes the letters and places them on the dresser. Then. Slowly. He unbuttons his flannel shirt, tempting me with his gorgeous, muscular body. "Give me one good reason why we shouldn't," he says. He holds his shirt to the side and drops it on the floor. "Just one reason, Salem." He steps forward. I moisten my lips and close my eyes. "Nothing? No answer?" A finger traces down the front of my dress and stops low between my legs. He can't wait, not until after dinner, not until after we talk about the letters, not for another minute … and I can't either.

But, I do love playing hard to get.

"One reason, beautiful. Tell me."

"You're leaving in four days."

"And?" He lifts my dress over my head and moans at the sight of my body.

"Because I fall hard for men when I sleep with them."

His lips pet my lips as he unclasps my bra. He slides his hand to my breast, caressing my nipple while his other hand unzips his jeans. "I don't mind if you fall for me. That would be a good thing, wouldn't it?"

"Not if you don't come back."

His thumb swipes my cheek, nudging me to look at him. "Who said I'm not coming back?" He lets a playful smile fly. "We're neighbors, Salem. I own the land behind you. It's not like you'll never see me again."

"God, don't do this to me."

"Do what?" he asks, lightly biting my chin.

"Make me fall for you."

"Then tell me to stop. Tell me you don't like it."

I grab the back of his neck and kiss him ... hard. His tongue explodes, full and warm, slick and excited like he's coming in my mouth. We kick off our shoes and recline on the bed, sharing closed-mouth smiles when our eyes lock.

This is crazy. I wanted to share one of my granddad's letters with him, and what I learned about the treasure. Now I'm so worked up and wet between my legs—my heart pounding, belly curling—that all I want is to be with him, right here, right now. Everything else will have to wait. *Everything.*

"Salem!"

Except.

"Salem, where's the fire extinguisher!"

"What?"

"Salem!" Joss yells.

I bolt out of bed and put on my dress, running down the stairs in a flash. Four of my guests follow, shrieking as they run out the door. "What the hell, Joss? What happened?"

"Where's the fire extinguisher?"

"Where's the fire?"

"One of the logs in the fireplace popped and spat out an ember. Your rug's on fire."

"Where is it?"

"Jim took it outside."

"Shit." I stamp out an ember on the wood floor before dashing to the front door. I pull it open and come face to face with Brad Brenner. "Double shit." I slam the door, appalled, and turn back to Joss. "Did you call Brad?"

"Of course not. Why would I?"

"Because of the fire."

"Salem, it just happened. He wouldn't get here *that* fast. And no, I didn't," she says snappishly.

He opens the door and walks in. Nate appears on the balcony, his shirt off, hair messy like we just fucked. He glares at Brad. Brad glares back.

"What do you want?" I ask. "I have a full house tonight and don't have time to talk."

"Did you know you have a fire out front?"

"Yeah, Brad. I know." My voice is fierce, my hand on my hip. "Joss, it's in my kitchen." She races to my private quarters to get the extinguisher. Brad looks up at the balcony. His legs part in a fighting stance. "Why are you here?" I ask, breaking the fixed stares.

"I wanna question your friend up there." He nods at Nate.

"What about?" Nate says, walking down to the lobby.

Brad steps forward and places his hand on his gun, invading Nate's space.

"What's the problem, Brenner?" Nate asks.

"Just a hunch."

"A hunch about what?"

"How come I can't find any connection to you and Grady. Or you to the Murphy family?"

"Because my mom was adopted. I'm not related to Grady by blood." His upper lip curls in disdain.

"Sure, that must be it."

"Why are you checking me out?"

"How about your mom?"

"My mom?" Nate's voice is tense. "What about her?"

"There's no record of her, not until she started school here in Tilford Lake. Where's she from?"

"Get lost." Provoked, Nate flips his hand toward the door for Brad to get out.

"Wait. Wait a second." I step between them. "Brad, what are you saying?"

"I'm saying it's unusual that the Murphy's adopted a kid without any record of where they got her from. And their adopted daughter has a son with the same background, no record of him before he started grammar school."

"Means nothing," Nate says.

"Okay. What hospital were you born at? I'll check it out."

"I wasn't. She had a midwife."

"That's convenient. How 'bout a birth certificate?"

Joss tears through the lobby with the fire extinguisher. Jim walks inside, his hand up for her to stop.

"It's out," he says, turning to me. "You gotta keep a screen over the fire so this doesn't happen again. The whole place could've burned down."

"I have one." I spot the fireplace screen set off to the side. "Whoever put the last log on forgot to put it back."

Joss holds up her hands that it wasn't her.

I spot the crocus crown on the hearth and wonder if Virginia did it. Then, with doubt, I wonder if it was an accident, or not.

Jim walks over to Nate as a backup for the situation with Brad.

"Brad, this is bad timing," I say. "Call me tomorrow."

"So you don't care about Eli anymore?"

"Of course I do."

"Then hear me out."

"You're talking trash. You know nothing about me or my mom." Nate knocks Brad's shoulder.

"Touch me again, asshole. Go on, touch me again." Brad pushes back, fear evident in his falsetto voice.

"That's enough," I cut in. "Just be upfront with me."

"I am. I'm telling you what I know."

"What you *think* you know." Nate's words pierce the room. "Dumbass."

"Dumbass?" Brad raises a brow. "Excuse me?"

"Time out," I mumble, pulling Brad by his coat sleeve to the front door. "I'll ask him about it," I whisper, "but I don't need a fight in here after everything else."

"It won't be a fight. It'll be an arrest."

"Stop it," I say through clenched teeth. "Call me tomorrow and we'll talk about this in private, but not now. I've got guests outside." He looks down at my chest. I'm braless from the mad dash, and my nipples are hard from the cold air coming through the front door. "Dirty pig." I smack him. "Don't you dare. I'll call Chief and file a sexual harassment complaint if you do that again."

"Nice, Salem. Real nice." He storms out and drops into the driver's seat of his patrol car, flipping me the bird. Snow and stones kick up from the car's rear wheels as he speeds down the driveway to the main road.

I wave my guests inside and warm a pot of tea for them, apologizing numerous times.

"My quilts better not smell like smoke," one says.

"That's right. Better not," says another.

"You all get half off your stay," I say, settling their nerves. They take their tea and march upstairs to their rooms in a huff. I catch snippets of their whispered complaints…

Can you believe this place? … Nincompoops run it… It smells like wet dog and smoke in here … I bet they have bedbugs … You sure this is the only hotel in town?

"It's a lodge, not a hotel," I whisper. "Sparrow Lodge."

"Hey, babe." Joss strokes my arm. "Why don't you finish your—"

"No, I'll stay down here. You can hang out with Jim if you want."

"Sorry," she says.

"It's not your fault. I'm the one who shouldn't shirk my responsibilities for dick." Jim laughs, but Nate's definitely offended. "This is my family's place. I can't forget what that means and why I'm here."

"Why *are* you here?" Nate asks.

"It's my obligation."

"Says who?"

"Says me."

I'm not sure what's happening here, but the sexual tension between us just wilted like a rotting willow tree. Is he angry with me? Or still irritated with Brad? Is he embarrassed by what he just said? Or insecure over what Brad said?

He looks down at the floor, his foot sweeping left, right. Whatever it is, he's not the same confident Nate. Something just bit him.

Wordless, skin pale, he goes upstairs.

"What the hell?" I say, somewhat ambivalent. I turn to Joss and Jim who're sharing a chair by the fire, entwined in each other's arms.

"Bummer," says Virginia.

I jump when she speaks, my heart lodging in my throat. Was she standing next to the reception desk the entire time?

"Is that still an expression?" she asks.

"Yeah." I sigh. "Bummer."

"What happens now?"

I shrug and walk behind the desk to bring my computer out of sleep mode, checking for new reservations. None. "I have some orders to place, and I need to dust the lobby."

"And order a new rug." She smiles.

"That too. I'll place an old one down for now."

She nods. "I'll let you be." She heads for the stairs, stooped over to convey her frail body carries the burden of the day.

"Virginia?"

She ascends the stairs one foot at a time, placing both feet on each step while holding the railing. Old age sucks.

My grandma used to complain that the older she got, the more invisible she became. She said people are blind to the elderly. I think that may be true in Virginia's case. I haven't seen anyone else talk to her since she arrived. It's sad, really.

Jim picks up the crocus crown from the hearth, and Joss ducks for him to place it on her head. I've not only noticed the lust in her eyes but also a spark of magic between them. She plants a kiss on his cheek, *a good omen of things to come.*

"You make this?" he asks. She shakes her head *no,* and a flower falls from the bunch. The recent nightmare of feathers floating from Eli's hand crosses my mind. Jim repositions himself and accidentally steps on it, *a bad omen of things to come.*

I turn back to the stairwell. "Virginia?" I call out.

"Yes, I'm listening."

"You think Nate's related to me? I mean…" That came out wrong. I look up at the dusty Christmas decorations on the beams, then back to watch her measured steps. "Do you have any idea who he is? Do you think he belongs here?"

She pauses on the top landing, using the railing for support. Her eyes roll back as if she's conjuring up an answer from some deep closet of her brain.

"Where a person belongs is a decision they make on their own, it's not about where you're born or who your family is. That man is in the right place if he's happy being here."

Seeming to age another year with each stiff-hipped step, she crosses the balcony toward her room, resting before she enters the hallway. She stares down at me one last time, her eyes red-rimmed, pupils as dark as Eli's were in my dream.

"But from what I've witnessed, Salem. I don't believe any of you belong here."

FOURTEEN

The clock over the reception desk stands at midnight. Sleep has become a challenge since I held Eli's key, examined Connor's stash, found Granddad's letters ... since I fell for a guy who may not even exist.

Nathan Harlow.

Sexually speaking, my desire to be with Nate is more than it ever was with my ex-husband. But should I be suspicious of him like Brad is? Brad, a guy I've known my entire life. Brad, who's becoming a dirty smarmball. Or should I trust my instinct with a guy I barely know, a guy who could be hiding something.

I look up at him. He's drunk. Nate is. Drunk and gawking at me, sitting cross-legged on the opposite end of the grungy rug I lugged out of the storage closet. The rug with juice stains and edges frayed—the moth-eaten, dust-laden rug that needs to be placed over the clothesline and beaten with a broom. It's making my nose twitch, but looks a touch better than the scuffed wood floors, which are sooty from the minor fire.

"Stop staring at me," I whisper.

He hasn't said a word. Besides taking a drink from his beer every so often, picking at the label, and scattering tiny scraps across the rug, he's close to stone-still. Like Virginia said—a fly on the wall—observing without interacting. If he's adamant about staying down here, so be it. Whatever his deal is, I'll act like I just don't care.

My focus turns to the spread on the rug. I have it all laid out: the stash, Granddad's letters, three sparrow keys, Virginia's flowers, *and* a glass of red wine—my aid in the detective work.

I pick up Eli's key, his tiny sparrow the last thing I ever expected to see, not to mention the sentimentality I feel when placing it with the other two. I put them in a line below the three crocus flowers, the fire casting an amber glow on the brass keys and painting the flowers a sunny yellow-orange. My fingers run across the lot, back and forth, trying to awaken the past.

"I understand your part now, Connor." I take a sip of wine. "*Wunderkabinett.*"

I never knew he wanted a display case full of his discoveries from the property. I have my granddad to thank for sharing Connor's plan for his nature collection, and for filling me in on how it came about.

I flip through the letters and slide one to Nate. He unfolds it without preamble. He hasn't bugged me to read them since the walk back to the lodge, but I can tell by the way he dives right in that the wait has been driving him mad.

His face is all shadows except the fire that lights his eyes. I notice slight changes in them as he reads, from hope, to surprise, to grief.

• • •

Grady,

Good to kick back with you last week. You look healthy, better than old Felix Whitfield. I feel ancient. Did you notice my stomach? Carol bought me a pair of them pants with the elastic waistband. Have you seen the commercials? They're on late at night when only us gray-haired men whose minds won't turn off *are awake. Two pairs for $19.95. Two pairs, Grady. The shipping and handling were outrageous, but they fit all right. Call me gullible, go ahead, I'll let ya!*

I told Carol about your bone project. She said you should've been an artist. She remembers you were good at it back in high school. Still could be one, you know. She's sending you the pamphlet for next year's craft festival at the Post. Do show off your work. Does no good sitting in that root cellar of yours. No good at all. You have talent, my friend. Don't keep it hidden. People should know of your gift. You hear me? Come out and play with the rest of us. We're not dead yet. We're smack dab in the middle of it all. The beginning may be over, but we're still far from the end. Ever think about that? What's left? Decades, years, or only days? I'm hoping for decades. I know you, though. You'd say we'll all be dead tomorrow. Cranky pessimist is what you are.

I'm teaching Connor all about it. Life and death. I told him about your project. The bones, the pretend tags you made with obscure animal names, how you pieced them together—the entire display of mythical creatures. What craftsmanship. It piqued the boy's curiosity. I mentioned it takes more than one to have a collection, more than one to start a Wunderkabinett like yours. Not one bone but a pile of them. Whatever he collects, I suggested starting with three, the number of good fortune. But knowing Connor, he'll take it to an extreme. He has one of them heavy-going science brains, a bit of a mystery at times. Not sure what's stirring in that head of his, but I do know he loves finding oddities on the property. A hunter. Unlike game hunters, a different mindset I'd suspect.

I repeated what you said, told him that the story of the objects is more important than the physical objects themselves. That what you say about it may be more meaningful than what people see. He liked that, Grady. The boy is nine, but he's interested in what you're doing. He declared the other day that his

*Wunderkabinett would be the best in the State, a draw to the lodge
if he's allowed to display it in the lobby. A genius, I tell ya. A genius
at nine. At that age, I rode my bike day and night, went fishing,
didn't read much. Have I mentioned that? You remember? Same
with my son, he was athletic, but not his boy. I'm afraid if he
doesn't stop parading around the herbal tea he's concocted from
plants on the property, kids will be calling him a sissy. Tea, Grady.
Not the same herbs we were always after in the sixties.*

*Gotta love him. That's all we can do is love our kids. You get
it? You hear me? I'll spare you my lecture about your grandson.
Just let him be.*

Felix

•   •   •

"Wunderkabinett." Nate smiles. He crawls across the rug to set
the letter back in my hand, then drops his phone in my lap. "Look
at it," he says. I pick it up ... the birth certificate of Nathan
Patrick Harlow is on the screen. "I asked my mom to take a photo
of it to get Brad off my back. What's wrong with that guy?"

"Everything," I mutter. "You don't have to prove—"

"You asked."

"Asked what?" I move a wisp of hair off his forehead.

"Asked Brad what he was getting at, what he meant by not
finding any record of us from when we were young. You asked.
Here's your proof."

"That's why you took off?"

"You were questioning me. I had to think of a way to prove
it to you."

"You don't have to prove a thing. And I *didn't* question
you, Brad did."

"What do you call it then? I saw your face. You have your doubts about who I am."

I shake my head. "Wrong. You're so wrong about that."

The weightless fug of smoke circles us. We exchange unending stares that become apologetic glances. A minute passes. My face feels flush. His eyes covet me, an expression that leads me forward. Reeled in and caught. I try to kiss him, but he turns away with a grin.

"You have to earn it," he says, moving back to my mouth, lips honeyed with drink.

"You tease. You're worse than me."

"Talk to me first. What else is in that stack of letters?"

"A lot. But I haven't read them all. I can't just rip them open all at once."

"I say go ahead and rip 'em open." He teeters back and sits cross-legged again, taking a long pull of beer. "Connor never mentioned his plan for his collection. I would've remembered that."

"Did you ever see Grady's bone collection? As a whole?"

"Nope. Just him cleaning them."

"What about my granddad? You must've met him."

"Not that I recall. What else did he say?"

I slide another letter to him, this one with an even bigger surprise than the last.

• • •

Grady and Gert,

When can Carol and I get another helping of that chili? Fantastic! Or, as my granddaughter would say, 'cool beans.' I don't know if that's the right expression given that the beans were so darn hot, not cool. Perhaps 'awesome opossum' works better. She also says that. Was it opossum chili? Whatever the secret ingredient was, do share. We ate the rest of it today for lunch. The best we've had. Thank you, friends.

I may stop by this week to return the Tupperware and to tell you about this in person. Long story short, one of the guests found a tooth—a child's tooth sitting on top of a tree stump! The tears on our faces when we got the news. The family was in the dark for two days. We kept saying it couldn't be Eli's. It's been too long. Couldn't be his. I was going to ask you to pray for us. Please, friends, pray. Can you believe it? Me of all people, asking for prayers.

Turns out Connor punched his little friend and knocked out a tooth. He got that squirrely Brenner boy good. Connor denies it, won't tell us what the fight was over. Not a peep is coming from that boy. So unlike him. The other one too. His daddy came over about it, wanted to find out what happened. You know anything? You see anything?

Connor's grounded now. You shouldn't see him in the pines again until summer. My son didn't even know he'd been out there. Birdbrained parents. Birdbrained boys. Foolish fight, I'm guessing.

But the good news, it wasn't Eli's tooth. Bad news ... where is my grandbaby? Those boys stirred up the past like it was yesterday. So much pain, if you could feel it for just a minute. There's no relief from it. None.

All the years Carol and I said we weren't much for religion, never went to church, tell us, have we made a mistake? Are we damned? I feel it now. Damned to hell. Could be the reason we're cursed. Could be why we lost him. Is it punishment? Do you believe that? What do you think? Tell us it's not true. Tell us abandoning religion hasn't cast a shadow over our lives. Tell us our little grandbaby isn't gone forever. Tell us.

My Eli ... the Whitfield treasure. Call me unrealistic, but you watch, you watch my friends. My treasure hunt will bring my grandbaby home.

Felix

. . .

"The Whitfield treasure is Eli?" Nate rubs his chin. "The hunt wasn't a marketing ploy to bring guests out to the lodge for business, but—"

"It was a treasure hunt to find my brother. My granddad kept that from us."

"Grady kept that from me, too. Unreal. And the fight?"

"Had no clue. No one ever told me about it. I must've been sent to stay with Joss when it happened, or I would've noticed the cops and all the commotion."

"Bet they were protecting you from the stress. Hard to know how a kid will react to someone finding a tooth on the property."

"True. But still, these decades-old secrets about Connor and my granddad are surreal."

"Maybe you only remember what you want. You could've blocked out a lot from when you were a kid."

"What, like amnesia? No way."

"Do you have a lot of memories of Eli?"

I shake my head and look over at the fire, the last log dying out. I bite my nail and think about the few memories I *do* have of him. One, when I was sitting in this same spot when I was a toddler. My favorite doll was on my lap, and Connor was playing on the floor with his plastic dinosaurs. We had just finished lunch, the afternoon sun had expanded through the back windows, and Eli was asleep in my dad's arms, his tiny hand attached to my dad's finger. They were on the floor with us, my dad humming a peaceful lullaby, rocking him. It's a sweet memory. That's what I have of Eli—sweet memories.

Nate fiddles with his cell, bringing up a music playlist. He selects a song I've heard before, but I can't remember the name of the band. He cradles his knees close to his chest and rocks to the music. A smile. I can tell he's thinking about me.

He turns shyly away and watches the fire in silence, drinking his beer while admiring the massive log mantel and two-story fieldstone fireplace, the main interior feature of the lodge. My mom sat next to it when she returned home from the hospital after giving birth to each of us. And it's where she wanted to be during the final weeks of her life. She said after she was gone, she'd be watching over me whenever I sat here. If I needed her, she'd be here in this spot. If that's true, if she *is* here, I want her to see everything I've found. These are her mysteries, too.

Nate turns up the volume on his cell, pulling me from my daydreams. I can't help but fall into the music, dipping my head to the intoxicating voice.

"It's called 'It's Been Awhile,' " he says as if he knew I was about to ask.

"I've heard it. What band?"

"Staind. Meatier than Hanson." He grins around his beer, his dimple back in play.

I step like a crab over the objects to sit within his reach. "I like it. It's like bar music."

"Bar music you slow dance to when you wanna knock a woman off her feet and get laid."

I blush. A strand of his dark hair hangs over his forehead, lips glossy from beer.

"What?" he whispers.

I run my fingers through his hair, my cheeks lifting, eyes smiling. "I've already been knocked off my feet, Nate." I blush hotter.

His forehead rests on mine. He puts his hand on my knee and our toes curl together. This setting, the solitude of us in this dark room alongside the fire, the song that lulls us but also turns us feverish; it's all too much.

"I'm lonely, Salem." He defeats me with his husky voice and blue eyes.

I touch his hand and say my next words without reluctance. I know what will come of them, and I know I want it now more than ever.

"I am too, Nate. We can fix that."

He looks up with a loaded grin, his head tilting to the balcony, to my private quarters, and back at me. "We can definitely fix that."

My insides catch fire, becoming hot and liquid, his hands already pulling at my shirt.

• • •

The rain from earlier has trickled to a stop. My bedroom window is bathed in condensation, the dim shadow of tree branches in a sleepy dance on the ceiling. Nate's magnetic, standing over my bed, eyeing my nude body. I do the same. Take in his tight stomach and the outline of his abs. I shove my hands under my thighs to keep from biting my nails. My fingers are cold as ice, feet rubbing quickly together in anticipation. His hands shake as he removes his black boxers and climbs on top of me.

A questioning look, his eyes focused, narrow, checking for any reservations about this before we begin. None. I tap the condom wrapper in his hand and pull the covers over our heads. Our breath mingles in the dark, his more pronounced than mine. I've thought about this. I know exactly how Nate will be in bed by the way he kisses: delicate at first, sweet as lemon pudding, sure to pleasure me before he comes.

But unexpectedly, he takes me without any need for foreplay. I squeeze my eyes shut with his first thrust inside, tingling sensations capturing me whole. He thrusts again, the motion sucking the air out of my lungs. I moan his name before his tongue slips past my lips, the bed erupting, pulled in by damp heat.

"Oh, God." He breathes.

I can sense his smile under the covers, guttural sounds growing louder, knowing it's all because of me. I'm not ashamed that I can't control my hands or the sounds that I'm making. Not ashamed of how wet he makes me.

He bites my chin, releasing a twirl of magical, lambent light behind my eyelids. The room disappears. The lodge. Past. Present. Only the two of us remain.

"Yes. *Yes.*" His muscles ripple and waves of heat pulsate through his body.

He sucks my tongue and sinks between my legs, making me come fast and hard. I pull him closer, grazing my toes along the back of his legs as he exhales a paralyzing breath into the passing night.

FIFTEEN

The morning starts with bitter cold sweeping in, winter back in the air. Nate's scent leaks from my pores. We stare at one another from across the sitting room. He and Jim drink their coffees and spread contagious yawns, while Joss and I wear horseshoe grins without a trace of regret.

Joss knew right away when she saw Nate and me this morning that we'd slept together, but waited until now to ask if it was a *tinsel night*. A phrase she's used since high school, meaning casual sex is a tasteless ritual, fake and cheap. Tinsel-like. Except her definition doesn't fit how she's been acting around Jim, and sleeping with Nate last night didn't seem casual or fake. The phrase was fitting when we were younger but has since lost its kick.

"It sounds old-school now, doesn't it? Time to rename it," I tell her.

"Jim's a good fuck so we can call it that."

I nod toward two women walking down the stairs. "Classy, Joss," I whisper. "Hold back on the f-word around my guests." She pops her cinnamon gum, curls dropping free from her ponytail, her white helmet under one arm and tan boots stained a deep purple from the grape juice processing plant.

The women admire the maps on the tabletops and gaze at the small, octagon window that's near the ceiling. Centered on the glass is a sparrow created from mica flakes. It shines like gold when the sun's out, dull now, bottled in a gray day.

"*Mica night* sounds better than tinsel," I say. More romantic. We'll call it that since all of us have a happy twinkle in our eyes."

"Still on that subject?" Joss pops her gum, tosses an eye roll. "Cheesy, babe. How was it, anyway?"

"You know … spectacular. Especially the second time."

If we were alone, I'd tell her how I kept thinking with amazement that *this is actually happening, I'm having sex again!*

"About time. You've got some catching up to do."

"To you?" I snort. "That'll be impossible."

Her delighted little cackle startles the two women. She mouths *sorry* to them before waving Jim over.

"Hey, I forgot to tell you, my granddad wrote in one of his letters about Connor and Brad getting in a fight. You remember that? Something big must've happened between them. Connor knocked out Brad's tooth."

Joss tilts her head to put on her helmet, struggling with the chinstrap. I help her snap it and lower her goggles over her eyes.

"Connor didn't fight," she says.

"That's what I thought."

She waves to Jim once more. "Come on, kiss me goodbye before I leave for work."

"Get your ass over here," he says, arm extended.

She presses her lips together, placing her hands on her hips. Her cheeks puff out and turn red. Joss's power trips are playful, but usually don't go over well with most men. Jim's one of the few who doesn't much care.

"Watch the language and get moving," she seethes through her clamped overbite, vying for control.

"All right, woman." He finger-combs his beard downward, dragging his feet across the room in protest. Like her, I can tell he's hamming it up.

Joss's hands are slapped away from her hips when he reaches her side, his macho grip moving in. He draws her forward and gives her a hard kiss.

"Coming back?" he asks, raising her goggles back up.

"Maybe." She smirks. "If you want."

"I want. I absolutely, positively want."

"Good. What're you gonna do today while I'm out working for a living?"

"You guys sound like an old married couple," Nate says, getting a dirty look pitched back from Jim … and more dirty looks from the older women.

"Searching for the treasure," Jim says, eyeing Nate before turning back to Joss. "I'll find it and share it with you."

Nate hasn't told him the treasure is Eli, and I'm not about to either. Jim's search will get him out of the lodge and keep him busy for the day.

"Martin's Bar tonight?" Joss asks.

"My room." He nuzzles her neck.

"Hold up. You said *I'm* whipped. Me?" Nate's powerful voice diverts the room, causing the women to click their tongues. We disgust them, too loud and too forward. Nate catches on, sips his coffee and unfolds the newspaper to disengage.

"Joss, get your coat. It's cold this morning," I tell her.

"I will. See ya, badass." She gives Jim a peck on the cheek.

"See ya, gingerbread."

I laugh. "Gingerbread?"

"Her eyes," he says, "look at her big brown eyes. Gorgeous."

If this is an act, it's a good one. I had him pegged as a varmint when he first arrived. Being quick to judge is the M.O. in this business. People come and go so fast that it's hard not to form an opinion about a guest when they first walk in. But Jim threw me for a loop. Could be all the sex that's sweetened him up. Could also be that he likes her, I should hope.

Joss flicks her eyes to each of us to say goodbye, but she doesn't make it out of the room. Her focus turns to the wavering ceiling lights.

The hairs on my arms stand on end. Nervousness swells in the pit of my stomach, the same feeling I had after my dream about Eli.

What the hell's wrong with the lights?

Nate sets the paper down and looks up. "What is that?"

"Power surge, I think." I draw in my bottom lip. "Maybe?" My unsteady voice isn't reassuring. The lights flash before diminishing to a pulsating glow. The coils in the incandescent bulbs move like blood pumping through a restricted vein, squeezing and releasing. "I'll check the fuse box. Joss, unplug my computer for me."

"Will do."

"Fuse box? This place is ancient," Jim says. "Light's are still on, by the way. It's not a fuse." He stares at the ceiling.

"Check it anyway." Joss unsnaps her helmet on her way to the desk.

The lights go out, colors fade to the cool spectrum, and faces grow pallid. Joss tosses me the flashlight from behind the desk, and I hurry to the laundry room off the lobby. The lights come back on before I can get the box open. When I do, no fuses are blown. Nothing has melted. Nothing blackened. Everything looks fine.

"It's not a fuse!" I holler.

"Told ya," Jim answers, the door chime stifling his words.

I walk backward and poke my head into the lobby, listening to the high-pitched notes singing from the front door. Closed, I might add. The door is closed. "Stupid hunk of wood. I swear that thing is possessed."

"Bogeyman's back," Nate says. He leans against the doorjamb to the sitting room and crosses his arms. "Or something's drawing out the power. I haven't heard any lightning though."

"Me either," Joss says.

"Got any guests who brought a toaster oven, a table saw, or a mini fridge with them?" His dimple shows, a joke that puts a brief smile on my face.

"Nope, haven't seen anyone bring in any of that."

"Could be a wiring problem." Jim joins us in the lobby. "I might be able to fix it, but don't sue me if you have a fire."

"A second fire?" One of the women stands, worried.

"This place is a dump," says the other. They leave their coffees on the table and squeeze past Nate and Jim. "Rose, pack your bags. We'll stay in the next town over."

"That's an hour from here," I remind them.

"I don't care. Didn't you hear me? Your hotel is a dump."

I slam my palm on the reception desk. "It's a lodge, not a hotel. A beautiful family lodge!"

Jim laughs at my minor meltdown, but Joss slips off her helmet and steps cautiously to my side. "Babe ... take ten." She sets her helmet on the desk.

"It's not a dump. And it's not gonna burn down!"

"Salem, it's okay. The wiring is fine. The lodge is fine. Everything's fine." Her fingers skim along my forearms to help me relax. "Nothing's going to burn down. Promise."

"It will be a cold day in Hell before I stay here again," one woman says. "I'm not ready to turn to ashes in my sleep."

"Goody, go. She doesn't need your business," Joss says to her.

The woman's eyes fly wide, finger pointed, deep creases between her brows. "Don't you get snippy with me, missy."

"Then stop being such a biddy."

"W-w-w-what? What? A what?"

"Shrew," Joss adds. "Hag. Old fart."

"Dear Lord." The woman gasps, holding her chest. Her friend takes her by the arm and spins her in the opposite direction. They toddle up the stairs like conjoined twins, blocking anyone from coming or going.

"This is so wrong." I rub my temples to block out my mom's voice in my head. Never works. I deserve to get a lecture after losing my cool, but with Joss, a good spat is in her blood. Doesn't matter if her target is sixteen or sixty, if they need to be put in their place, she'll do it.

Two other guests come out of their rooms and watch from the balcony. They whisper as if conspiring against me, then exchange concerned looks with the two women walking up the stairs.

"I'm calling AAA. They'll send out a hotel inspector."

"It's not a hote—" Joss covers my mouth before I can finish.

"Go for it. This lodge is a landmark in these parts," Joss goads them on, keeping me out of the argument.

Crackling and popping noises spill out of the outlet by the sitting room. The women shriek and climb faster. The chime begins another short jingle, only this time the door actually opens. Jim takes rapid steps to meet the unwanted guest walking in.

Brad Brenner.

Nate stands straight, puts his hands in his back pockets. More crackling. Another shriek. Smoke floats out of the outlet. Lights flicker. And in the midst of it all, Brad plods past Jim and sticks a flyer in Nate's face.

"This you?" he asks. "Matthew Fields."

"What?" Nate looks at the flyer of a missing child, a vein bulging on the side of his neck. "Back off, Brenner. Doesn't look anything like me."

Brad looks at the photo. "This kid went missing when he was six. Yeah, he looks just like you. Same age. And this one. See this." He holds a second flyer in Nate's face. "A girl who would be your mom's age now, missing from the same town a few hours north of here. Tell me it's just a coincidence. Go 'head."

"Brad, get out." I point to the door, leaving the safety of the reception desk. "Leave!"

"Rose, hurry. Faster," one woman says. "They might have guns!"

"Lord, I don't want to get shot," says the other. "Please Lord, I don't want to turn to ashes or get shot!"

"The lodge isn't on fire and no one's getting shot!" I yell, noting the small amount of smoke rolling out of the outlet. I signal to Joss to run and get the fire extinguisher.

Nate slams Brad hard in the chest, likely hoping to knock him off his feet. The jolt sends Brad back, but he's quick to steady himself and pull his gun.

A woman gasps. "Run, Rose. Run!"

Nate freezes at the sight of the barrel. I demand Brad put it away, but I've become nonexistent to the male testosterone permeating the room.

"Get out, Brenner." Nate's face burns red. "Get the hell out of here with that gun."

Jim catches Nate's right arm and pushes him back. He steps between him and Brad, his hand up for Brad to lower the gun.

"Jim, get back," Nate says.

"No, I've got this." Jim pivots to throw a punch, but Brad anticipates the move and ducks. He grabs Jim's legs and tackles him to the floor.

"Put your hands behind your back. Hands behind your back, now! You're under arrest for assaulting a police officer." Brad cuffs him in one swift action.

"He didn't even touch you, I did," Nate says.

"I can handle it!" Jim yells. "Don't get involved, Nate. You've got more to lose."

He runs his fingers through his hair, helplessly watching as Jim is yanked off the floor and led to the door. "I wasn't gonna punch him, Jim. You know that. You know that about me. It was just a shove."

"It was the gun, Nate … Get my wallet and meet me at the station."

"Brad, let him go!" Joss shouts. She hands me the fire extinguisher, grabs her helmet, and follows them outside. "Brad, stop!"

Ollie barks and paws to get out of the confines of my bedroom. An audience of four women forms on the balcony, their mouths open, wrinkled hands clenching the railing. Nate swears as he passes them on his way to his room.

Stunned by the domino of events that just wiped us all out, I'm unable to speak. I'd like to think I don't appear shaken that the world around me is crumbling, but that's doubtful. Honestly, I'm beside myself. The room is polluted with antsy faces staring down at me, and my hearing is lost in the magnitude of stress, stuffed to the max with cotton balls.

This lodge has been the center of my existence forever. Doesn't matter if the yard is an overgrown pigsty, the front sign is cracked, and only the sparrow is lit. The structure *is* the heart of the Whitfield family, it's what's important, something that can't be replaced. I had the sense it would be a comfort until the day that I die. But it's no longer a sure thing. This morning it's become as fragile as a glass ornament dangling at the outer edge of a pine branch. When it drops, I won't be fast enough to catch it. The collapse appears to be imminent.

I look to the fireplace for reassurance from my mom, her guidance absent. The response I want is merely my own thoughts and words imitating the woman I'll never be. I could stare for days at the last place she was alive, but she'd never come back. Steadily watch the emptiness of the room for a sign, but there'd be none.

Biting my nail, I see her gray hair first, then her Robin's-egg blue robe and bootie slippers. Virginia Pullman. Normally the first guest up and moving about in the morning, today she's the last. She missed the spectacle.

Then again, Virginia is a spectacle.

Carrying a small cardboard box, she stops in front of me, face to the door, hesitant to leave.

"You okay?" My voice is broken and tight from anxiety.

"Not today, Salem. Tomorrow." She places a folded slip of paper in my hand, eyes milky when she looks up. "I'm afraid my feet will get cold."

Her slippers whisper across the wooden floor. With one hand on the box and the other glued to the door handle, she waits as if she expects me to stop her. I should ask where she's going, if she's checking out today, or if she wants a cup of tea, but part of me says not to bother her, while another part wants to hug her. Virginia is the first guest who I'd happily invite to stay for eons. An apparent lost soul who belongs at Sparrow Lodge, like Joss, like Nate, like me.

She looks at the photograph of my family above the door, her hand falling from the handle. Her head tilts as she blows the photo a kiss. I see myself reflected in the glass, superimposed over Eli.

"Virginia?"

She opens the door and crosses into raw silence. No pretty jingle. No parting goodbye. Just the door closing, Ollie whimpering, the women departing from the balcony, and Nate in a whirlwind, leaving me alone with a burning plastic smell in the air.

The slip of paper handed to me by Virginia is the size of a fortune cookie message. I unfold it and finger over her exquisite penmanship, back and forth, sifting over the letters until the words sink in.

I'm not sorry.

SIXTEEN

Tilford Lake's electrician, Frank Ennis, arrived an hour ago to a cold and smoky lodge. My voice was edged in panic when I called him. Better now. A competent electrician at the lodge is reassuring that it won't burn down. My brain believes that. Same as when Connor broke his arm when he was eleven. I thought he was going to die until the doctor came into Connor's hospital room. Then everything was fine. A skilled professional would keep him safe. Just like Frank will protect the lodge. Positive thinking.

I work a glob of hand sanitizer into my palms, eyes on Frank as he kneels in front of the outlet, scratching his butt crack with a screwdriver. The same screwdriver I just picked up for him when it dropped next to my foot. How many times he's used it for scratching his butt is unknown, the sanitizer a necessary safeguard just in case. I concentrate on his face when he looks over his shoulder, but the crack scratch … it's one of those things that's hard to ignore, like a piece of food stuck between someone's teeth, or Joss's boobs creeping out of her low-cut shirts.

He takes two chocolate donuts wrapped in cellophane out of his toolbox and tears the package open with his teeth. I have to say, not all the people in Tilford Lake are stereotypical small-towners, but Frank and his butt crack, eating chocolate donuts on the job ... I guess there's always a few who fit the part.

"The ground wire wasn't properly attached," he says. "How long has this extension cord been plugged into this outlet?" He takes a bite of one of the donuts, chocolate on his lips.

"About a month."

"What was plugged in here before that?"

"Nothing."

"Is it necessary?"

"Probably not." I hug myself, rubbing my upper arms. It's hard to admit I'm at fault. This is different than neglecting the playground and the pool. "Guests were complaining that the room was dark in the morning. I added a few lamps to the coffee station, but I ran out of outlets. The coffee pots and hot water are now on the extension cord. I plugged the extra lamps into the wall where the appliances used to be."

He licks chocolate off his fingers. "You notice the pinched cord?"

"No."

"I went over this with your mom a few years back. Use extension cords sparingly. Plug the small appliances back into the outlet and get an adapter for the lamps. The other problem with the flickering lights was the space heaters. Those are energy hogs."

"Like I said, I didn't see my guests bring them in, only walk out with them."

He nods. "Add the info to your website. And tell people when they check in that they can't use 'em. Could cause a fire."

"Okay."

He stands and pulls his jeans high over his gut, the remaining donut clamped between his teeth. He takes it out to speak. "Last thing. The sticker in the fuse box says you're past your routine inspection date."

"Is that bad?" I bite my fingernail. "Shoot, that's bad. I know it is. I've fallen behind on a few things."

He chuckles and looks around the lobby, spotting the tattered replacement rug, the pine garlands on the beams, and for sure he saw the charred rug on the front lawn when he got here. "Well, it's not good. I have the rest of the morning free. Can do it now or come out the beginning of next week. Tuesday morning?"

"Now's fine."

He scratches his double chin, eyes on my flat hair, oversized hoodie, and sweatpants. After a night of sex and not showering this morning, I must look frumpy.

"You know, Salem. My daughter needs a job this summer before she heads off to school, in case you need an extra pair of hands to get the lodge in order."

"Thanks. I'll think about it."

"She's a hard worker."

I continue biting my nail.

Ollie opens one eye. He watches Frank gather his tools and head to the laundry room. Loafing in his dog bed, he's satisfied with the ample behind-the-ear scratches he got from Frank earlier in the day. With a roll onto his back to stretch his stumpers, his fuzzy squirrel toy tumbles off and makes a lively *squeak*. It only takes a nanosecond for Olls to be on his feet to search for the source of the noise. I pick up the squirrel, squeak it, set it back on his bed. His tongue rolls out to say thanks. Ollie lives for hugs, a warm bed, and a full belly. Easy to please, I always tell people.

"You're adorable, buddy."

He sets his chin on the squirrel and closes his eyes.

"Talking to me?" Frank asks.

"No, sorry. My dog."

"Oh."

My chest shakes with silent laughter. Frank's the one man in town that the older women gossip about. "He's a catch," "Nicest man in Tilford," "His wife's damn lucky, damn lucky," they say.

I can see it. Frank has a stable, decent paying job. He's overweight, but jolly, and has a big, toothy smile that ignites plump, raspberry cheeks. The kids in town think he's Santa. And subconsciously, that could be why so many women find him attractive, seeing that Santa is the most lovable guy on the planet. That said, Brad fits the same description, but there *is* a significant difference between the two men.

One's charming. The other's a skunk.

The flyers Brad brought of the two missing people are on my desk. They have nothing to do with Nate. I checked the names online after everyone left. The boy was found years ago: a parental abduction. And the body of the woman who vanished was recovered in the woods after a bear attack. Brad's grasping at straws, desperate to knock Nate out of the picture. All I can say is—good luck!

Ollie raises his ears, his droopy eyes set on the balcony. I look up.

A creak.

I hold my breath and wait to see if I hear it again. Seconds pass. *There. There it is.* A creaky floorboard, coming from the room next to Virginia Pullman's, the room above my living room. Same spot Nate and I heard the other day.

Room 2.

"Frank, I'm going upstairs for a sec. Holler if you need me."

"All righty."

I choke down a breath and climb the stairs, begging the sound be nothing. Or something easily explained, like the wind, or the age of the place. Old wooden buildings are known to creak, pop, and rattle. Or it could be the temperature drop. Wispy snowflakes are multiplying on the windows. Thermal contraction. Could be that. An evil spirit trapped in Room 2 also crosses my mind, but common sense snuffs out the absurdity of that one. But something's in there, something other than a ghoul.

Adrenaline drives my feet, the creaking louder, faster. Blood rushes to my head as I turn the key. I open the door and see the empty rocker swaying in the corner, its curved legs creaking on the hardwood floor.

I sniff the fresh air, the room chilly from an open window. It must've been stuffy in here last night, smoke from the lobby drifting into this room, my guest upset. My guess, she cracked the window as a precaution to keep her quilts smoke-free.

A thin layer of snow swirls on the floor under the open window, the flakes gracefully skating like they're on a frozen pond, a movement that delays evaporation. I walk in and close the window, my fingers melting the ice flowers on the glass.

The creaking stops, the room now hushed.

I rap my knuckles on the dresser on the way out, dismissing my superstition that ghosts inhabit the lodge. Sweat has gathered in my armpits and behind my knees from the incident. I can't account for the creaks Nate and I heard the other day, this room unoccupied at the time. Odds are it was the temperature change.

I lock Room 2 and open Virginia's room. This will be the third time today that I've gone in here, confused by how spotless she left it. She made the bed and folded the towels as if she didn't expect me to wash anything before the next guest checks in. No luggage or toiletries, nothing in the closet, not even a single piece of trash in the wastebasket. Virginia Pullman handed me a puzzling note and then she disappeared. She didn't mention staying another day but left her car in the driveway. And I didn't see which direction she went, whether she hit the road east, west, or wandered into the forest.

The tension in my shoulders jumps a level when Frank drops a tool.

"You okay?" I call down, closing Virginia's room.

"All good. Only worry if the donut rolls out of my hand." He chuckles.

"Roger that."

I puff my bangs off my forehead, my gaze falling to Nate's room. He hasn't called. Joss either. And no return calls from Brad or Doreen at the station.

I walk over and lay my hand on his door, left open when he raced out. He was too busy to notice, stuffing wallets and keys inside his pockets, hopping on one foot to tie his boot. He kissed me and said not to worry. But I am worried, especially about Joss. I don't want her to do anything foolish like I've pondered doing all morning. With his door open, I'm so tempted to step inside and break the rules, tempted to find out what the stack of papers is on the dresser. Tempted to do other things: sniff his pillow, dab his cologne on my wrist, wrap myself in his soft flannel shirt. Tempted to use his shower and share his towel.

I'm of two minds about it. Nate's a guest. Guests are respected. Guests deserve privacy. But his naked body was pressed against mine. He was inside me. Only fair, I get to go inside his room.

Only fair.

My nose leads the way, pulling me in, devouring the vanilla and cinnamon scent hanging in the air, the same way Frank devours his chocolate donuts. My mouth salivates, greedy for another kiss. If he caught me touching his clothes, licking the rim of his beer bottle … God, I've never been a stalker girl. It feels wrong. Wrong, wrong, wrong. But the restless energy rolling off my body hampers those feelings.

I can't help but smile. A slow forming, wicked smile. I love being bad. Love it!

I flop on his bed and kick my feet, flip on my back and snort his pillow like it's a drug. With the pillow held to my chest, I roll back and forth, still high from last night's sex.

"I can't wait for us to fuck again."

"Salem?" Frank knocks on the doorjamb.

"Ah!" I jump up, toss the pillow toward the headboard and straighten the comforter.

"Oh, Lordy. Never mind!"

"No. No." I walk up to him, and he steps back. "I'm just cleaning the rooms."

"Call it what you want."

"Frank, wait."

"Sorry 'bout that." He hurries down the stairs. "Might wanna close the door before you ... before you do that solo female pampering. That's what my wife tells our daughter."

"I wasn't ... it's not ... don't think that I was ..." Dammit. I set my hands on the railing. "Frank, what did you need?"

"All good." He waves a hand. "I'm just fine."

"Ugh." I look down and away, then cover my face with my hands. Somehow I make it back to Nate's room, sit on the edge of his bed with my fingers wedged between my legs, heart racing. Bad karma. That's what I get for coming in here. Bad, bad karma. Now Frank thinks I'm a pillow sex enthusiast.

"Frank, I wasn't making out with the pillow!"

"Nothing to be ashamed of."

"I swear!"

I force myself to breath steady, toughen up, pretend I don't look and sound pathetic. But my reflection in the mirror over the dresser shows the truth—face red-hot, eyes mortified—I may die of embarrassment. I'm acting too young for my age, like a callow teen experiencing puppy love for the first time.

"Let me know if you need anything, Frank." I try to sound calm.

"All good."

I take a few drawn-out breaths and pick lint off my sweatpants, kindling a memory of my mom. I have a heavy heart for her today. And the lint doesn't help; it's always a trigger for my dad and Connor's wake. The day my red sweater shed on everyone who offered condolences. The hugs transferred from me to my mom, and the lint passed to her black dress. She picked off each piece one by one, a way for her to disengage, to stay in denial a little longer. It got her through until the lint was gone and she resorted to picking fuzzy pieces off my sweater. A red pile grew on the carpet of the funeral home, resembling an erupting volcano. Like then, this is turning out to be one of those sludgy days. Gloomy and lethargic with lasting burdens worse than bubblegum stuck in my hair. Sour cops, vanishing guests, tense friends, a wounded home. A slap across the face or a kick to the shin would be a welcome distraction.

My phone lights up my hoodie pocket. I take it out and see Brad's number on the screen.

"Brad, where are they?"

"Officer Brenn—"

"Knock it off. Are they at the station?"

"Took 'em to Hell. All of 'em." His excitement flips a switch inside me. My hand curls into a white-knuckled fist.

"Does that mean Jim's in jail? And Nate? What about Joss?"

He laughs.

"This isn't funny. It's not funny, Brad. Your little scheme isn't working."

"What scheme?"

"To get me to doubt Nate. I'm not falling for it. Now stop it and tell me where they are."

"Hang easy. They're fine. I drove Jim past the station a handful of times, purposely stalling out by the front door to hear the wimp apologize. Then I dropped him off at the diner. Joss and Harlow tailed me the whole way."

"They're at the diner?"

"Everyone's happy eating Simon's daily special. Meatloaf today. Want me to bring you a plate?"

"No, I don't want you to bring me a plate. So you didn't arrest him?"

He laughs again, a belly laugh, callous and unpleasant. "What I did was show him who's boss around here."

I roll my eyes. "And who would that be? Chief?"

The loud squeak of Styrofoam rubbing together makes me cringe. Must be his takeout box.

A sniff. A suggestive moan. "Uh, smells sooo good."

"Brad."

He blows on his food and takes a bite. With a sharp intake of breath, he says, "Hh-h-hot."

"Brad."

"What?" He exhales and slurps his drink.

"Jim's not the type to apologize."

"Like you know him so well."

"Better than you. I doubt you let him go just like that."

"Told you, I was showing him who's boss." He blows on his food for several seconds, chews, takes another swig of his drink to wash it down.

"Bullshit. Tell me what happened."

"Can't, I made a deal. It's null and void if anyone finds out."

"What deal?"

"None of your business."

"Is money involved?"

"Can't say."

"Jesus, it is, isn't it? Did you take a bribe?" He blows on his food. "Brad, you're the one who'll end up in jail."

"Now *that's* bullshit. I haven't been in trouble a day in my life." He talks with a mouthful of food. "The other party is the one who'd go down for this, not me."

"You think?"

"That's right."

"You've never done *anything* wrong. Ever?"

"That's right."

"Then what happened between you and Connor? Why'd he hit you?" His line falls silent. I look in the mirror and see myself biting my nail. My hand drops to my side. Outside Nate's window, the snow is heavy, descending over the yard, entombing Annabelle the hippo. I watch her disappear, waiting for Brad to talk. "Connor didn't get into fistfights. You did something wrong. What was it?" I push.

He swallows. "Who told you he hit me?"

"My granddad." I hold the cell away from my ear, flinching from another round of abrasive laughter. "It was in a letter, doofus. I know you think I'm losing it, but my granddad doesn't talk to me from the dead."

"Sure, Salem. This time I'm calling the loony bin to pick you up. No joke."

"Brad, he wrote about it. It was in a letter he sent to Grady Murphy."

The laughter stops. "What did it say?"

"That Connor knocked out your tooth, but neither of you would say why."

"My lips are sealed. Let it rest."

"I won't. Start talking."

"Don't hold your breath."

"You have to tell me."

"Says who? Look, before Connor died, he asked me to watch over you if he got into college, and that's what I'm doing.

That's *all* I'm doing. It's what I've always done, check in on you to make sure you're okay."

"That's the only reason you've kept in touch with me?"

"And just so you know, those phony private detectives are nothing but trouble."

He snubs my question. I figure he's tugging at his collar to get more air.

"Nate's not phony. And don't you dare change the subject. What did you do to rile Connor? He never hit anyone. You must've hit him first."

"Forget about it." He hangs up.

Brad and I argue like brother and sister, but the tension between us has spiked since Nate and Jim arrived. It's something I'm on edge about. I put my cell back in my hoodie, fuming over this. If I could get a good look at Brad's face, I might be able to figure out how he feels about the fight. See if his eyes show remorse or if he's still harboring rage. Maybe I'll be able to hear it in his voice. I pull out my cell and call him back.

"What?" he answers.

"Don't avoid this conversation and don't hang up on me."

"Salem, what happened between Connor and me was between us. We worked it out. That's it."

"It must still upset you, or you'd talk about it."

"Nope."

"Then what's the big secret? I won't let up until you tell me. I'll keep calling."

"I won't answer."

"I'll come to your house."

"The only time you leave the lodge is to get groceries or to walk your fat dog."

"Ollie's not fat. He's big boned!" I slam my palm on the bed several times. "Don't talk about him that way."

A painfully long pause. "Sorry." This time I hear the regret in his voice. He knows better than to say anything bad about Olls, especially since he's overweight himself. "This is getting out of hand," he says.

"I know it is." I lower my voice. "Think we can have a conversation like two civilized adults?"

"All right, look … I threatened Connor once when we were kids. I was gonna rat him out for something, but he made sure I walked the threat back and didn't tell a soul."

"He made sure by knocking out your tooth?"

"He didn't plan on that happening."

"Why'd you threaten him?"

"Because I wasn't prepared for what I saw…"

He hesitates like a little boy too scared to ride his bike over the crest of a steep hill. I have a sneaking suspicion the fight had something to do with Eli or the key. My mind can't piece together any other possibilities.

My eyes comb through Nate's room as I wait, stopping on the stack of papers on his dresser—my original reason for coming in here. "You gonna talk, Brad?"

"I'm thinking."

I get up and flip through the stack. Medical bills, some from twenty years ago, addressed to Gertrude Murphy. Gert. She was sick for years. Bills like these are familiar to me. My mom's cancer meds cost over ten grand a month. The chemo and other treatments emptied her retirement savings, along with all the money she got after my dad died. On a janitor's salary, Grady and Gert must've been broke. I'm surprised a few of these were paid in one chunk. A check sent for twenty grand, another for ten. Where'd they get the money?

"You still waiting for me to say something?" he asks.

"What do you think?"

"Salem?" Frank calls up the stairs.

"Who's that?" Brad asks.

"Frank Ennis. He's doing an inspection." I leave Nate's room and look over the railing. "Yeah, Frank?"

"Can I get into your private quarters?"

I walk down the stairs. "Is that what you needed earlier? You should've just asked."

"I was about to." He blushes, chocolate on his chin. I give him a big smile to let him know I've moved on from the humiliation. He swipes his forehead with the back of his hand in good fun, saying, "Phew."

"Brad, hold on a sec."

"Brad Brenner?" Frank asks.

"Yeah."

"Shit," Brad grumbles. "Don't tell him it's me."

Frank grabs my cell. "Brenner? Kayla said you asked her out to dinner." His voice hardens. "She's just a kid, you hear me? A kid!" He points to the cell. I nod to go ahead and use it. He takes it into my quarters as he works, but I can still hear the yelling from out here. It's not uncommon for lonely Tilford Lake men to ask out high school girls. But Brad's a cop. His reputation is quickly spiraling the drain.

I look out the front window at Virginia's snow-veiled car, the last few days of warm weather proving to be a tease.

I imagine Virginia's walking through the forest in her robe and slippers, her gray hair iced, her nose sore and red. By the time I notice Frank handing me my cell, I sense the severity of the situation. If someone didn't pick Virginia up this morning, then she's out in this weather, and she's certainly not dressed for it. Plus that note, that note she handed me. *I'm not sorry.* Were those meant to be her last words?

"Brad."

"I gotta go, Salem."

"Wait, I need you to come out here. I think one of my guests is missing."

"I told you, they're at the diner."

"No, an older woman who was staying here for a funeral. She left this morning, but her car's still here."

"A funeral? There haven't been any funerals in Tilford Lake this week."

"You sure?" I walk into the sitting room and sort through the pile of papers, turning to the obituaries.

"I'm positive. We get notices at the station when there's a funeral."

"Oh my God."

"What?"

I stare at the paper from two days ago, my head ducking closer and closer to the page. The front door chime sings as I read the name.

"Fixed it," Frank says. "The battery was just about dead."

I can't comprehend what Frank said. The chime sings and fades, sings and fades.

"Oh my God."

"You just said that. What is it?"

I thought of Virginia Pullman as wise and kindhearted, reminding me of my grandparents. I was convinced she was the sanest person at the lodge, here for a family member's funeral, a funeral she attended two days ago. But with the obituary listed in the paper, an obituary for Virginia Pullman, I now know that she's unsound, the one who's most flawed ... and quite possibly, the most cunning one of us all.

SEVENTEEN

Late afternoon brings thickening darkness of snow clouds and moisture. I sit in Casper's Funeral Home, waiting for Wayland Casper to finish brewing a pot of tea. When we were kids, Joss and I made fun of the unfortunate name of his business, believing it was home of the cartoon character *Casper the Friendly Ghost*. Joss even dressed like Casper one Halloween, stood in the front yard of the funeral home, waving to passing cars. Her dad grounded her for a week, disrespecting the dead and all. Then the place became too real, the name Casper no longer friendly, more of a dreaded nightmare, coming here for funeral after funeral.

"How you been, Salem?" Wayland sets the tea tray on his desk and pours two cups. "Sugar?"

"No, thank you." He hands me mine and I take a sip: citrus-flavored, orange and lemongrass, a sweet licorice aftertaste. "I've been okay. Busy."

"Not here." He smiles. One of his top, front teeth has a small chip in it. "It's a blessing when I can say work has been slow."

I unzip my coat and force a polite smile, taking a whiff of the stale air. The funeral home has an odor that will impregnate my clothing and hair, an aromatic mix of Frankincense and rose incense, combined with the musty scent of old books. It's similar to the smell of a church, and inside Casper's, the odor clings to the vintage wooden chairs, dark green carpeting, and velvet brocade drapes. I may need to shower a second time today to wash away the memories that shadow the scents.

"Good tea." I raise the cup to thank him before placing it on the saucer on his desk. It's been a year since I've seen Wayland. Last time was at the bank. His hair is grayer, crow's feet more developed, and sweater vest much tighter around his ribs. The inevitable signs of aging have arrived. In common with Nate and Frank, he has a friendly and robust voice, only more distinguished. It's perfect for an NPR-like radio station, fitting his Subaru and gourmet tea personality. He also appreciates face-to-face conversations, mentioning how important eye contact and body language are in his line of work. More personal. Less cold and distant than when families prefer to make online arrangements. And not unlike the lodge, Wayland has multiple visitors each week with little or no chance of forming friendships or long-term relationships. Another example of a "revolving door" life, fresh faces that come and go, no way to stop the spin.

"You said business has been slow, but Virginia Pullman was here this week. Right?"

"Correct." His perfectly groomed brows and hazel eyes lift with excitement. He leans forward and spreads his fingers on the desk. "Look at me. My fingers are shaking because of her. Strangest experience I've had in my twenty years of running the family business. Peculiar woman. Too eccentric to have grown up in Tilford Lake, as she said."

"She grew up here?"

"As she said. Her parents lived in that stately Queen Anne next to the courthouse. After they passed, Dr. Abrams bought it."

"Wow, the gigantic green beast? The one with six bedrooms?"

"That's the one. But Virginia didn't live there long. She moved to California after high school and got a degree in

Mathematics. She had a job as a human-computer until the seventies. Then she taught at a university out west."

"Human-computer? Wait, I'm confused. She told me she was a live model in New York City."

Wayland rocks in his high-back chair, holding his index fingers in a steeple formation. "Well ... I didn't believe most of what she said, especially after she explained why she was here. It was unorthodox. I was waiting for her to say she had been to Mars."

"She said she was in town for a funeral. She went to it two days ago, but this morning I found *her* obituary and funeral arrangements in the paper. Was that a mistake? Was it for a family member with the same name?"

"No, no mistake."

I wring my hands, my nerves nearly shot. "You're saying Virginia had a funeral for herself?"

He nods. "A living funeral. I've read about them, but never thought someone would ask to have one here."

"That's crazy. *She's* crazy."

"I'd call her ... quirky." He tilts his head with a smile, raising a finger. "A complex personality you can never decode. More of a genius than a nut."

"Geniuses usually are nuts."

"True." He laughs.

We pick up our tea and drink at a sedate pace, the time spent processing the experience with Virginia. His chair squeaks. A strand of my hair falls over my cheek, still damp from the shower. I tuck it behind my ear. His chair squeaks again.

"Wayland, her obituary didn't mention any relatives. Who came?"

"No one. She sat with a pile of photos in her lap, staring at an empty casket. It was just her."

"Did she say why she was doing it?"

"No. And I didn't pry. Is she still at the lodge?"

"Her car is. She walked out this morning and left me this note. I haven't seen her since." I take the slip of paper out of my pocket and slide it across his desk. He has a curious look when he reads it. "What do you think it means?"

"Hard to tell. People her age often go through a stage of repentance when they know they're close to death. She didn't look sick, but that doesn't mean she isn't."

"Yeah, but why'd she give this to me?" I take the note back and stare at her words.

"No one came to say goodbye, Salem. It's possible she doesn't have any family. There're countless lonely people in this world. It's the epidemic of our time, right along with the opioid crisis and mass shootings." He takes a quick look over his office, stopping on a row of family photos on the bookshelf next to his desk. "After my dad died, my mom succumbed to loneliness. I'd ask her every morning if she was okay, and she always answered with the same quote. It's etched in my mind forever." He sits motionless, his eyes close. " 'When you have nobody you can make a cup of tea for, when nobody needs you, that's when life is over.' " He opens his eyes. "Sad, isn't it? And now that my mom is gone, they're the first words I say to myself when I wake up each morning."

I look at my cup, circling the rim with my finger. I'll remember that when I make tea for my guests. "Who said it?"

"Audrey Hepburn. Her favorite actress." He taps his lips in thought. The chair squeaks as he swivels. "You know, you might've reminded Virginia of someone she once knew."

"I did feel a connection to her … did you happen to see the photos in her lap?"

"No, but"—he glances at his family photos once more—"she boasted that back in the day she dated every man in Tilford Lake. My dad was one of them. And old man Martin who owns the bar. She even had an affair with Joe Clayton the same year he was married. She was proud of her promiscuity."

"How could you tell?"

"She grinned when reminiscing about them."

"Great, so we have a genius slut on our hands."

His body jiggles as he laughs. "Maybe so … she also mentioned her best friend was Gertrude Murphy."

"Gert?" The room instantly feels claustrophobic. My fingers tremble and the teacup almost slips from my hand. I pull my Sparrow Lodge sweater away from my chest so I can breathe, the logo separating from my heart. "Gert Murphy?"

"They probably went to school together."

"M-maybe," I stutter.

"Virginia didn't respond when I told her Gertrude had passed years ago. But I'm sure she already knew."

I smooth my sweater against my chest. The strong funeral home scent seeps deeper into my pores, enters my bloodstream, and clogs my veins. The smell will be harder to wash away this time.

Something led Virginia here, and it wasn't family. The note, *I'm not sorry*, she's not asking for forgiveness. Like Wayland said, she's proud. Arrogant even.

"Thanks for the tea." I stand. "I should go, it's getting close to four."

"Got a big crew coming in tonight?" He pushes his chair back and waits for me to zip up my coat.

"Not sure. The guests who had reservations left early or are MIA. Josselyn Arriaga is staying with me for the week, but she's at work until five."

He puts his hand on my back and leads me to the front door. "Have you reported the situation to anyone at the station?"

"I talked to Brad."

He sighs. "Was that your only choice?"

"Yep. Too bad, right?"

"It is. I heard Chief is on vacation. Let's hope the screwball can handle being on his own for a few days."

"Logan's working the opposite shift."

"He's not much better."

I set my hands on the push bar of the steel entry door and duck my chin into my coat. "Brad said I should call him tomorrow if Virginia isn't back. He'll come check out her car and the area."

"Why is he waiting so long?"

I shrug, scrunching my nose from the cold when I open the door. "He's super busy eating meatloaf."

• • •

It's nice to have a plowed driveway when I return to the lodge. Big Boy's Plowing & Towing is one of the more reliable services in Tilford Lake. The guys are out to do the job within hours of a substantial snowfall. But a job done quickly isn't always one done well. They usually bury my maroon Jeep Cherokee—a beater that was my high school graduation gift—under a giant pile of snow. Today Virginia's luxury car got the brunt of it, the model and make no longer identifiable under its coffin-ish shape.

I park next to Joss's Nova and step into the wet snow that clumps like mashed potatoes. Joss bangs her heels together on the porch, waiting for me to open the front door. She's wearing Nate's coat, which is ten sizes too big and down to her knees.

"Where'd you go?" She asks, taking off her helmet and fluffing her hair with her fingers. Its fan-like appearance looks like the top of a palm tree. "It's friggin' cold. What happened to spring? We got, like, a foot of snow today."

"I know. Where's your key?" I open the door and let her inside.

"I keep it on a separate chain from my car keys. It got left behind when I ran out this morning." She holds out her arms. "Nate was gracious enough to lend me his coat."

"What about Jim's coat?"

"Too small. Hey, can I light a fire? It's cold in here, too."

"Go ahead, less work for me." The chime overhead chirps a short melody. I smile at the sound, kick off my boots, and hang the coats next to the door. "Frank Ennis fixed my electrical problems."

"Goody. Hope it wasn't anything major."

"No. How come you're not at work?" I check my cell. "It's not even four." Joss gives me her *don't nag me* look. "Let me guess. You couldn't last the whole day without sex."

She grins. "I'm playing hooky so I can see Jim. I worked half a day, then told Sheila I have monster cramps."

"Bet you got an earful from her."

"Two earfuls. She complained about hiring women at the plant. She said we take off too much for medical stuff. Then Sully Newman cut in and said he needed to leave because his hemorrhoids were driving him nuts. Hemorrhoids, Salem. He said that in front of me. I walked out arm and arm with him. If Sully gets to leave because of his ass, I sure as hell can leave because of my ovaries."

"Except you were lying." Ollie hears us come in. He barks and scratches to get into the lobby. "Coming Olls!"

"Sully could've been lying about his ass. He's probably sitting on a hard stool down at the bar right now," she says.

I open the door behind the reception desk, and Ollie charges toward the front door to go outside. "Do your business and come right back," I tell him. His roly-poly middle squeezes through the door before it's completely open.

After Joss gets the fire lit, she relaxes in the leather armchair with her feet on the hearth to dry her soggy socks. Ollie comes back inside and sits with us next to the fire. I tie a purple bandana around his neck, telling Joss about Virginia, my trip to see Wayland Casper, how nothing makes sense, how tired my mind is from trying to come up with answers to all the riddles, how I just want to sleep for days.

"You can crash when our men leave," she says.

"Where are they?" I slouch in the chair, checking my phone. Still no return call from Nate.

Joss checks hers. "I don't know."

"What happened with Brad? Did Nate bribe him?"

"Who told you that?" She squirms.

"No one. Brad said he couldn't tell me why he let Jim off, but it sounded like that's what happened."

"Oh."

"Oh? What's oh?"

She tries to bury an unwarranted smile behind her phone.

"Joss?" I duck my head to look into her eyes, but she turns away. "What did you do?"

She sinks back, shaking her head in defense. "Nothing."

"Bull. You can't lie to me. Did you bribe Brad?"

"I wouldn't call it a bribe."

"Then what?" I stand and stare down at her with my hands on my hips. "Fess up. How much did you give him?"

"It's not a bribe…"

"Joss, how much?"

"Okay … but it's not a bribe. We have a date. I told him I'd go to dinner and then to the bar. It's harmless."

"It's not harmless!"

"Salem, don't get so upset." She repositions her bra.

"Does Jim know? Did you piss him off and that's why he's not here?" I stamp my foot before she can answer. "Dammit, Joss, a date with Brad?"

"What can I say? I like the guy."

"I hope you mean Jim."

She puckers her lips and throws multiple kisses. "Love you, babe. Don't be mad."

"Don't distract me. I *am* mad."

"Mwah!"

"Stop it." I smile. "You're awful."

"But you're smiling."

"Because you're so rotten!" I throw my hands in the air. "You're grounded."

Her cheeks balloon when she tries to stifle a laugh.

"When is this date anyway?"

"Tonight." She glances at her cell. "At six."

"Is that why you left work early? To be with Brad and not Jim?"

"Nope."

"And somehow you think Jim's not gonna find out? This will end in disaster."

"It won't."

"There'll be a fight and it better not happen here."

She stands and puts up a hand to stop. "I'm taking Jim with me."

"What?"

"Brad needs people to hang with. Haven't you noticed he's spent the past few days calling attention to himself? He's bugging us on purpose."

"Going out with him won't fix that."

"It might. He's downright miserable like the rest of us, that's why he eats nonstop." She raises her shirt and grabs a roll of fat. "It's depression. What else are we gonna do in this rinky-dink town besides eat and go to the bar?"

"Brad's looking for more than dinner, Joss. You know that. You shouldn't play with people's emotions."

"He'll be happy about it."

"Does he know Jim's going?"

"He will."

"Neither of them knows what's going on tonight?" The door opens and Jim walks in. "You're in deep shit," I whisper. "This will blow up in your face."

Her eyes expand to full moons, begging me to keep my mouth shut.

"Hi, sweet gingerbread." Jim tracks snow inside and sits on her lap, his black hair caked in a clumpy porridge of flakes. Joss brooms it off and slicks his hair to the side, then kisses him, hard, with tongue ... lots of tongue.

"Horny lovebirds," I tease. The sight is enough for me to give them a moment alone. I feed Ollie and collect my granddad's letters from my living room, then come back and sit across from them, flipping through the letters to find the ones I haven't read.

"You're cold. Where's your coat?" Joss rubs Jim's arms.

"Gave it to Nate. The sleeves are up to here on him." He karate chops a point on his arm below the elbow before reaching under her shirt to play. She screams and swats him away.

"Stop it. Your hands are freezing!"

"Come on, warm me up."

"Where is he?" I cut in. "Where's Nate?"

"Are those, *those* letters?" Jim turns. "Your granddad ruined my entire day. I can't get Nate to come inside. He'll have frostbite if he stays out there much longer," he starts mumbling, *"out there in a blizzard, no hat, dimwit just keeps digging and digging."*

"What are you talking about?" I ask.

"Nate. Your granddad. You know." He looks at Joss with a warm smile, and they fall into another session of sideswiping tongues. I roll my eyes. Ollie comes out, and I swear he rolls his eyes, too.

"Enough." I pat Jim's leg. "What about my granddad and Nate?"

Joss's feet point inwards as they kiss. After two more pats to break them apart, Jim finally pulls back. He waggles his eyebrows at Joss before answering me.

"The letter Nate's wound up tight about. We've been at the cabin all afternoon because of it."

"Which letter? Why didn't he say anything to me?" I pull out the two letters I showed him last night, rereading each one, searching for what I could've missed.

Jim stands and looks through the stack. He stinks of liquor and sweat, his hands red from the cold, beard spotted with green fuzz from his sweater. "Nate has a great poker face. I suspect he didn't let on because he's protecting you. Best private detective in upstate New York, if you ask me."

"He said we'd work together." I continue reading. "What's he digging for?" And then I find it. The part of the letter about Grady's hobby, the bones, his Wunderkabinett ...

You need to show off your work, my friend. It does no good sitting in that root cellar of yours.

"A root cellar," Jim says.

"I see," I whisper. A chill enters the room.

"Nate said he doesn't remember any root cellar on the property."

It's a chill like I've never felt before, creeping under my jeans and up my legs, warning me to not move from this spot.

"He said he's not coming in until he finds it."

Then a second biting chill outweighs the first. A chill that sneaks up my neck and invades my ear, howling, *Go, Salem, go. You have to be there when he finds me.*

EIGHTEEN

"Eli, wake up." I nudge his shoulder. He lifts his head off the pillow, eye boogers and dried-up drool showing a good night's sleep. "Hi." His midnight hair sticks out at the sides. Together with his reddish-brown pajamas, he looks like a woolly bear caterpillar. "Woolly." I pinch his cheeks and he giggles. "Get out of bed, woolly, woolly bear." He kicks off the blanket and raises his arms to be picked up. I try to lift him under his arms, then around his rib cage, but he's too heavy. "You're four today, Eli. Too big." I snap the blanket off the bed and spread it on the floor, twisting one end in my hand. "Ta-da! Magic carpet ride. Hop on."

He slides off the bed and sits cross-legged on the blanket, wraps the fabric over his legs, then points to the door. "Go, Salem, go!"

"Happy birthday to you," I sing, my parents joining in from the living room. "Happy birthday to you," we sing. I drag him on the blanket down the hallway, through the doorway, and into the living room. His eyes sparkle when he sees the mountainous pile of presents on the coffee table. He's unable to get to them fast enough, stumbling along the way.

"I'm four." He turns to Mom with four fingers held high. His baby teeth stand out to me now that I've lost my front ones. But Mom promised they'd grow back.

Eli rips off the forest animal wrapping paper and squeals, "A dump truck. It's yellow!" He pushes it across the room, bumping Boo's tail.

"Watch the cat, buddy," Dad says. Boo hisses and jumps onto the windowsill, then out the open window.

Eli picks up the truck and looks at Dad. "Can I go play outside?"

"Let's open your other gifts first," Mom says. She sets her camera on the windowsill and waves me over. With a short lick of her finger, she washes cinnamon toast crumbs off the corners of my mouth. Her saliva smells like coffee and maple syrup.

"Did you eat pancakes this morning?" I ask.

"Look up," she says. She pulls my hair into a ponytail and winds it into a topknot.

"Ow. Not so tight," I complain.

"I can never get it to stay."

"I don't care."

"But *I* care." She sweeps the stray hairs behind my ears and playfully musses my bangs. "You're so pretty." I make a scrunchy face and she laughs. "Silly girl. Go get Connor for me. He's out back. Tell him he's missing all the fun."

"But if I go, then *I'll* miss all the fun."

"Hurry." She pats my bottom. "I want the three of you together for photos."

Eli walks up to Mom and hugs her leg, his head tilted way back to look at her face. "Mommy, I want cake for breakfast."

"After dinner, when Grandma and Granddad are here," Mom tells him.

"Now," he cries.

"Eli, look." Dad brings him a gift. "Look at this big present. I wonder what this could be."

I run out of the room and open the two-ton wooden door between our private quarters and the lobby. The bronze bell on the reception desk *dings* as I enter the room, my eyes meeting a guest's. "Hi." I flash my toothless smile. "My dad will be right with you." My flip-flops slap across the floor, through the escape hatch, and down the back steps. I hopscotch along the path of round patio stones to say hello to Annabelle, duck under her low-hanging belly, stamp on an ant-covered Popsicle stick, and throw myself onto the lowest playground swing with my trademark belly flop. "Connor!" I call out, arms dangling. "Come watch Eli open presents!" My hair falls free of the topknot and my ponytail hangs to the ground. I walk the swing forward and put my weight on the rubber seat, raise my legs and glide freely with the force of gravity, backward and forward, like Dad's pendulum. My flip-flops fly off. My toes dig into the sand. "Connor?" I stop the swing and look around the yard. At a small distance, I see him under the tall pine that's closest to the lodge. "What're you doing?" I walk up to him.

Kneeling in his robe with his back turned to me, he says, "Almost finished."

"With what?"

"My gift."

Connor always wakes up early. Dad says he gets lost in the outdoors with no sense of time, that he moves through the day like we're not even here, that like an animal, Connor was meant to roam free. Dad says he won't place limits on his boy genius. That's why Connor gets to stay outside after dark. I don't mind. Dad says I'm different. I'm pants … passive. Sitting in the lobby with a coloring book spread on the floor and my box of crayons is more fun than picking slimy night crawlers or knocking down wasp nests with Connor.

"What is that?" I kneel next to him.

"A paracord survival bracelet. Making it for Eli."

"Looks like rope."

"No, it's parachute cord, stronger than rope." He pulls on it. "Granddad gave me a whole bunch that day Grandma gave you the pinwheels." He checks the size on his wrist. "He said it was used in the suspension lines of parachutes back in WWII." He trims the ends with his pocketknife, then takes out a lighter and melts each end.

"What are you doing that for?"

He presses his thumb into the cord. "It makes the ends wide so they don't slip through."

I touch it and he slaps my hand. "We're not supposed to play with fire," I say.

"*You* can't play with fire. I can. And it's not playing."

I notice the nasty sunburn and peeling skin on the back of his neck. I poke it and he slaps my hand again. "Sorry."

"Stop bugging me."

"Mom wants you inside for pictures."

A branch snaps and Connor's head jerks toward the forest. He lays his hand on my chest to stay still. Seconds pass. He stands up straight. Listens. Sprints away.

I follow, fighting to not slip on the dewy grass. "Wait. Wait up."

He stops in the field behind the pool, next to the trail that zigzags into the pines. A wooden crate bumps up and down, set between a large rock and a pile of old fence posts. Not a blink comes from Connor. Not a breath. Not a shooing of the fly on his cheek. He watches me through the corner of his eye, stares at the crate, then back at me. I'm scared but don't know why. And then I'm embarrassed about being scared. Connor's not. He's wide-eyed, eager for excitement.

"I think I caught it." He grins.

"What?"

"The woodchuck that's been eating up Mom's flower garden."

"Connor," I whine, "I hope it's not Boo."

"It's a live trap, Salem. Nothing's dead."

"I know." I know that. Connor wouldn't kill an animal. Even so, I don't want Boo under one of his crate traps. "What are you gonna do with it? Take it to Granddad's to live?"

"No. I told Mom to put a fence up to protect her flowers, but she hasn't, so I need to trap the woodchuck and talk to it." He steps forward. "I'll tell it to find a new home. It has until August to move out. Then I'll cover its burrow."

"You can't talk to animals. I'm not dumb."

"Sometimes you are."

"Shut up, poophead."

"I'm telling Mom you said that." He peeks between the slatted sides of the crate. "Nope, not the woodchuck." He flips it over, and a rabbit scurries toward the edge of the forest, past nesting boxes attached to the first row of trees. "I know that's you, Ralph. I've caught you before!" He laughs with his head thrown back, suddenly lost in a bluebird flying overhead. It lands on a nesting box and sings, *tu-a-wee*. "Good morning," Connor says.

Tu-a-wee.

"Good morning," I say.

Tu-a-wee.

"I wasn't talking to you." He smiles as he walks past me, inspecting Eli's bracelet.

"I know you weren't." I wave at the bluebird. "She's pretty."

"It's a boy."

"*He's* handsome."

"That box belongs to a sparrow. The bluebird should leave it alone and go back to the pole boxes in the field."

"Maybe he's renting a room from the sparrow for the weekend like people do at the lodge." I giggle, but Connor doesn't laugh. "Mom said you act as old as Granddad sometimes."

"They're disappearing." He pays no attention to my remark.

"Who are?" I skip next to him.

"The tree sparrows."

"Is that why it isn't in the nesting box?"

"No, there are plenty of sparrow species using the boxes, but the tree sparrows only visit in the winter."

"It's summer."

"I'm just saying they're disappearing."

"How do you know if it's not winter?"

"You ask way too many questions."

"I don't think they disappeared. I bet they're on vacation."

"They're not finding seed in the fields, Salem. I've been watching."

"For how long?"

"Would you stop it?"

"I thought you and Dad built the nesting boxes last year to help them out."

"We did."

"And you give them seeds in the feeders."

"I do."

"Maybe you need to build bigger feeders." From the window, Mom waves to hurry. "We need to get inside."

He ties his robe. "Don't touch my trap, okay?"

"I won't." I skip ahead then walk backward until we're side by side again. "Are you taking the woodchuck away after you catch it?"

"I already told you, no."

"Why?"

"It has babies here that'll starve. I'll make her move them on her own."

"How?"

He sighs. "Questions. So many questions."

"I like asking questions. Tell me how you'll get it to move away from Mom's flowers."

"All right. I might put a radio out here at night and upset it with noise. It will find a new place to go, over that way." He points past the lodge. "In the field across the street. Doubt it will go in the forest." He looks over his shoulder. "But if it does, Grady will catch it and eat it."

"Yuck! That's what my friends at school say. He eats rats. That's why he looks like one."

"I was only kidding."

"But my friends say…"

"Is the cake out?"

"No. After dinner."

"Eli will cry until he gets it. It'll be out before lunch." Connor swings the bracelet on his finger. "You like it, Salem? I can make you one."

"Love it. Can mine be purple?"

"No."

"Yellow?"

"Nope, only army green. Think Eli will like it? It's eight feet long if he takes it apart."

"Why would he do that? It's pretty like it is."

"To use it." He tugs my hair. "To put his hair in a ponytail, like yours."

"His hair is too short. *And* he's a boy."

"Granddad used to have one. I saw pictures."

"Dad said that's because he was a pippy."

"Hippie … a hippie. Eli could also use it to hang a pot over a fire."

"We're *not* supposed to play with fire."

"Or make a tourniquet."

"What's a turkey kit?"

Connor swings the bracelet faster. It flies off his finger, landing on the steps of the escape hatch. "He can use it as a belt or for shoelaces." He picks it up and hides it in his robe pocket.

"Salem."

"No, he can't. Eli's shorts have elastic. *And* he can't tie his sneakers. Mom buys him Velcro ones."

"You have no imagination."

"Yes, I do."

"Salem."

"Then I'll unknot it and teach him how to jump rope."

"I like that! Teach me, too." I skip through the escape hatch and into the lobby. "Will you, Connor?"

"Of course. Brad's big sister taught me. It's super easy."

"SALEM!"

• • •

My memory breaks. I'm halfway through the forest, using tree trunks as my guide amid the absent moon.

"Salem, I've been calling you." Joss grabs my arm. "Slow down for a sec so I can catch my breath."

My last memory of Eli—on his birthday no less—is a memory of Connor. I wish I had more time with Eli, remembered more, but Connor is always in the forefront. And if I don't remember much about Eli, Eli wouldn't remember much about me, if anything at all. I've tricked myself into believing that someday he'd wander home. He doesn't have memories of the lodge. He has no memories of our family. This *isn't* his home.

And now Nate … Nate's digging. Nate knows. Nate knows he's not coming home.

"Nate's digging, Joss."

"Salem, you listening?"

"Huh?"

"I said it's freezing out here. Put on your coat and your mittens." She pushes them into my chest.

"Thanks."

"Jim said he's digging for Grady's animal bone collection."

"That's right." Jim catches up to us. "He called it wonder crap."

My throat constricts. "Wunderkabinett. Don't make light of this."

"I'm not," he says.

"I know he's digging for Eli."

"He's not."

"Well, he's not searching for Grady's bone collection out in this weather, that's for damn sure. He knows Grady killed my brother. He's searching for the root cellar because that's where he'll find Eli."

"Salem," Joss says quietly.

"Nate came here and he's digging because he knows." I grip my coat snug under my chin, turn and throw myself forward to find the felled tree. "We always thought it was Grady"—tears well up in my eyes—"deep down we all thought the same thing. Didn't we?"

"Salem, go back to the lodge. Jim and I will get Nate."

"No."

"She's just as stubborn as he is," Jim says.

My skin shrinks around my bones from the cold. Branches slap my face as I press on. I push them away, letting them snap back as I pass.

"Hey!" One strikes Joss. "I'm behind you, you know."

"Sorry." I reach the stream and shuffle my feet forward over the tree trunk, inch by inch, my arms out for balance.

"Good find," Jim says. His hair, beard, and green sweater are a slab of snow. The abominable snowman comes to mind. "I had to drop down the bank and balance on icy rocks to cross the water earlier."

"My granddad cut the tree down when we were little."

"Must be rotted out by now."

"No. Connor said it would last a good fifty years." My arms swing in a circle, blood pumping.

"Careful, Salem," Joss says.

"One at a time." I hop off and wave them across, continuing the slog to Grady's cabin.

The forest is in complete disarray: pine branches low from the weight of snow, rocks and stumps lost in white, my tracks from the other day gone missing. And my head … my head is a pure tangle of confusion.

Eli might be out here.

Is it possible Grady put him in the root cellar after the police searched? Or could it be that no one looked because no one knew it existed? Granddad would've mentioned it to the cops if he knew. He would've. I just know it.

Terror, real terror of what I'm walking into hits me. What if I see bones? What does the murder mean if Grady is dead? Did Nate know anything? Did he see it happen? Did he know Grady killed Eli but never knew where the body was?

"Salem, wait!"

I pass the fort Nate and Connor built. It's now a square wall of snow, the bliss of childhood defeated by nature.

Connor was first born, a leader, brilliant, the one I looked up to. Eli was a toy, not human to me, cute and cuddly like my stuffed animals. Who was I among them? And who am I now without them?

"Salem, are you listening? Don't go another step without me. Wait up so I can help you."

I begin to run, taking wild steps through the fierce wind and snow, plucking my feet up high and thrusting them down again. I'm close. I'm at the crest of the hill that leads to Grady's. But suddenly I feel like my life will end when I reach Eli, that his loss has kept me alive. The last Whitfield, the one who's safe if

Eli's out there, the one who'll wither and die once he's found. My job to stay and wait for him is over.

"Salem, stay back!" Nate shouts from the bottom of the hill. He parked his truck at a distance behind a tree that obstructs the driveway. High beams light the property. Hundreds of small holes dug in the frozen earth are visible.

I stumble when I see Brad standing next to Nate. He raises a hand for me to stay away. I walk slower and slower, grabbing hold of a tree trunk to stop myself. My insides ignite and rise in my throat. Shovels lay on the ground. A bush was cut back. And a door set into the hill is propped open with a branch.

Nate walks toward me. I shake my head, a silent prod for him to say he hasn't found anything.

But he doesn't.

"Say something," I tell him.

He doesn't.

His hair is stiff, his face white. There's no reassurance in his body language, no optimism in his walk, no hope left in his troubled voice.

"Salem, stay there. I'm coming to talk to you."

No, I say to myself. I step closer to the tree, wanting it to suck me in so I can withdraw from the forest, from this scene, from what Nate's going to say. A car pulls up the driveway, parks behind Brad's vehicle. It's Logan, the other Tilford Lake cop. Two cops, an open door, Nate coming to talk to me.

No.

"Stay there," Nate says.

"Why?" I step forward. "Say it, Nate. Why?"

Joss bounds in front of me. She seizes my shoulders and blocks my view. "Look at me," she says. "We're going back to the lodge. You don't need to be here."

Jim runs past us and meets Nate in a private huddle. Their whispers ricochet through the pines and coil around my neck.

Bones ... It's him ... Get her out of here...

"Go back, Salem."

"Joss, there's nothing at the lodge." My vision spirals like a kaleidoscope, teary eyes distorting the forest. "I'm not walking away from him."

"It could be someone else."

Broken and drawn, her cheeks sag, a gloom that forces her to lower her head and set her lips firm. She knows that's not true.

My family, the Whitfield curse, they're all dead. I'm alone in this. Alone to bury the one who was lost before anyone else, the baby, the one who should've lived the longest. Eli's remains are only yards away, I can hold him if I want, but that would make this all too real. There's still the possibility I'm dreaming. A chance that I'm not the unluckiest person in the world.

Joss squeezes my shoulders. "Babe, I'm sorry." There's a sudden tremor in her hands.

"How do they know? Ask Nate how he knows it's Eli. Is he in his rocket ship pajamas? The blue ones?"

"Salem." Nate's voice is low, apologetic. He holds me, but I'm numb to his touch. Words are mute. Joss and Jim speak, I watch their lips move, hear nothing. Snow lands on my face; I sense nothing. Joss waits for me to break down, howl and weep, but I give her nothing. My eyes stay fixed on Brad, his flashlight, and the river of light shining down on my brother's cold and lonesome bones.

I shed my mittens. Reaching under my coat collar, I pull out Eli's key—a comfort I knew I needed to bring with me. I secure it in my hand and thumb his initials, finishing the hike down the hill.

"Salem, wait."

"Let her go." Jim places his arm across Nate. "Think how you'd feel in this situation. She has to go."

I repeat in my mind that there's still a chance. But I know from experience that when people fade out of my memory, they never come back. Eli faded away when I was a child. I couldn't hold any memories of him in my mind. He can't come back. And as I walk closer to the root cellar, disappointment and heartache roil inside me.

I slip off my coat, ready to lay it over him to keep him warm. I think about the reason why this happened. How it came about.

"Don't touch him," Brad says. "You can go inside, but don't touch him."

I raise Eli's key to a tear pooling on my chin, then slide it to my lips for a kiss. The key pulsates from my shivering fingers like it's come alive.

When I enter the dank root cellar, I feel the same anguish that I've seen on the face of a gray fox in a coil spring trap, forlorn, desperate. The separation from family, the seclusion under the earth, his bones misshapen, skull in pieces ... how he must have suffered, it rips my heart from my ribs. I don't touch him or stare. I only cover him. He's in a galvanized steel tub in need of warmth. He hated being cold. Even during the summer months, he'd sleep in winter pajamas.

Those are missing.

My emotions surge while waiting for Chief to call with instructions for Brad and Logan. They won't listen to Nate, even though Nate knows a hell of a lot more than they do. He insists they call in a crime scene unit or a detective from the city.

Oblivious, Brad keeps repeating that there's no crime scene to investigate, that he probably wasn't killed in the root cellar, that he was likely put here long after the fact, that's why he's allowed me to go inside. Probably, likely, is what Brad says.

I block out the arguments and the ignorance, send Jim and Joss back to the lodge, and wait in the icy crypt next to Eli. I sit with him among shelves lined with dusty Mason jars, next to large bins labeled for potatoes and onions, among the dirt floor and concrete block walls, next to a wooden table with Grady's animal creatures on top, and tubs of bones below. Is there another person's skeleton in the tubs? The thought of that makes me sick. Sitting underground with the moldy, death-like odors makes me sick.

I want Brad and Logan to move Eli. Lift him out of this grave and take him to the station. I insist. I tell them I'll carry him back to the lodge if they don't move him. I insist again, and they agree when I start to lift the steel tub by myself.

Chief calls back with instructions and advice from area agencies: Rein yourselves in… Don't let anyone disturb the scene … Don't jump to immediate conclusions … Take your time and think … Clear the scene … A detective is being assigned and is on her way… Don't touch a thing until she gets there…

Like Nate had suggested: call in someone else. Except I've already convinced Brad and Logan to put Eli in one of their vehicles. I want him out of this godforsaken place. I want him inside a warm building, near people, surrounded by voices. I need his remains protected. But I'm overwrought with guilt as they drive off the property. My parents wouldn't have done this. They would've held him for hours. I gave him away. Irrationally, I pushed him from a place within half a mile of his home.

I shout for them to bring him back. Scream and kick the snow next to the fetid root cellar. "Bring him back." I turn to face Nate, struck by the whispering wind.

Bring him back.

NINETEEN

"Wait and see," Nate says for the millionth time. "You don't know if it's him."

"Is that why you had that look on your face when you saw me walking down the hill?" My eyebrows shoot up. "Because you didn't think it was him?"

I add another log to the fire. Flames ignite and cast a glow onto the lobby floor where Joss and Jim have spread a blanket and are falling asleep. Joss, a true friend, chose the floor over one of the beds so she can be within earshot, just in case I need anything. But at four in the morning, she can't hang in with me much longer. After apologies and hugs throughout the night, swollen eyes and pockets full of used tissues, we're beat.

"I thought we'd searched every inch of Tilford Lake. All these years, and after finding him, I didn't even hold him. I didn't touch his hand to let him know I was with him. It was so fast, Nate. I forgot to tell him someone who loved him was there." I rub my forehead. "Everything happened like a dream. Why didn't I say something to him?" I drop onto one of the leather chairs in a daze, Nate in the one across from me, our legs slipping under blankets. "The last time I saw Eli was years back. It's hard to picture him that small." I close my eyes to push my thoughts away, to clear the scene of the root cellar. "This isn't how it was supposed to turn out." I whip my hair back and forth to get the smell of dirt and mildew to wane.

"Initial reactions don't mean a thing," Nate says.

"That's not true. Everyone felt it. We all knew when we were out there. Hard to imagine it's anyone but Eli."

"That's the problem. We're imagining and not being realistic."

"*I'm* being realistic. You're not. That was my brother. *Is. Is* my brother."

"With no teeth or hair, it will take time to identify—"

"Please"—I press my fingers to my forehead—"please stop. I don't want to think about why his skull was in pieces. I saw him, Nate. I know."

He leans forward. "Find the hope that you lost."

"Why? So it can be ripped away from me again?"

He drops back and puts his feet on the coffee table, rubbing them against mine. "Brad and Logan are imbeciles." He tries for a smile.

"No kidding."

"They made a mess out of everything."

"I know. I wish you were a Tilford Lake cop instead of one of them."

He shakes his head. "I'm not cop material."

Jim quickly sits up to object.

"Keep your mouth shut," Nate warns.

"He's heard that one before, Salem."

"What did I just tell you?"

"Everyone's always on his case about becoming a cop. I've been pushing him since high school."

"I'm not the type," Nate says, his voice firm.

Jim lowers back down and places his arm over his eyes to block the light of the fire. "I'd love to know what you think 'the type' is."

"Anyone but me."

"Wraaang." He uses a loud nasally voice. "That's ass-backward and you know it. Live the dream, Nate."

"I am."

"Then live a bigger dream. You're better than stalking guys cheating on their wives and tracking people down. You've always been better at everything. I could never keep up with you."

"I'm *not* better at everything. And being in situations like this one isn't how I want to live my life."

Jim props himself up on his elbows. "Then why'd you come? You knew you'd find her brother's remains. You knew."

Nate shakes his head incessantly.

"You knew exactly why you were coming here ... besides trying to hook up with your first crush."

"Drop it."

"You've talked about Salem since we were ten."

"Jim, don't push me."

"I don't push you enough. Now tell her why you have a quiet job hiding in the shadows."

Nate's feet hit the floor. "Lay off. If I were a cop, I'd get pushed into situations I have no control over."

"You're right." Jim puckers his lips and starts to whistle. His head rocks to a made-up tune, an act to annoy Nate. He tugs his ear, whistles more. Then suddenly stops and looks directly into Nate's eyes. "Better to hit the bottle than to save lives and live up to your name."

"Goddamn you, Jim. One more word"—Nate holds up a finger—"one more, and I swear."

Joss spreads the blanket over their heads, making Jim disappear to help end the battle. "Leave him alone," she says in a sleepy voice. Jim kisses her and his outline shifts alongside hers.

"He said you knew you'd find Eli," I say to Nate, accepting what Jim said as the truth. "Did you see something when you were a kid?"

Nate stares at me for a minute before lowering his head. "No. You've asked me that already." He draws circle patterns on the arms of the chair.

"Grady gave us bad vibes."

"Who's us?" He looks up.

"The kids in town. You had the same gut feeling as the rest of us, or you saw something."

"I didn't. I saw him cleaning bones, but I never saw the bones pieced together like the animals in the root cellar. I didn't know he made all those mutilated creatures until I read your granddad's letter."

The image of a two-headed chipmunk with a rat's tail gives me cold shivers. And the spine made to look like a centipede, and the rabbit … the rabbit skeleton with tiny bird skulls for feet.

"The cellar is intact compared to the cabin, doesn't seem like Grady was the one who cleared his place out," he says. "It's more like people came and stripped it, but no one knew about the cellar or it would've been cleaned out like the rest of the property."

"You're probably right."

"You know anyone who could've done it? I wouldn't mind getting back some of my gram's stuff for my mom."

"Joss and I can ask around. Kids using the cabin as a party house might've felt like everything in there was fair game. But it could've been anyone."

I look from one end of the lobby to the other. Sixty years of family possessions under one roof. Three generations. What happens to everything when I die? Who will take the furniture, the clothes, the mementos? Will the photograph above the door end up in a landfill? Will the lodge get torn down? I'm too young to have to think about such things, and too old not to worry about it.

I tuck my blanket under my chin for comfort.

"Sorry, Salem." Nate's voice emerges as a faint whisper. I can tell he's referring to Eli. I answer with a quick nod, a little sad he's dropped the *wait and see what the detective says, wait for more evidence, wait for DNA results.* "Wish there was something I could do." He puts his feet back on the coffee table, pressing his toes against mine. He sits quietly, his hair as dark as the hour, and limp from being out in the snow.

"You found him, Nate. That's everything my family ever wanted."

"*If* it's him."

I look up at him through my eyelashes. "Thanks for saying that. I'd feel better if it were you at the station with Eli, not Logan or Brad." My insinuation that he should be a cop is unintentional this time.

Nate keeps his eyes on me. The orange glow of the fire sends glimmers along his cheekbones, but there's an expression of unspeakable pain in his tired eyes. I watch his throat as he swallows thickly.

"People always say that, you know. That I should be a cop, or they ask why I didn't want to be one, like it's the same job I have without the paycheck and the benefits. It's not. They're two separate worlds."

"Just tell her," Jim mumbles. "Chicks dig damaged men."

"Go to sleep."

"Just helping you out, making it easier for her to find out you're messed up."

"I'm not mes—" Nate stops mid-sentence, takes a goliath breath. I can hear him processing his response. He pinches his nose and says, "Jim. This isn't the right time."

"You're afraid," Jim says.

"That's not it."

"It *is* it. And it's okay. I keep telling you to be open about it and you'll feel better." Jim's hand slithers out from under the blanket. He feels for the 6-pack a foot from his head. Without looking, he grabs a bottle and flings it in the air toward Nate. "Good catch," he says when the bottle doesn't break.

Nate puts half the beer away in three gulps. Jim might be right. The men I've known locked their emotions away. Especially fear. They projected themselves as powerful animals in wealth and actual strength. My ex-husband with his motorcycle, the toys he bought to compete with his friends, how he acted like a hotshot and bossed me around. He was a dictatorial ass who hid his feelings. It was all about power, central to his existence.

"Your face is red like it was when you were tearing apart your living room," Nate says.

My ex-husband believed that being a tough-guy with authority led to happiness. His emotions didn't extend beyond that. I say there's more to life than always being happy. Everyone needs to let the bad in to have a deeper appreciation of the good, experience fear to gain self-confidence. I told him that once. I did. And he laughed.

"Salem, talk to me."

I pull my sweater cuffs down to keep from biting my nails. I'm disappointed in myself for thinking about him. "It's bitterness this time … and maybe it was last time. I can't remember."

"About?"

"Men. Nothing important."

He slides his palms down his thighs and claws his knees. "We suck, don't we?"

"Not you. And I mean nothing important compared to the rest of the night. I'm just overthinking my past."

His hands slide back up, the tension easing in his shoulders. "Exactly why the stuff about being a cop doesn't matter, not with everything else going on."

I smile and he smiles back, lifting his blanket for me to come over.

Joss turns away from Jim, and an outline of a loving spoon position forms under the purple and white polka-dotted blanket, the same colors as the crocuses lining the drive. As I nestle alongside Nate, I notice the wilted crocus crown resting above us on the fireplace mantel. Its beauty has died, but Virginia's intent to awaken love has tunneled into our lives.

Nate pulls me into an embrace and kisses the top of my head. His masculine scent of sweat and sandalwood masks the stench of the cellar, providing some relief. We hold hands under the blanket, but my mind wanders away from his touch.

I was courageous when I walked down the hill and into the dark cellar. Connor would've been proud. But after a glimpse of the brutality, the air turned so cold it pricked the inside of my nose and throat. It was difficult to swallow. I couldn't find my breath. The voices outside erupted into the small room, causing my eardrums to ring. Then my eyes stung. I kept looking up to see the moon, but only saw soil overhead.

•   •   •

"Look up, Salem," is what Connor said the night after Eli went missing. "You see it?"

"See what?" I looked up.

"The moon. It's the easiest object to find in the sky, except when the skies are gray."

"Oh, I love that song about gray skies. Grandma sings it to me all the time. You are my sunshine…"

"I'm talking about the moon, not the skies. You know it formed when a chunk of Earth got torn away by a big impact."

"Yeah?"

"Did you know?"

"No." I shook my head. "Maybe another chunk got taken away last night and Eli's on it. If we see another moon, he might be there. Then we can go get him."

"He'd be dead."

I looked to see if our parents were nearby. I saw them along the edge of the forest. "Connor, don't say that," I whispered.

"He couldn't breathe, Salem. Not on the moon."

"Oh, then he's definitely not there."

Connor looked around then hugged me, something he started doing more often after that night. He even sat through me singing the sunshine song with only minimal complaints about my flat voice.

"Love you, Salem," he said.

"Because I make you happy?"

"Sometimes."

"You're supposed to say when skies are gray."

"Yep, greatly"—he spread his arms wide—"hugely"—he spread them wider—"you make me monstrously happy ... when skies are gray."

• • •

Showers of sparks from cracking firewood float into the chimney. I sit up and hug myself.

"It's okay, beautiful." Nate massages the nape of my neck, guiding me back to his side. "Close your eyes," he whispers. He yawns and stretches his legs, causing me to yawn and stretch mine. My head lowers to his shoulder, in range of the steady beats of his heart.

I take longer, deeper breaths as the early morning drones on, finding relief when my limbs grow heavy, and I fall into a velvety sleep.

TWENTY

One fall night when the moon bloomed bright and large, Connor let me use his pirate hand telescope to scan the sky. Convinced Eli was up there, I tried to find him, but he was hiding and wouldn't come out. I sat on the front steps and peeped through the tiny hole, copycatting Connor's pose when he'd use it to watch birds nesting in the tall pines or to scout for boats on the lake. The telescope worked for him. He found extraordinary magic with it. I saw only the dead of nightfall and heard only a biting silence that greedily gnawed at my spirit.

No color. No movement. No Eli.

After that, I daydreamed about *my* disappearance. If Eli could vanish without a trace, when would I wake up and be in a faraway land? What would become of me?

When I awoke this morning, my belief that this was possible became a reality. Not when, *when* would I disappear, but what has already become of me? Where have I gone?

Some would say I dried up after graduating from high school, fettered with iron shackles in my marriage. Others would say it was after my mom died, that my limbs took root inside the lodge, making rare silhouetted appearances in the front window. I breathe, but that doesn't mean I exist … something to mull over. It doesn't have to be. This girl can break free, sow pink into her cheeks, not settle on a prearranged course. It doesn't have to be.

"Salem, you there?" Joss asks.

"I'm thinking."

I balance my cell between my ear and shoulder and open the front curtains. Dust motes cascade in the bright sunlight. I squint, grappling with mid-morning. The spot on the front porch where I sat with the telescope years ago is slick with black ice, a hazard that hinders my escape.

"You like the yellow or the red?" Joss asks. "Yellow or red, babe."

"Lemon or strawberry?" I question her vagueness.

"Yeah."

"The white powdery donuts with the jelly filling?"

"Yeah, come on. I'm holding up the line."

I blow at my bangs and switch ears. "You know, I'm not all that hungry."

"You gotta eat."

"Are there any bagels?"

"Nope."

"Muffins?"

"Nope. I'll get you a red one."

"I've got frozen waffles here I can eat."

"Donuts are healthier ... three reds, one yellow," she orders. "You think Nate likes red?"

"Is that strawberry?"

She ignores my question.

"Hello?"

"Jim ... hey, Jim. What kind does Nate like?"

"Joss, get whatever you want."

"Wait, grumpy. What about a drink?"

"I'm fine with what's here."

She smacks her gum. Twice. I bet her hand is on her hip. "Am I bothering you? Are you and Nate in the middle of a hot fuck or something?"

"Hey, Joss. Can you hear me rolling my eyes? Hear that? I'm doing it again. Listen."

"Yep." She smacks her gum. "That's really special."

I put my hand flat against the windowpane. Exterior frost crystals turn to liquid under my palm and trickle down the glass. "Food and sex are the last things on my mind." A delicate outline of my hand remains when I pull away. "Whatever you want to get is fine."

"A red jelly and a coffee, coming right up."

I end the call, rubbing the sleep from my eyes. Nate is in the shower. Ollie is taking his after-breakfast nap. Virginia, still unaccounted for, and my other rooms sit empty after the four women took off to stay in the next town over. Granddad is my remaining companion. His neatly stacked letters are on the reception desk, soliciting my attention. With only two left to read, I pick one up, slip into the armchair next to the fireplace, and unfold the cream-colored paper.

• • •

Grady,

I saw a ghost. No, really. She opened age-old wounds. I called to tell you about her. Still not answering your phone? Pick up when I call. It could be a life or death situation … like Virginia Pullman!

Vixen Virginia, back here in Tilford Lake. Said she was in town to visit a dear friend. Was it Gert? Did she stop by your place? Do tell, but not in front of Carol. Her face was beet red when I said I ran into Virginia. She started asking a heap of heated questions. Where did I see her? How long did we talk? Was anyone else there with us? When is she leaving? Did you do anything I should know about, Felix? Did you?

It's painful here. Carol told me to "talk to the hand." Have you heard that one? She picked it up from our granddaughter. I *found out talking to the hand does NOT mean I should talk to the hand. Tried that and got nothing back, now Carol's giving me the silent treatment. Thought she'd be over it by now.*

I should've made an about-face when I saw Virginia at the bank. Does she still have an account up this way? Odd, isn't it? She hasn't lived here for years. Guess that's beside the point. I'm digging myself into a deeper hole thinking about her.

Then again, how can I not think about my past? You tell me. You know the story. That sneaky woman showed up one night just days before the prom, waiting for me in my parents' backyard. I know you've heard it, but let me get it off my chest one last time. It's eating me alive. That dirty, lousy, fink of a woman.

Virginia was waiting by the trashcans next to the garage. Hadn't a clue she was there. I went out back to haul the cans to the front for morning pickup, and she blinded me with a flashlight. Scared the bejesus out of me. After I blinked the white spots away, I saw her waving the light across her breasts. Topless! She was taunting me topless, Grady! Nearly ruined my life. I swear I didn't touch her. Didn't matter, though. I was guilty. Guilty of cracking a smile, couldn't help myself.

She said not to tell a soul I'd turned her down. Fine with me. It would've ended right there if it weren't for that weasel next door, Nicky Turner. He saw me handing her her blouse. Rumors spread like a lit wick of dynamite. Then Carol heard and came stomping over to toss her prom dress in my face. She said I'd broken her heart. I was seventeen, first time I'd seen a woman in the flesh, and it was the wrong one! Always stays with a man, doesn't it? What a drag it had to be Virginia. Was I the only one who didn't have a crush on her?

By the way, thanks for talking me down from the high school roof after Carol told me to go to hell. What a week that was. You had started your maintenance job, the first day, I recall, came out carrying a broken chair to the dumpster. You looked up and shook your head, said, "Felix, you jump, and I'll be the one who has to clean up your guts, and they don't pay me enough to shovel innards off the sidewalk."

Ha! Your morbid sense of humor, I almost rolled off the roof laughing.

Virginia hasn't changed, by the way. She said her husband is the pilot of Air Force One. Same as in grammar school when she said she took her parents' private jet to the North Pole to visit Santa, and in middle school when she told everyone she was spending the weekend with her Aunt Jayne. Jayne Mansfield.

Lies! Lonesome woman, wouldn't you say? No family. No ring on her finger. All that money couldn't buy her a husband. She'll say anything to make her life more interesting than it actually is, a pure attention seeker.

Sorry to tell it like it is. Best to keep this between us and not mention my words to Gert. She'd defend Virginia from sunup to sundown. I remember she lived in the Pullman guesthouse when she was a tot. Her mom was their cook. Is that why she always liked Virginia? She's a good woman, Grady. I love Gert. Loyal like my Carol. Don't want to cause a rift between the four of us by saying anything to upset her. Maybe Virginia even took to Gert as the sister she never had. Is it why she's out this way? Does she know Gert's cancer came back?

Wish we could help. Money's tight, but we can whip up a nice meal to bring over. Gert like barbeque meatballs made in the crock? Let us know. We'll stop by soon and try to cheer her up.

Be well, my friend.

Let's all be well.

Felix

• • •

On the way outside to meet Brad, a black squirrel barks a short, sharp *kuk* and twitches its tail for me to stay back. Trapped in the metal bird feeder on the front porch, the mischievous little thief gorged on half the seed.

Ollie steps out and tilts his head in curiosity. "Pudgy rodent. Look at him, Olls. He ate half the food in the feeder. Now he's too fat to get out." Ollie barks. "I know, buddy. The metal cage was supposed to be squirrel-proof." A second bark, loud and friendly. "What?" His rump sways as Brad's patrol car comes up the drive. "Yep, there's your friend. He said he was stopping by."

Nate steps outside with my granddad's letter in his hand. He's wearing only a small bath towel around his waist and unlaced boots with no socks. He leans over and plants a kiss on my lips. After I stare stupidly at the skimpy towel, I force myself to look away and into his eyes.

"Your granddad's letters are gold." He hands it to me. "Any thoughts about Virginia?"

"Yeah. The note she gave me might have something to do with my granddad." I take it out of my pocket and show it to him.

He reads it and hands it back. "She's not sorry for what?"

I shrug. "I don't know. Could be the situation he wrote about in his letter."

Brad steps out of his car and gives a wave that I don't return. He stops on the bottom step of the porch before quietly making his way up the stairs.

"Watch for ice, Brad."

He takes off his hat and pats his sandy blond hair into place. "Anyone else here?" His eyes sweep the open doorway.

"Joss and Jim are out getting food."

"Any guests?"

"My guest is missing. I told you that yesterday. Virginia Pullman. Remember? Her car is under that pile of snow." I point to the mound next to my Cherokee. "And my other guests left when you pulled your gun in the lobby."

Nate cups my shoulder and draws me closer, either a dominant show of power over Brad, or to offer emotional support. Surprising such a simple gesture makes me feel loved.

"Just doing my job."

"By provoking a fight with phony flyers?"

"They were real."

"The cases were solved." I cross my arms. "It doesn't matter. What happened to Eli? Where is he now? What did the detective say?"

"Eli's at the station in the evidence room. Chief threw a fit when he found out we moved him from the cellar."

"Tell him I made you do it."

He snickers. "You kidding me? That'd be even worse."

Our heads turn to the swinging bird feeder. The caged squirrel sends out another *kuk* and swats its tail, disturbed by Ollie sitting below him.

"I'll let you out in a second." I turn back to Brad. "What did the detective say?"

"Nothing, yet. She arrived when I was on my way out."

"Oh." My shoulders fall.

"Chief called in a few more people. He sent me out to meet them at the property." He looks down, shuffles his feet. "I thought I'd stop by to see how you're doing first. Need anything?"

"Yeah, I need you to find Virginia."

Nate taps the letter. "An attention seeker," he reminds me.

"I know." I uncross my arms. "Find her. She didn't go far without her car. She can barely walk. And in this snow…"

"Yep." He puts his hat back on. "That all?"

I step forward. "No, that's not all. Tell me why Connor hit you."

"Trivial kid stuff. Water under the bridge."

"Brad." I take his arm and soften my voice. "Please? I always remember Connor as a caring big brother. Now I'm picturing him as a bully. What happened?" Brad blinks at my hand on his arm. His cheeks flush pink. "Please," I repeat.

He lifts his head and focuses on Nate. I watch him contemplate telling me about the fight, but I know he won't with Nate within earshot.

I glance over my shoulder. "Nate, there's a pair of pliers in the cabinet in the laundry room. Can you get them for me? I need to twist off the wire on the feeder door to set the squirrel free."

"Yep." He holds the ridge of the tucked towel at his waist and walks inside.

"Well done," Brad says.

"We've got a minute. Now talk. Was the fight about Eli?"

"No, Shelly."

"Your sister?"

"I caught them kissing in the woods."

"What?" My jaw drops.

"Connor's hand was fumbling under her shirt. It hurt to see that, you know?" He twists his fingers, breathing faster.

Brad's the jealous type over women *and* men. He'd not only feel betrayed by Connor, but anxious that he might lose him. In high school, Brad fell a year behind in French and was put in the same class as me. He had a crush on a girl who sat next to him. But when the girl's boyfriend stopped by the classroom to surprise her with flowers, Brad clawed his desk, crumpled his papers with one hand, and broke his pencil with the other. His jealousy is over the top. Another reason women don't like him.

"So you hit Connor over it, and he punched you back?"

He shakes his head. "Connor never hit me, Salem."

I look down at him suspiciously, squinting in the bright sunlight. He seems embarrassed, and I'm embarrassed for him.

"Your sister clocked you and Connor took the fall so no one would find out. Is that it?"

"Well," he says, resting his arm on the porch railing in a humiliated stance, stooped over, head down, "that's right. The dorky, fat, wedgie kid got beat up by his sister, and his best friend saw it all."

A total sadness I've never felt for Brad falls over me. And it's *not* a feeling I want to have for him. It makes me wonder if Connor hung out with him because he genuinely liked him, or because he pitied him like I do now. I told Brad that wasn't the case, but now I just don't know. A dreary thought to digest. It might even be true of my granddad's friendship with Grady, and why Gert and Virginia were friends.

"Connor was *my* friend, not hers. And to see the two of them like *that*." He rubs his hand up and down the railing. "She kept her tongue swirling in Connor's mouth even when I threw a rock at her."

I snort. "You threw a rock at your sister? No wonder she punched you."

"I missed."

"Of course."

"On purpose."

"Uh-huh."

He turns around and heads for his car. "Shelly hit me because I said I was going to tell our dad." His voice has a hard edge to it. "He'd ground her for it. We were just kids. She shouldn't have been making out at that age."

"Ah." I nod. That's why people don't feel sorry for Brad for long. He's nothing but a big baby. "You're not a kid anymore, Brad. You don't have to throw a fit and storm off."

"Bite me!"

Nate stands tall behind me. "Need any help?"

"Nah. He's leaving."

"Don't you dare tell anyone, Salem. Not a word." Brad points at me but he's quick to retract his hand, a stunned reaction to his own words. Awareness has sunk in. He shouldn't be acting this way with everything else that's going on, or at all. "Sorry," he says, his head turning to the side as if he got slapped. I pity him again.

Nate begins twisting the wire off the feeder. The distressed squirrel shouts out an alarm call, chattering and flicking its tail. Ollie growls at it, and I offer scratches behind his ears until he simmers down.

"Almost got it?" I ask.

"A few more turns," Nate says.

"Keep me updated every hour about Eli," I call out to Brad. "And find Virginia for me."

"Bradley." Doreen's high-pitched voice enters through his walkie. "Bradley, you there?"

"I'm here, Doreen."

"Bradley?"

"Doreen, go 'head." He puts his arm on the roof of his patrol car and rests his forehead on his sleeve.

"Chief is coming in."

"He's on vacation. Tell him we got everything under control."

"Bradley."

He exhales. "What, Doreen?"

"He wants you back at the station. He said, *pronto*."

Nate opens the door of the feeder and steps back. "Got it."

"Cool." I pull Ollie inside and close the door to the lodge so the agitated squirrel can hightail it out of here.

Brad scratches his forehead with his thumb before he's back on the walkie. "I'm supposed to meet people at the Murphy property."

The walkie clicks but her voice dies under static. Nate and I stare at Brad, listening in on the conversation.

"Can you repeat that?" He straightens his back.

"Chief is coming in."

"No, what you said after that."

"It's not the little Whitfield boy."

I walk to the edge of the porch and wrap my arm around the post. The squirrel jumps out of the feeder and dashes through the front yard, rejoicing in its freedom. It bolts past Brad at lightning speed, bounding from tree to tree through the glittering snow.

"Come again?" Brad asks, looking up at me.

"The detective said they're animal bones pieced together to look like a child's skeleton. She left here laughing up a storm."

"I knew it." Nate grins.

"Yes!" I grin wider than him.

Brad rubs his forehead. "Chief ... is he fuming? Is that why he's coming in?" There's no answer. "Doreen?" He drums his fingers on the hood, suddenly stops and holds them flat. "Fuck." He hurls his car door open and drops heavily into the front seat. After multiple smacks of the wheel, he starts the engine, puts the car in reverse, and backs out of the long driveway, not bothering to take the time to say goodbye.

"Bye, Brad!" I beam.

"It's not him," Nate says, his mouth close to my ear. "It's not him, Salem."

I turn and grab him by the nape of the neck and look steadily into his eyes. A flush climbs up my chest and burns into my cheeks. My life just did a complete 180 in a matter of seconds. All traces of the punishing night have washed away. I slip my hand under his towel, and he stifles a groan against my lips.

"Let's go inside and celebrate," I whisper.

He sets his forehead to mine, his dimple awakening next to his full lips. "Yes, let's do that." His voice is deeper than usual, thick with want. He runs his fingers across my waist, then casually reaches for the door handle. "We're going to take this one slow."

TWENTY-ONE

Unlike my nightmares, there's no need to tear through the forest on a frantic search for Eli. Pines no longer grow denser and darker as I continue to wend my way closer to Grady's. The ground is no longer littered with dead branches but glazed in an expanse of blinding white.

Chickadees take flight from ice-rimmed branches. Their rapid departure creates plummeting mini-snowballs, specking Joss and Nate's dark coats. Far ahead, Jim leaves a single line of prints for us to follow. The *slap* of his snowshoes, offbeat and low-pitched to ours, conjures up a memory of the last time my family used the shoes for a winter hike—the Christmas before my dad and Connor died—the shoes a gift to the family from my mom. She led the way that evening. We followed her to the eastern side of the property, out of the trees and through the field dotted with bird feeders, past two sparrows Connor called by name, and over to the lake to enjoy the sunset. Vibrant pinks, purples, yellows, and oranges, skated over the partially frozen water. For once Connor didn't give us a lesson on the season's sunsets and why they're more beautiful in the winter. Now I wish he had.

I set off on a short jog, twenty, thirty, forty feet, wasted in nothing flat from lack of exercise. My lungs burn with each breath. Embarrassed, I keep my back turned to Nate and Joss, waiting for them next to a young red pine.

Rime ice on the windward side of the tree begs to be poked. I prod the spiky crystals, splay my hand on the needles, and carry out a two-finger piano run along a low branch. It dips from the tension, a whirlwind of excess snow kicked up in my face. I wave it away then sidle between two branches to the fresh snow stuck to the trunk, soft enough to finger two hearts, a house, and my name ... the same imagery I'd sketch into the playground sand with a stick. It's a silly activity, but one that makes my whole face smile.

The forest returning to my childhood kingdom, harmless and unblemished, is precisely what I need today. Finding Eli, then to learn it was a fake skeleton of a boy pieced together from animal bones, and now the renewed hope ... it's all too much to process. I'm still sorting through my feelings of why my reaction was surprisingly tame. I cried but didn't wake with the same devastating thoughts boring into me that I couldn't go on without him. Not like the experience with the rest of my family. Not how it was when my mom died, and a freight train roared in and crushed me. Not how my deep and deafening cries for my dad and Connor swallowed the forest life whole. Not like any of that.

"Hey, ho. Out of breath from someone's morning wood?" Joss teases, making the juvenile "finger in the hole" gesture. I elbow her side to get her to stop. "What?" She grabs my coat, stumbles, and wobbles on my mom's snowshoes like an unsteady drunk. "Why'd you take off?"

"No reason."

"Sure, sounds believable. No reason to run full speed ahead until you almost have a heart attack. No reason at all." She continues to steady herself on my arm as we walk alongside an impenetrable thorn thicket.

"I had thoughts I needed to get out of my head, that's all."

"Told ya," she says to Nate. "She's obsessed with her family. They're all she ever thinks about."

"Not true."

"You should be thinking about Nate."

"Maybe I was."

"Maybe, but doubtful."

I give her a long stare. "You've been lucky, Joss. Wait till you lose your parents or one of your sisters. It's not something that ever leaves you. It just doesn't."

"Sorry," she whispers. "Did I put you in a bad mood?"

"No, I'm actually in a great mood today."

"Are you back to believing Eli's bagging groceries in the next town over?"

"He could be. Or he could be a bartender, or a chef, or a construction worker. Doubt I'll ever know." I bend down and tighten a strap on her snowshoe.

"Why are we going to Grady's then?"

"To inspect the root cellar. It was too dark to get a good look last night."

"Aren't you creeped out by it? I can go if you want to wait back at the lodge."

"I'm good."

"Babe, really?"

"She's curious," Nate says. He pops his coat collar to protect his neck from the cold and puts on a pair of sunglasses. A glowing smile holds steady on his unshaven, ruddy face. A smile that pulls my own cheeks high. He takes my hand, and we step a little faster to catch up with Jim.

"That's right. I'm curious." I swing Nate's arm, his skin warm and rough under my fingers.

"We're also going so I can get a sense of how much I'll be able to take home with me on this trip." He squeezes my hand.

"And I want to do it before the cops grow brains and realize they should be out there searching the cellar before us."

"Oh, yeah. I didn't think of that," Joss says.

"I'm banking on the fact that they didn't either. I want to dig through it before they take off with something I haven't seen."

We reach the top of the hill and begin the hike down to Grady's root cellar. From my granddad's letter about the Wunderkabinett, I had pictured two or three creatures made of bones, but there were at least thirty in there. Connor collected in threes but stopped. Maybe he got tired of it, outgrew the fascination. But Grady must've worked on his collection for years, even decades.

"Why do you think Grady made a skeleton of a kid?" Joss asks.

"It had something to do with him wanting to fix his face," Nate says. "I think the deformed animals are supposed to represent him ... his birth defect and the way he saw himself mangled and not human. And the human-like skeleton was his dream, but he never got it right. That's why the skull was in pieces."

"You're guessing," she says.

"I'm not guessing, I'm deducing." Nate hisses in a breath. "Another hole in the roof." I look up at a dead oak branch spearing the cabin roof. "Jim and I might have to tear this place down so no one gets hurt."

"I can help," I offer.

"Blaaa!" Jim dangles an animal skeleton out from behind a tree. Joss and I jump back as Jim's laughter rocks the forest.

"Don't touch my stuff." Nate grabs the skeleton. He tousles Jim's slick hair until his deep side part disappears.

"Don't touch my stuff," Jim mocks, fussing to fix his hair. "Can I have it? It's like some rat-fox-fish creature."

"What would you do with it?" Joss asks.

"You know, display it. Put it on a bookshelf or my kitchen counter." With his snowshoes off, he steps closer and grabs her hips. "Or it can be our bedmate."

"God, no, Jim." She sticks out her tongue, red-stained from the strawberry jelly donut. "I'm not a three-some kinda girl."

"Too bad." He rubs her nose.

Nate and I pull on our snowshoe straps and release our boots. He takes off his sunglasses and heads toward the cellar, his hand on my back to keep me close. I swallow a smile, remembering the thump of his heart last night while we sat side by side next to the fire, and his low moans while we fucked through the late morning hours. He kept kissing me even after he came.

He props open the root cellar door with a branch, and I peek inside. Adrenaline blazes through me as I wait for my eyes to adjust to the dark.

"Ever see *The Texas Chainsaw Massacre*?" Joss catches my hand and pulls me inside.

"No."

"We're safe. No one's gonna get sawed to pieces," Nate says, hunched over from the low ceiling. He shines a flashlight over the skeleton creatures. "Like Salem's granddad said in his letter, this is art."

"Art? Pfft." Joss laughs. "How can you call this art?"

"How can you not? Take it you've never left Tilford Lake."

"You sayin' I'm a hick?"

"I'm saying don't be so judgmental if you have no experience."

"Look who's talking." Jim sniffs. He wipes his runny nose on his coat sleeve. "What do you know about bones and living in the woods? We're from the city."

"I wouldn't call Vinland Falls a city." Nate directs a side-eye at Jim. "You've seen the fishing lures my dad made. Don't you think those are art?"

"No, they're lures."

"Really?"

"Yeah, a tool, like a fork."

"My mom has them on display in a shadow box in her living room."

"I know. So what? Because they're on the wall instead of inside his tackle box, they're suddenly art?" He picks up a short piece of barbed wire. "Let's take this back with us. I'll hang it in my apartment and call it art." He smirks.

Nate shrugs. "If it means something to you, why not?"

"Bullshit." He pitches it out the door.

"Understanding bullshit is why I breezed through college and why you dropped out. If you want that wire to be art, then that makes it art. How about your tats?"

He touches his chest. "Don't put me on the spot like this."

"Why?"

"Because you don't have to act all high and mighty just because you have a college degree."

Nate grins. "Just getting you back for last night."

"How? By making me look like an idiot in front of the women?"

"I don't think you're an idiot," Joss says.

Jim punches Nate's shoulder and steps past him. "You're lucky we're family," he says. He digs through a pile of loose bones in one of the metal tubs and pulls out a beaver skull. "Dang, look at this thing." He turns to Joss. "You're right. It is like *The Texas Chainsaw Massacre* in here. Wonder if Grady ever made any furniture or wind chimes out of this stuff." He looks to Nate, but Nate's too busy examining a deer hide lashed to a wooden frame to answer.

"The tiny bird-frog is kinda cute," Joss says. She pats the skull, and one of the front legs drops off. Trying to put it back in the socket triggers the head to plop on the table and roll to the ground. With her hands raised, she mouths *sorry* to Nate and steps silently away.

Nate squares his jaw for a second but doesn't much care. He turns back to the deer hide and glides his finger across the top. "There's something about this thing."

Jim puts down a turtle shell and steps closer. "Is this gonna be another art lecture?"

Nate stares between the strings lacing the hide. He slants the frame away from the wall and nods at Jim to grab an end. They move it to the other side of the room. The light from the open door exposes writing carved into the concrete block wall. Words etched with a sharp object, a penknife, or a nail. Words never meant to be seen by us.

"Whoa," Jim says. He steps closer and reads the top line aloud.

"If you're going to do something, do it well. And leave something witchy." - Manson

Nate frowns.

"There's another," Joss points. "Are these serial killer quotes?"

Jim snaps a photo of it with his cell. "Manson didn't kill anyone."

"Murder by proxy," Nate says.

"Whatever." Jim twists his lips.

Nate turns to me. "You doing okay?"

"So far." I stride past him and read the next one.

"We've all got the power in our hands to kill, but most people are afraid to use it. The ones who aren't afraid, control life itself." - Ramirez

I look at Nate. "Ask me again if I'm doing okay."

Joss links her arm in Jim's. "The detective who left needs to come back and see these."

"They're just quotes," Jim says.

"Right, just some serial killer quotes knifed into a wall. No big deal."

"This one's more like instructions," Nate says. He puts his hands on his knees and leans forward to read it.

"I separated the joints, the arm joints, the leg joints, and had to do two boilings. I think I used four boxes of Soilex for each one, put in the upper portion of the body and boiled that for about two hours and then the lower portion for another two hours. The Soilex removes all the flesh, turns it into a jelly like-like substance, and it just rinses off. Then I laid the clean bones in a light bleach solution, left them there for a day and spread them out on a cloth and let them dry for about a week in the bedroom." - Dahmer

Nate holds the flashlight on it so we can take photos with our cells.

"Instructions?" Joss questions. She stares at the creatures in the room. Her shoulders tighten and she shrinks into Jim. "Gross."

"Chilling," I say, "but they're not just quotes or instructions. They're like Virginia's *I'm not sorry* message. He wouldn't have taken the time to etch the words into the wall if they weren't significant."

"Salem, we're talking about Grady here," Joss says.

"I know." I point at the last quote, hardly visible, in lower case letters along the bottom row of concrete blocks.

"Yes, I do have remorse, but I'm not even sure myself whether it is as profound as it should be." - Dahmer

Jim moves forward. He reads each quote a second time then fingers the Manson text. "This is the best one."

"There are no *best* ones," I counter.

"But I can like it if I want. No harm in that." He rubs his beard. "I'll draw a thumbs up icon next to it and claim I've unearthed the first Facebook wall." He's the only one who laughs. "I'll call it art."

Joss unwraps a piece of cinnamon gum and shoves it in his mouth, opens one for herself, blows a bubble and snaps it between her lips. "Lame joke, Jim. Bad timing."

"Fine. But seriously, this is wild."

"Wild?" Nate raises a brow.

"I'm just sayin' everyone has an obsession. I'm on a Viking kick, and my last girl read a ton of books on Jack the Ripper, seems like Grady was into serial killers. Good for him."

"Good for him? No. On top of all this other stuff?" I tilt my head at Jim. "Special guy I had living behind me. It's not normal. The bones were plenty to deal with. Now this?"

"The one about remorse isn't so bad," Jim says. "I bet it's about the animals he killed."

"Or about not being at his wife's side when she died." Nate glares at the quote. His voice pitches as if to ask if we agree.

I offer him a thin smile. I absolutely would *not* leave my mom in the end, even when she said she didn't want me to watch her die. But some wouldn't have the strength to stay. Everyone deals in a different way, there's no handbook for it.

"Your grams may not have wanted Grady there, or Grady couldn't bear it." I meet his eye. "Not everyone can watch a loved one die."

He smiles and takes a black flask out of his coat. After a sip, he passes it to Jim. "Did you?"

I nod.

Jim passes the flask to Joss, then to me. Bill Harlow engraved in silver lettering winks when it catches a ray of sunlight.

"Your dad's?" I ask.

"Yep."

"Drink slowly, not like the gulp Joss took." Jim wraps his arms around her and kisses her shoulder. "Sip it," he insists.

"I'm not a virgin drinker," I inform him. The liquor burns my throat and causes a waterfall to spill from my eyes. "Rum. Not bad." My voice is raspier than an old man with a cigarette habit.

Joss looks up and down the wall. "You think"—she touches the Ramirez quote—"there're bodies behind here?" The sudden sound of my cell causes her to shriek in fright. "Salem! Don't do that!"

"I'm not calling myself, Joss. I didn't make it ring on purpose." I take the cell out of my pocket. "It's Brad. He might have news about Virginia."

"Tell him I'll pick that skeleton up from the station," Nate says. "Make sure he doesn't put it in the trash."

"Okay."

"And tell him real men don't pull weapons in a fight," Jim adds.

"You can tell him that yourself." I step outside, away from the musty stench emanating in the cellar. "Hi."

"Salem."

"What?"

"I'm out front. You here?"

"No, I'm at Grady's. You won't believe what's in the cellar."

"Don't touch anything."

"How come?"

"Chief wants to search it." A pause. "He said…" His speech is tired like he hasn't slept in days. "Look, I can't screw anything else up. Can you just come back to the lodge? I don't want to drive over there and get trapped in another round with Harlow and Gaines. No one's ever known about the cellar, so we gotta have a look."

"Take it you got chewed out for not thinking about that sooner."

"Chewed out and spit out. Now it's back to work, but not with *them* there."

Nate comes up behind me. I point at my phone and then the cellar so he knows the cops are coming. He makes a quick about-face, heading back inside to finish examining the room before they show.

"Any news about Virginia Pullman?" I ask. The *crunch-crunch* of snow under my feet harmonizes with the *zip-zip* of my coat as I walk to the front of Grady's cabin.

"No. I haven't had time."

"What about Logan? Can't he look?"

"He's off until tomorrow."

"The station could use a cop who can handle two things at once."

A fierce exhale pummels my eardrum. "Fuck off, Salem."

"That's your response to everything."

I put my hand on my hip and crane my neck to see the busted cabin roof, then look over at the dead oak tree, its shadow has the tiny structure in a chokehold.

"Brad, I know about Joss. That deal you two made."

"So?"

"You took a bribe, and it wasn't even a good one. If you think Joss is going to—"

"Keep it to yourself."

Windblown footprints wander up the broken porch steps and into the cabin. They're too small to be from any of the men who were on the property last night. And the lack of any treads shows a boot didn't make them. A slipper is more likely.

"Tell Joss to be at the bar at eight. She still owes me," he says.

"Oh, grow a pair." I hang up, shoving my cell inside my coat.

I pass over the bottom two steps and stride to the third, the cabin door partially open.

"Virginia?"

I hold steady, suddenly less buoyant. Her eagle eyes home in on me from all directions. She spies from the forest, the roof, and the windows. No, she's under the porch.

"Virginia?" I swing around, check the driveway, scan the high pines. "You here?"

I'm apprehensive when I shouldn't be. She's just a harlot, a lying harlot.

The iced door creaks and groans as I push it open. Snow swirls across the roof and descends through the two nature-made skylights. Sundrenched flakes settle on a piece of twine strung across the living room, a weathered line that shimmers when it sways, beckoning me inside. I pass the cardboard box Virginia was carrying, open and empty.

The items she left were meditatively planned out for this dead room.

The contents of her box: photographs. Black and white photographs clipped with clothespins along the twine that spans the length of the room.

I step forward and look at each one up-close, my pulse quickening, heart hammering.

One boy in each shot with dark hair and a bright smile. A boy about the age of four, in foreign rooms of a foreign house, with bunnies and sheepdogs, toy cars and building blocks, ice cream cones and cakes. He swims, and swings, and runs, and jumps. Photographs of a boy who never ages, not ten, or sixteen, or twenty, but a handsome little boy who is forever four, free of friends and relatives in every shot. A boy who wraps himself in flowing curtains next to a soaring window, and peeps over the back of a sofa with long eyelashes and Whitfield eyes. A boy in black and white who makes me feel so all alone.

Fat tears fall. I pluck the twine out of the wall and roll the line of photographs into a messy ball, shoving the heap back inside Virginia's box.

"Salem, you ready?" Joss calls out.

I grab the box and barge outside, my eyes darting. I shout at Virginia to come out, to show herself, to explain. Near the dead oak, a family of deer leaps away, while Nate, Joss, and Jim stare speechless and bewildered.

TWENTY-TWO

"We'll drive through town and stop at the diner to ask about Virginia. Someone must've seen her." Joss closes the passenger-side door of Nate's truck and rolls down the window. "Sure you don't want us to call the station?"

"Is that supposed to be a joke?" I pick up a snow shovel and help Nate dig out Virginia's car. "An old woman left my lodge in a robe and slippers two mornings ago, hasn't come back, and the cops don't seem to care. They haven't even started looking for her. Why go to the station?"

"To tell them about the photos."

"No, they'll say I'm crazy and overreacting like they always say. I'm tired of hearing the same crap from them. I'm done. I'll find out what's going on. *Me.* Not Brad, or Logan, or Chief. The only thing they're good for is getting in the way."

"Cool it." She raises a hand. "Do you want us to kidnap Virginia if we see her?"

I look up. Joss smiles.

"Don't leave it to the Tilford Lake cops, Joss."

Her smile drops. "Is that a yes?"

I take a deep breath in through my nose and get back to shoveling out Virginia's car door.

"Babe? You didn't answer me."

"Just pull up next to Virginia, open the door, and she'll jump in. I guarantee it."

"Like a dog?"

"She lives for attention."

"Yeah, like a dog."

"Jim, careful with my truck," Nate says. "Put it in a ditch and you'll be the next person who disappears."

Jim leans across Joss. "Hey."

"What?" Nate tosses a pile of snow away from the trunk before he looks at Jim.

"I love you, man."

"Good. But that doesn't give you permission to scratch or dent my truck."

Jim kisses the dash and rubs it lovingly before he backs out. Laughter promenades down the driveway, muffled out when Joss closes the window.

"She'll get fired if anyone from the plant sees her in town."

"She's playing hooky again?"

"Supposedly, she has the flu."

"Jim's the same way. His motto of 'women before work' always comes back to bite him in the ass."

"Oh, great," I gripe.

"Huh?"

"The door is frozen shut." I tug on the handle. "I can't tell if it's unlocked or not."

Nate leans against the door and throws his weight into it, breaking the ice around the seal. "Can you get me some hot water?" He pulls out his wallet and uses a credit card to chip away at the remaining pieces. "Not too hot, I don't want to shatter the glass."

"Be right back." I go inside, fill a pitcher, and bring it out to him.

He pours it over the rubber seals, puts his weight against the door twice more, and says, "Open Sesame." His fingers wiggle with the magical phrase. He tries the door and it opens. "Guess it was unlocked." He sinks into the leather driver's seat and spins the air fresher that hangs from the rearview mirror. "Smells like peaches."

"Peaches and cream."

"You know your air fresheners." He checks the center console. "Empty."

"The freshener is in the shape of an ice cream cone. See the orange the white swirls. What else could it be?"

"True. Good eye, Salem. You should come on a job with me sometime." He fingers the roof, checks under the visors, surveys the back seat, then opens the glove box. "Car manual for a Cadillac sedan, registration, tissues, and a flashlight." He shines the light around, then steps out and looks under the seats. "Her car is spotless. Not even a hair. Let's try the trunk."

"Her room was spotless, too."

"Yeah? You always go in people's rooms when they're out?"

"No, not ever … or not usually," I correct. My cheeks flush with thoughts of Frank catching me with Nate's pillow. "I had to see if Virginia was all right. In case she fell or…"

"Or died?" He scoops icy chunks off the top of the trunk.

"Yeah. It's the same as what we're doing now."

"Did you find anything?"

I thrust my shovel into a snow bank and leave it there. "Nate, she even emptied the trash. I couldn't believe it." I blow on my hands, the ice burning cold. "Can you tell I'm a wreck?"

He leans his shovel against the car and takes my hands in his, squeezing my fingers to warm my skin. "Change comes about fast, doesn't it?"

"That's for sure. Alive, dead, alive, dead. I didn't expect any of this to happen."

He places soft kisses on my wrists, gentle-eyed and considerate. "An endless emotional spin."

I nod. "The weight of my past is exhausting at times, but Eli's worth holding on to. This is, too." I gesture toward the lodge. "I know I say that a lot, but I'd never give it up."

"You must daydream about taking off."

"Sometimes. But those thoughts are always short-lived. I can keep doing it. I'm here for him and the lodge. Things will get better." I pause, stare down at my hiking boots, tap the top of my boot with the heel of my other. "Sorry. Joss is right that I'm always thinking about my family."

"A lot of us do." He shrugs. "Bet most people have family on their minds ... and sex. Hopefully not family and sex at the same time."

I laugh. We pick up our shovels and continue to dig, the rear end of the car budding out of the snow.

"I told Joss once that I'd rather have Eli's disappearance be like the abrupt turn of a rickety, old roller coaster. At least that's quick. Your stomach hollows out for only a second, but with a missing person everything moves at a crawl."

"I get that. Always 'what-if' scenarios, but never any substantial evidence."

"Exactly. What if a car hit him and the driver panicked and hid his body? Each day is a guess." I stab the snow. "Twenty years later and this is the first week of change." I touch his arm. "Good change. The past has come back. You. Virginia. My granddad's letters, the keys, the stash, and now the photos, I'm confident the release of all these secrets is for a reason."

He runs his fingers through his hair. I'm lost for a moment in his blue eyes, so utterly sensitive to his charm. His sexy dimple teases his cheek, a hint that he's aware of my fixed stare.

"What?" I ask, taken with the scent of his cologne on my skin.

"Nothing. You're just … you're amazing, Salem." He smiles.

I smile back. "Pop the trunk, Nate."

"You got it, beautiful."

• • •

"Two suitcases and her purse," I tell Joss, "a winter coat and a pair of boots. Nothing else was in the trunk. She's still in Tilford. She's not going anywhere without her car and her things."

"We looked. We asked. No one has seen a woman walking around town who fits her description." Joss spreads the photographs of Eli across a tabletop in the sitting room. I place a cup of tea in front of her, warning her not to spill it on him. "I'll be careful." She motions me to sit next to her. "Salem, these had to have been taken by a professional photographer. They're so much better than the ones you have of him. No offense."

"I know. They're gorgeous pics. I can see every tiny detail, like the fine hairs on his face. The family portrait over the door in the lobby was shot by a professional, but I have only a handful of others that aren't blurry or taken from ten feet away." Joss's eyes follow my finger to a mole on Eli's chin. A mole I don't remember. "These close-ups are remarkable."

"Some look staged, like this one of him with the two sheepdogs. Did your mom ever take him to a studio?"

"What? No. Why would she take him and not me and Connor?"

She holds up a handsome headshot of Eli. "Because this little guy was much cuter than the two of you. I think your mom liked him better."

"Amusing." I twist my lips, my voice dry.

"I'm trying to make you smile."

I bite down on my lower lip and flash a top-toothed smile.

"See, that wasn't so hard, was it? You look like a beaver, by the way." She tucks my hair behind my ear. "Babe, these could've been taken by someone in town, maybe when you and Connor were at school. Virginia could've known the person and wanted to get these to you."

"Doubtful." I pick up a photo of Eli biting the head off a chocolate Easter bunny. "See his hair? It's different lengths in the shots. And this one was taken in the spring." I put the photo down and tap another. "This one, this was summer. He's swimming. And in this one he's wearing a turtleneck, leaves are falling from the trees."

"But he doesn't grow up. He can't be the same age in every shot, not unless they're Photoshopped. Someone took these before he disappeared, otherwise…"

"Otherwise what?"

She takes a hard look at the photos. "Otherwise, there'd be pictures of him past this age."

"In other words, he may have died at four. Right?"

"Or this photographer never saw him again. What did you say Virginia did for a living?"

"No clue. She's lied about everything aside from her name."

Joss uncrosses her legs and pulls down her skintight black skirt, her deep cleavage exposed in a low-cut top, one that laces at the neck but is unlaced. My hole-in-the-knee jeans and pilled sweater are vegetative by comparison, but better suited for the night. If I were meeting Brad at the bar, I'd fend him off from the get-go with a stinky shirt and baggy jogging pants, eat an onion sandwich beforehand. No makeup. No perfume. And I'd be sure not to touch up my nail polish where I bite my nails.

I sip my tea, my attention back to the photos. Eli appears happy, but the images are totally tragic. Tragic by circumstance. Tragic that his haunting eyes are on me no matter which way I turn the photos.

"You're coming with Jim and me to the bar. Nate, too."

"Nope." I sneer. "I'm not getting in the middle of this."

The water in Jim's room above us shuts off. The shower door swings open and slams shut. Bottles clatter as if he cleared the bathroom counter with a quick swipe of his arm. I watch the ceiling and touch the side of my neck, pausing in thought. "The shit you get yourself into, Joss. I swear."

"Jim's okay with it. It's just a night out with a friend."

I laugh. "Yep, you, Jim, and your bestie, Brad Brenner."

Her mouth opens. She's considering a hardnosed comeback when she notices I'm pondering the idea of going out. For a second I feel sorry for her. She shows signs of shame, eyes down like a scolded kid, her shoulders slumped.

I check the time on my cell. 7:30. "I have to wait until eleven to make sure no one's coming in tonight."

Her eyes brighten a little. "Have you seen the snow? The quilt show is over, and no one in their right mind will be driving into Tilford Lake tonight."

"Well, Nate's taking a nap. I don't want to wake him."

"That's no surprise after your second workout this afternoon."

"Third."

"Third? Really? He's a keeper."

"I know."

She nudges her chair closer and takes my hand. "Salem, come on. You have no new reservations, no guests besides Nate and Jim. Why not come out with us to the bar? It's been too long."

"Because I hate it there. Besides, I have to figure out what to do next with all this." I wave a photo in the air.

"We can make plans over a pitcher. It'll be easier to figure out what to do after a few beers." She caresses my hand. "Babe, the photos aren't going anywhere. Neither is Virginia. You have her purse behind the reception desk, and I bet her car keys are in there."

I nod. "They are. I looked."

"Good. Lock up and head out for a night before the spring weather returns and you get bombarded with guests." She lifts her fallen bra strap to her shoulder then tugs the bra down to get her boobs where they need to be.

I try to picture what it'd be like to have an ordinary life and a regular nine-to-five job. Would the dull days bother me like they do Joss? Or like most people, would I even be aware? The positive of Sparrow Lodge is that it *is* unusual. It keeps my mind alive. There's no need to stare at the television in boredom or kill monotony with drink.

Please, Joss mouths.

She gives up on me for a second to put on a fresh coat of plum-colored lipstick, smearing it across her full lips. She presses them together in a smoothing motion before taking a drink of tea, leaving thin, vertical lipstick lines on the white rim. They look like my palm lines Virginia fingered the day when she asked if I had a good friend, and then said, "Don't lose her."

I look at Joss and smile. Being small-town girls, I know our dating pool is shrinking. And for Joss, I know she hopes one night things will change. I know she wants to say the best day of her life was something other than prom night. I know this is true. I know everything about her. I know she wants to remind me the guys are leaving after tomorrow, and she wants to tell me I have too many responsibilities, that I no longer take fun seriously.

I also know Joss doesn't want more from life than what this small town has to offer. She likes to be where everyone knows everyone, where she can be a big slutty fish in a small pond, where she sticks out like a sore thumb and wouldn't have it any other way. Her needs are simple: a pair of jeans that actually fit, one story to always treasure, and a true friend—a friend who'll go to the bar with her when she asks.

"All right, Joss. When do we leave?"

TWENTY-THREE

Martin's Bar is cramped and seems smaller than the last time I was here, but the stench of armpits, stale beer, and cigarettes are the same. Smoking isn't allowed inside. It drifts in from the back door that leads to the parking lot where a makeshift smoker's lounge—complete with plastic lawn chairs, a string of lights, and a fake palm tree—has been cobbled together by the locals.

"You guys wait here." Joss unravels her scarf and flips her hair off her shoulders. "I see Brad in the back. I'll tell him we're here."

"You mean, *warn* him we're here," I say. "He still doesn't know we're coming."

"He does now," Jim says.

Brad's mouth sets in a hard line when he sees us. He stands with hesitation. Joss waves. He stays rigid.

"Give me a couple minutes." She kisses Jim on the cheek. "Behave."

"I'll try my best."

She elbows her way to the back of the room, past men whose pick-up lines have to do with working at the plant. Like, "Sit with me, I make *grape* company," and, "I got *canned* today because I can't *concentrate* after seeing your *juicy* lips around town." And the worst one, "If I take you to the back seat of my truck, will you let out a little *wine?*" Tanked-up women laugh. I roll my eyes.

Brad crosses his arms and falls into his cop stance. He's at the unlucky table, the one that's a defunct, tabletop arcade game from the '80s. Under a dartboard and next to the restrooms, it's where I vomited on my twenty-first birthday, where Joss and I got drunk the night I found out my mom had cancer, and where I came apart at the seams the first time I saw my ex-husband clumsily cup a woman's breast, which he insisted was an accident.

"I can tell you don't like it here," Nate says.

"What gives it away? Is it because I'm biting my nail or cutting off the circulation in your hand?"

"Both. Want to leave?"

I continue to gnaw at my nail, not in the right headspace to drink tonight, perfectly willing to be the designated driver. "The noise gets to me, that's all. Sorry about my bad habit." I hide my hand in my pocket. "I know its nasty."

"No sweat. It's trivial. Now, if you picked your belly button lint all the time, *that* could be a deal breaker."

I laugh and swing his arm. "You're so good at helping me to relax."

"Look at that badass cop." Jim lifts his chin, his gaze set on Brad. "He got all dolled up for Joss. What boyband you think he's in?"

Brad's curtained hairstyle is gelled to look wet.

"Don't forget she did this for you," Nate says. "If you hadn't swung at—"

"I was helping you out."

"That's what she's doing for you."

Jim shrugs. "I can still make fun of his hair if I want."

"You mean if you want to act like you're ten." Nate takes off his wool coat. The muscles in his arms are hard through his tight-fitting thermal. He slides his sleeves past his elbows, a treat for my nose to hunt out his warm cologne amid the other scents in the bar. Men like Nate know they look good. There's no need to tell them, a craving smile is enough.

"Look at him throwing a fit," Jim says.

Brad slams a chair into the table. He tosses his hands up in protest, his elbow knocking into a woman serving drinks. She steadies her tray with both hands, stopping the beers from toppling over.

"Watch it, butthead," she says loud enough for the entire bar to hear.

Ryan Sherwood, a guy I went to high school with, pushes past us to get inside. "Butthead Brenner!" A Star Wars nut with a head too big for his body, he could pass as a bobblehead. "Yo, looking good, pal. You buy that gel by the gallon?" He slips off his coat and elbows Nate in the gut. "Sorry, loser."

I put my hand on Nate's chest. "Trust me. Don't."

"Yo, witch," Ryan harasses. "Did Martin finally make a space in the lot for you to park your broom?" Laughter follows him throughout the bar. He settles in at a table with two women.

"Nice guy." Nate keeps his cool.

Joss slings her coat over a chair, a drifty smile on her face. She heads to the bar with Brad, two fingers up for us to wait two more minutes. Jim responds by holding up one.

The older men hunched over barstools are quiet, their hands shaking when they lift their beers, possibly age-related or from alcohol withdrawal. After claiming the same stool for decades, I can tell who sits where by the size and shape of the curves permanently molded into the sparkly red vinyl.

The men sprout upright when Joss enters their space, the guy next to her pivoting to check out her ass.

This is where Joss shines in all the wrong ways. Where she's queen of the room with the swing of her hips, her boss makeup, "can't miss it" hair, and bouncy boobs. The men she's slept with, almost every guy in here, still gawk, still drool, and still make Joss feel like she's the most sought-after girl in Tilford Lake. This is her showtime, and Martin's Bar is as good as it will ever get.

Joss, me, the other locals, we're aware there's no future in Tilford, but moving to another small town isn't the answer. Wherever that town is, it'll have that one guy who manages the plant, and he's the guy with the best rims on his truck ... and there'll be a funeral director who knows everyone by name ... and a family business run by an actual family ... and a two-page newspaper that gives everyone their fifteen minutes of fame. And every small town is infected by the gossip plague. Not to mention so-and-so's wedding will become the bank's permanent marquee message unless the high school football team wins a game, or someone joins the military. Tilford Lake, Gilman Woods, Perty Ridge, and the like, they're all the same. Forgotten places found only when someone is lost. And being lost is how we like it, the answer to why we stay. We're not city-bred, we're bologna on white bread. The trick to survival is avoiding the liverwurst.

"The fuck you doing blocking the doorway?" Ryan calls to us.

Foul-smelling liverwurst like Ryan Sherwood.

"This ain't your bar. Go back to your own town."

I look up at Nate. "I take it he wasn't here last time you guys came in."

"Definitely not."

"All set, babe." Joss bangs two mugs together to get my attention.

"Hi, Brad." I'm the only one who greets him.

"We're not finished." Brad follows Joss, cradling mugs and a pitcher. "We're not finished talking about this."

"Let me help you with that." Jim takes the pitcher and two mugs from him, cocking his head slightly to the side for Nate to follow.

"In a sec," Nate says.

"Suit yourself. I'll hold the table."

"This blows. You want me to leave so you can hang out with your pinhead friends?" Brad asks.

Nate clenches his jaw. "We're all friends here."

"You still owe me. This isn't what we agreed on. I get two dates now." Brad's bloodshot eyes flare. I smell alcohol on his breath. "Two dates."

"That's not the best way to win a woman over," Nate says.

Brad sways like he's wicked fuzzy. "Know-it-all. You s-s-suck."

"Take it easy, tough guy." Nate grips his shoulder.

"Get back here before I drink it all!" Jim raises a mug.

"Shut your face," Ryan warns. He pushes out from his table and motions for one of his friends to come over. They eye Jim before turning to us. Their approach unlocks a torrent of blood to riot through the darkness of my veins. My heart joins the rampage, unlike my legs, which are fixed in place. This is *not* going to end well.

Nate moves in front of me, but Ryan sidesteps us and goes straight for Brad, shoving him out the front door with a cold face, the face of a man who wants to take a hard swing at somebody.

"Really, Ryan?" Joss chases them outside. "The guys are here with *us*. You won't lose your chicks to them."

The noise in the bar diminishes to church-like silence. A crowd forms by the front windows. Nate and I look at one another and follow them out the door.

"Is this on you?" Ryan punches Brad's shoulder, enough of a jolt for his mug to slip from his hand and sink into the snow. "You bring them here, Brenner? We don't even like *you* coming 'round, now you're bringing in two more men. What gives?"

"I ... I didn't come here with—"

"I-I nothing," Ryan taunts.

"Isn't this the guy who asked Frank's daughter out?" Ryan's friend says.

"Kayla? No way." He grabs Brad by the throat. "Sicko, you like teenage girls? That's my little cousin."

Brad's on his tiptoes, face ten shades of red, slapping Ryan's hands for a quick release. Jim rushes through the door, cracking his knuckles and rolling his shoulders, ready for a fight.

"Don't." Nate places his arm across Jim's chest.

The gun sticking out the back of Ryan's jeans has control over us. No one's setting foot between Ryan and Brad.

"What are you, like thirty? Asking out a high school kid? You that hard up, Brenner?" Ryan shakes him. "Have you ever even gotten laid? Get yourself a fleshlight or something, ya putz."

"Ease off," Nate says.

The neon sign above the door targets a flash of red onto Ryan's gun, a marker to stay back. Brad's arms drop to his sides. There's a loss of hope in his eyes.

I believe we're all figuring out a way to pull Ryan away, but Brad is the one who cuts the suffering short—a dark spot growing across his crotch and down his right leg—as if his day could get any worse.

"You pissing?" Ryan steps back. "Despicable, man. You're such a waste."

The embarrassment I feel for Brad worsens with the nervous laughter that leaks through the front windows. People are used to Ryan's sudden fights, used to seeing him get his fair share of punches, but not used to the other guy having such an extreme reaction. It's a situation so awkward it can't be undone or unseen. And Joss's tactless cackle doesn't help. I throw a hard look for her to stop, but it's too late, Brad heard. He collapses in the snow, and an air of melancholy takes possession of him. With his hands over his wet pants, he curls into a fetal position and admits defeat.

"Let's drink," Ryan says to his friend. He snarls at Nate and Jim on his way inside, and as expected, gets a round of applause when he opens the door. As long as it happened to Brad and not any of them, they're not bothered by it.

Joss takes Jim's hand and leads him to the door.

"Where are you going?" I ask, tilting my head toward the lump on the ground. "Don't you see this?"

"Salem, he pissed himself."

"And?"

"And what do you want me to do?"

"We can't just leave him in a snow drift to die."

She rolls her eyes. "He's not gonna die."

"He needs a ride home," I snap at her. The cold night air pushes through my coat and across the back of my neck.

Nate crouches next to him and taps his shoulder. "Get up. Let's go for a walk."

"Go to hell." Brad rolls toward the street, same as when he'd fall off his sled as a kid and wheel down our sledding hill, same clumsy movements, the same frustration of failure. He sticks his face in a snowbank and a stirring wind blows a dusting of snow over his legs, leaving only his torso exposed, reminiscent of my toppled over hippo in the backyard.

"Jesus, Brad. I'll get my car," I say. He throws a toddler tantrum by kicking at the snow. "Stop it. We're trying to help you."

"Babe, this is so lame. You promised you'd hang out tonight," Joss complains.

"I didn't promise anything."

"We only see each other if I come to the lodge, now you're gonna try to save Brad Brenner after he's been such a dick to us?"

"Open your eyes." I smack her forehead with my palm. She almost chokes on the surprise. "Joss, I don't care who it is, I'm not leaving *any* person collapsed in the snow."

She points at Brad. "He's used to this. Just wait, he'll get up eventually."

"Is that a joke?"

"Look, he won't even show his face. Let him be. He'll get lonely and crawl back inside on his own."

"I'll pretend you didn't just say that."

"Nate, let's go." Jim holds the door open.

"You go. Take Joss inside before there's a second fight out here."

"Salem, where you going?" Joss calls to me.

"To get my Cherokee!" I round the corner and hustle down the street to my SUV, the seat still warm from the drive over. My cell rings as I turn the ignition ... Joss.

"Can you wait one minute till I get back?" I ask.

"I'm mad at you," she says.

"Is that so? Well, I'm disappointed in you."

"Salem."

"No, it's one thing for us to be disgusted with Brad, but another to leave him like this. What if he passes out and freezes to death?"

"He's playing you. He's not that drunk."

"Maybe so, but I'm not taking that chance. He could get hypothermia."

"God's sake, you need to let the past go and get out more."

"Excuse me? You need to get your shit together."

"Meaning what? Settle down and pop out a couple of kids?"

"Meaning there's a huge difference between being blunt about the way someone's acting and being downright mean to them."

She hangs up.

I hang up.

I park in front of the bar and spread Ollie's blanket on the back seat. Nate helps Brad up and guides him to the blanket before joining me up front. "Drive," he says, "away from the bar."

"I'll take him home."

"Not yet." Nate looks at the wilted mass in the back, shakes his head, and points to drive.

I pull away from the bar and drive to the main square, three blocks away. Storefronts sit abandoned, sidewalks are empty, and the streets are dark. My crooked right headlight illuminates the buildings on Nate's side, the way cops point beams down dark alleys at night. Talking is avoided. Nate picks at the cracked armrest. I keep my eyes on the snowy roads. Brad stares out the window.

I drive twice around the square. Three times. And four. Hard snow crunches under my tires. Flyers stapled to trees flap in a straight-line-formation, a battle to flee in the wind. I see more and more of these flyers hanging throughout town, the ones that advertise the new main attraction for Tilford: AA meetings.

I ease up to a stop sign. A lone flyer manages to break free from a tree. I watch it twirl away, nearly clapping for its freedom, excitement that's short-lived when a plow rolls the sheet of paper into darkness. Torn. Smothered. Dead.

"Someone say something," Brad finally speaks. "Tell me what a loser I am."

Nate rubs his forehead. "You shouldn't let guys like that have so much control. You gotta fight back."

"Right. That coming from the guy who's a cross between a professional football player and a model."

"Hey, you didn't think twice about standing up to Jim and me this week."

"I had my gun on me then."

A gust of wind rocks the Cherokee. Nate grips his knees, his knuckles white. "Grow some balls, Brenner."

Brad leans toward the front. "I think I'm gonna puke."

"No." I dig behind my seat and pull out Ollie's travel water bowl, drop it in his lap. "Do it in there, not on my floor."

He rubs the nape of his neck and falls back. "Not for real, Salem. I meant my life sucks."

"Oh, cry me a river. Whose life doesn't suck?"

"Fuck you."

"Fuck me?" I pull over and park alongside a buried curb. "Stop acting this way. You're self-sabotaging your life."

"Fu—"

"Don't! Don't tell me to f-this or that. F-off. F-you. F-whatever!" I scream. "I'm sick of hearing it. You've been reckless all week, you've been eating nonstop, and you've been on Nate and Jim's case for *no* reason whatsoever. Now you're starting to act helpless."

"I've always been—"

"Let me finish!" I scold. "When was the last time you were positive about anything? It's destructive, Brad. You've given up. You're gonna wind up a lonely old man with no friends. You think I want that to happen to you? To any of us? I don't." I inhale a lungful of air and dive back in. "You know, I don't think Connor asked you to look out for me when he was planning on going to college. I think he wanted you to come to the lodge so *I* could look after *you*."

"Fu—"

"I said, don't say that. Don't be so quick to swear at me and reject what I say."

"What the hell do you want? You go ahead and tell me what's good. I'm listening," he yells back. "What do I have to look forward to? You think maybe a horde of single women will come through town this summer? Maybe they'll like short, dumpy cops. Can't wait."

"Don't be so melodramatic," Nate says.

I squeeze the wheel until my fingers ache. "You think sex is the key to being happy? That's messed up."

He snorts. "What do you base it on? Wait, I forgot, you're not happy either."

"You're wrong." My voice bites. "The lodge makes me happy. And I have Ollie. I'm thankful for a lot of things." I touch Nate's leg. "A lot."

"Don't try to make a fairytale out of your rotten life."

"You prick." I snap my head around. "Don't make me come back there."

Nate puts his hand up, his face set in lines that make him look twenty years older. Hot air from the vents flutters his hair and causes Brad's urine to come to room temperature, a stench I clear by cracking the window.

"I think I'll take you back to the bar," I say in a lower voice. "I don't need this. I've had a hard enough week as it is."

Brad puts his hands over his face and the seat swallows him in. Joss was right; a lot of this is an act. He must enjoy making a scene, likes the attention, wants the company. An argument, a fight, staring at my chest, arresting Jim … conflict is preferred to boredom. Joss noticed it because she's the same way.

I pull behind the bar and park in front of his pickup, a sense of relief to be rid of him. Then dread: Joss is mad at me. And trepidation: I don't want to go inside. And unease: Brad's not getting out.

I adjust my mirror to look at him. Maybe peeing his pants wasn't an accident, maybe that one thing wasn't a sick show to get attention, and maybe, just maybe, the tear rolling down his cheek is real.

"It's good to be a cop, Brenner. Something to be proud of," Nate says unexpectedly.

"What would you know of it?" Brad asks.

Nate takes out his flask, offers him a drink. It's passed to me and back to Brad multiple times, eventually ending in Nate's hands. He stares at it for a minute, his finger tracing his dad's name. "My dad was a cop, one of the best in Vinland Falls." Brad shifts in the seat, sitting taller. "You probably already know cops aren't much appreciated."

"Not much," Brad whispers.

"Doesn't matter. It's not why you become one." Nate takes a sip and screws the cap back on the flask. He wipes his lips on his forearm. "You became a cop because of Connor." Brad raises his head. "That's right, I know. I get it. If you were the cop who got the call that day Connor went in the water, you would've gotten to him. You would've gotten the police boat out of dock quicker than the other officers. And you would've warmed his body the way he taught you years earlier. I know because he talked to me about survival skills when we were kids, years before it happened. I'm sure you knew what to do, he told you at some point. He knew everything, and he passed what he knew along to anyone who'd listen. That was Connor."

"Yeah," Brad chokes up.

"And because of that, you would've been better than the other cops who were there. You could've saved him."

Brad swallows hard. I bite my nail to stop my lips from trembling.

"And that's all good, Brenner. Next time you say your life sucks, why don't you remember that. Remember that's who you are. A cop. The one thing you should be proud of no matter what. That's what's good about your life. And if you don't think so, turn in your badge and find a different job. Let someone else who'll value it more than you take over, someone who'll take it seriously." Nate turns and points at Brad's face. "Someone who won't let my dad and other officers' deaths be in vain. Cause, you know, some cops don't come home because they get shot." He speaks shallowly from his lungs. "And you're sitting here bitchin' about nothing. What a joke. Be happy with what you've got, asshole." He breathes faster. "You put your life on the line to protect others, and you do it for your friend. Go ahead and tell me what's better than that. Tell me why you think your life is so goddamn awful. You tell me. *I'm* listening."

The back door to the bar opens and Ryan comes flying out with his hands all over a woman. Nate doesn't flinch. Even when the tires on Ryan's car spin as he drives off, Nate's focused solely on his dad, this conversation, and Brad.

"Wait here." Brad gets out and rushes to his truck. He opens the passenger-side door, slips off his boots, drops his pants, and shoves his stocky legs into a clean pair of jeans. Of course, only a guy like Brad keeps spare clothes in his vehicle.

After his boots are back on, he reappears next to Nate's door. Nate rolls down the window.

"I wanna buy you a drink," Brad offers.

"Yeah?"

He nods, sticks his hands in his pockets.

"Find anything at Grady's?" Nate asks.

"Nothing. Not yet."

"Not ever. Still think I'm the victim of an abduction?"

"Nope."

"Give me a sec." Nate rolls up the window. He has a crooked smile as he takes another drink. "You're not coming in, are you?" he asks.

"No, I just can't deal tonight. But you should go."

"You want me to come back to the lodge with you?"

I look past him at Brad standing outside the back door under the fake palm tree. The string of lights turns on. He looks up, his face lit, one side of his lips curling into a half-smile.

"You remind him of Connor." My voice is weak.

Nate lifts his eyes to mine. I rake my fingers through his hair until his breathing slows.

"You're a good person, Nate. He's not used to that."

He leans forward. I taste his breath in my mouth before our lips meet, and let out a soft moan before he whispers that he'll miss me.

"Be back to pick you up in two hours. Tell Joss ... um ... tell her I..."

"I'll tell her to just deal with it."

TWENTY-FOUR

"Hold on, Olls. Let me get Granddad's letters."

I gather the letters from the coffee table next to the fireplace and follow Ollie into the kitchen. He sets a paw on the cabinet where I keep his food.

"Not now."

He attempts to pry it open with his nose.

"You had dinner at six, remember?" His ears perk up. His tongue rolls out in excitement. From the day I brought him home, he's been killing me with cuteness.

I set the letters on the counter, spotting my granddad's handwriting on the back of the last one I read. It's a P.S. I didn't notice before. Ollie paws my leg, but selfishly, I make him wait.

Grady, before I forget, you have that set of keys I gave you to the back door of the lodge? You never dropped by when Carol and I lived there. Always welcome, but never took me up on my offers. Now you're a decade too late, my friend. Time to toss them.

Tom asked if I'd handed any out to our friends, said he's thinking about changing the lock. Why, Grady? My son thinks my friends are criminals? That I hang out with a bunch of hooligans? I told him not to touch that door. Keep Eli's door intact.

Back to the point, remind me to give you a new set for our mobile home, just in case we wake up one morning surrounded by gators. Carol's still troubled by Annie Merchant's horrible death down in Florida. Don't laugh, Grady. It's up to you to come and save us if the gators come. We're counting on you. And don't get any crazy ideas in your head about making a gator skeleton to leave in our yard, like the headless elves you left on our roof last Christmas. Some things just aren't funny. No gators. You hear me?

"Headless elves?" Ollie cocks his head. "Granddad kept the best secrets. I swear Olls, his letters shed light on Connor's stash and the nature boxes, Grady's bones, Virginia, and that the treasure hunt was to find Eli. Now the two nickel-plated keys and the headless boy. All answered thanks to Granddad Felix. Isn't it bittersweet?"

He lets out a whimper while pawing at the cabinet.

"Whine at the front door when you need out to go potty, not at the food door for snacks."

He barks and paces in the hallway with a slow tail wag.

"All right, if you're not going to listen." I pour a cup of food into his stainless-steel bowl, licked shiny clean from his last snack. "Chew it, Olls. Chew it." He takes pleasure in a back scratch and a pat on his rump. "You want to chill out to some relaxing music?" I head to the living room, suffering an ultimate mega-blast to my ears when I turn on the sound system. "Remember to turn it down next time, bud," I tease. The lowered music crosses the singing of a phantom door chime.

Was that the music or the front door? Ollie has no visible reaction. Though, he should've. He should've reacted if it was the front door chime.

"Hello?" I step into the hallway and listen. Check my cell. Eleven. Time to close for the night. I put my cell away and watch the light stream in from under the lobby door. No shadows. No movement. No one.

Ding.

Someone.

Ollie lifts his head, has a hard decision to make. Eat or greet a guest.

Ding-ding.

He sticks his snout back in the bowl.

Ding-ding-ding.

Food wins.

I start to move, but my chest cramps. I picture my feet trapped in concrete blocks. My mouth taped shut. Murmuring ensues on the opposite side of the door until the chime goes off again. Then. Silence falls.

I keep my ears open. It's times like this I wish I had a gun. My ex had a cabinet full … I just need one. One as I touch the door that leads to the lobby. One as I grip the cold handle. One as I swing it open to discover an empty room. I scan the lobby, the stairs, the balcony.

I'm alone.

No one is in view out the front window. No car within the circle of the porch light. But boot prints lead to the door and back out. Mine, Nate's, Jim's, I'm unable to tell them apart or if any are new. I turn the deadbolt and step back.

"Virginia? You here?"

The ringing in my ears steals the sound of silence. Without a fire, without any guests, without music or Joss, the lodge is too quiet, too ominous, and damn unsettling.

I scan the room. Darkness taunts me. If Virginia's here, she's uncomfortably close, her eyes staring into mine, her compressed lips smiling. I blink to focus on the shadowy corners, see motion that isn't there … a blur out the corner of my eye.

There's something behind the sitting room doors.

I think curtains move.

A creak.

"Hello?"

No one.

Anxiety is like snow. Suffocating. Pervasive. My muscles constrict as my body turns cold. My arms and legs tingle with a numbing sensation. To be swallowed in anxiety is to inch closer to the edge of a cliff, the landscape a muddled haze below. Fear settles in soon after. Every minuscule sound magnified, every heartbeat felt. Not a drop of saliva remains in my mouth. I don't remember walking behind the reception desk, checking the computer to see if I'd missed any reservations. Dissociation. I'm focused on dead air instead of business.

Ollie's paw tapping the lobby door pulls my wandering mind back to the present.

"Just a sec, Olls."

He howls impatiently.

"Okay, okay."

Ding.

I jerk my head to the top of the desk. The bronze bell vibrates.

"You won," a child's voice says from below.

Tiny fingers hook the ledge, a tuft of midnight hair sprouts out of the darkness. A boy. *The* boy. The boy from the photos pulls himself up. He leans forward and balances his belly on the desk, his eyes the color of silverfish. In his hand is one of the sparrow keys, the leather cord circling his wrist.

"You found me. You won."

The hair on the back of my neck stands on end.

"It's your turn to hide."

I have no particular destination when I sprint out of the room. Air doesn't come to me. Like a nightmare, I can't scream, I just run. *Go, Salem, go!* My legs become jelly then take on weight. *Go, Salem, go!* I scuttle down the hallway past Ollie, turn and scuttle back.

Slam the door to the lobby.

Lock the door to the lobby.

Never want to go back into the lobby.

Ding.

"Oh God! Oh God! Oh God!" My cell shakes in my hand.

"Pick up. Pleeease, pick up." Nate's cell goes to voicemail.

Ding-ding. "You found me. Come out and play."

"Pick up, Joss … Joss?"

"What?" She's short with me, angry still.

"He's here!"

"Who?"

"Eli! He's here. You gotta help me. I swear. I swear it's him!"

"Salem … I'm fucking tired of this."

"HE'S HERE!" I stomp.

She sighs. "What does he look like this time?"

"He's little. He's four."

She hangs up.

"No!"

I call Nate back. No answer.

The chair from behind the reception desk drags across the hardwood floor, making a painful screech. The front door's deadbolt is unlatched and the door opens. Heavy boots tread inside.

"Ahem." A suitcase drops.

Ding.

"I want to do it," the boy says.

Ding-ding-ding-ding-ding.

"She found me and now she's hiding."

Ding-ding-ding-ding-ding.

"Anyone here?" A male voice that sounds like a warm, low-pitched cello burrows into my heart. Even in the night, if I were sound asleep, I'd wake and instantly recognize it.

"Hello?"

I make a choking sound as if I've been punched in the gut. "Connor," I whisper. "That's your voice."

"Where'd you get that cord on your wrist?" the man asks.

"Over there."

"Put it back. It's not yours."

Connor's voice sounded just like that when he was older, low and masculine, but gentle, the sharp contrast of a grizzly bear to a lullaby. I open the door a crack and see the boy putting the key on the hook behind the desk. It dangles and clangs alongside the other two, tinkly as sleigh bells.

A man with messy, black hair looks up when he hears me.

"Hi." He smiles, unzipping a down vest.

"Hi," the boy echoes, unzipping a blue puffer coat. "I see you. I found you. My turn to hide."

"We're not playing hide-and-seek right now." The man lifts the boy and puts his bottom on the desk. He licks a finger and cleans food off the side of the boy's mouth. Same as my mom did when we were little. I open the door wider. His high cheekbones and thin, pointy nose match his tall and slim frame.

They stare at me. Twin smiles grow. Their matching haircuts—tousled top and short sides—are striking, but it's the icy-gray eyes and thick eyebrows that make every Whitfield stand out in a crowd.

"I'm looking for my mother," the man says. "Virginia Pullman. Is she here?"

TWENTY-FIVE

Stay calm. Remember to breathe. Put the jumbled cartwheel of thoughts in order before sunlight comes through the front windows.

Under the glare of Nate's watchful eyes, I glance up at the quiet balcony and back down at my stirring feet. "I'm worried about you, Salem," was what he said all night, and has continued to say into the morning hours. "He's here," has been my response.

Nate reclines in one of the chairs next to the fire, lifting a fleece blanket for me to come back to him, back to the spot where I've stayed all night, the spot where I can keep the balcony under surveillance.

"Please," he says.

But I don't come.

"She's lost her mind," Joss grumbles, her spicy temper rising with every step down the stairs. This is how she barged in last night, going up to her room without asking for an explanation. Livid. Cold. Hurt. "You've *never* left me stranded before. We had to walk two miles from the bar last night. Two miles! What the hell's wrong with you? We couldn't catch a ride because everyone at the bar was drunk. And I'm *not* getting in a car with a drunk." She waves a hand in front of my face. "Hello?" She turns to Nate. "Has she moved since last night?"

"She slept next to me in the chair, but not well. She insists Eli's here."

"And supposedly he's still four," she says.

"The boy *is* about four," I argue.

"And you gave a four-your-old a room?"

"A man. A man came in looking for Virginia Pullman," I say to them. "He got a room for the night. He's up there. He's here."

"So this *man* is Eli, but you didn't say anything to him?"

"He didn't recognize me."

She laughs. "Of course he didn't because it's NOT him."

"I think it is."

"You think? And you thought the boy was him. And now they're here, up there, but you've done nothing?"

"What was I supposed to do?" I look her square in the eye. "Run up to him and say, Eli, Eli, it's you! This isn't a movie, Joss. I was completely tongue-tied."

She stands in front of me and cradles my cheeks. "Did you hit your head or are you on drugs?" She shakes me by my shoulders. "Are you in there?"

"Stop it." I push her hands away. "Don't give me that condescending look, like I'm lying."

"Not lying, spinning tales."

"I'm not. His license says he's twenty-five. He's the spitting image of Connor and my dad. And his son looks exactly like Eli did when he was four."

"You say that about every guy and little boy you see. You've been doing this forever to get attention, admit it."

"What? Of all things, Joss."

"It's true. Since the day we met, I knew you were like this."

"Like what?"

"Broken."

"I'm not—"

"Quit it. You're the worst of all of us. Even worse than Brad."

"That's not true. I'm not entirely broken."

"Okay, if it will make you feel better, you're only half-broken, babe. How's that?"

"Like I give a shit."

"You do. Giving a shit is what's in your head morning, noon, and night. And still, you live in the past. Good for you, that's great, but not great for me. I can't do this anymore. Not until you move on," she lashes out.

"Hey, you don't see me with my boobs slipping out of my shirt or peeing my pants and rolling in the snow. Move on? Who's still stuck in the past acting like kids? Not me," I hit back. "Talk about broken. You move on. I don't need attention like everyone else."

"You need far more attention than the rest of us."

"Decompress, you two," Nate cuts in.

Joss throws him a look to stay out of it. "Whatever." She flips her hair in confidence that she's better than him. "I'm not putting you down, Salem. Your far-out stories are fun sometimes, but not when you leave us two miles away at the bar!"

"This *isn't* a story. This is my life! There's a car out front on the other side of my Cherokee. Go look." I point at the door and suck in a hot breath.

"You're ridiculous. You have a hunk sitting here who you probably didn't even sleep with last night. Face it. You don't want to be happy. You'll do everything possible to ruin a relationship because you're afraid. Afraid of being abandoned, and afraid everyone's gonna leave or get taken away from you. There's no car out there." She points. "I promise you that. You made it up."

"Not true."

"It *is* true. You're addicted to chaos because it's all you've ever known. When life is good, you either find or make up some crisis to turn everything upside down so you don't have to move forward. It's the only way you know how to deal." She puts her hands on her hips. "It's better to push everyone away and stay holed up in your lodge waiting for Eli than to have a good time with your friends at the bar!"

"That's *not* true."

"I'm still here," Nate says. "Salem and I are cool. We don't have to have sex every night."

"See Joss, that's what *you* don't understand." I puff my bangs away from my eyes, an alarming heat rising in my cheeks. "Real relationships aren't based on spreading your legs. Nate and I talked all night. You know anything about that? When you can get close to a guy just by talking to him?"

"I've been close to guys with my mouth."

"I'm sure." I smirk.

"Shut up, Salem."

"Don't you have to go to work or something?" I ask.

She turns a cold shoulder and crosses her arms.

"Salem, you need to stuff a sock in it," Jim calls down from the balcony. "Joss isn't going to work. She got fired for taking off to help you out. That's a good friend, so stop treating her like cow cud."

"She called in sick to spend time with *you*, not me."

"Excuse me?" Joss spins to face me. "What did you just say?"

A door opens behind Jim. A blurry shape runs alongside the railing. I bite my inner lip, nipping at a piece of torn skin with my teeth. He's coming. There's the little one. Little Eli. He's here.

Joss gasps. "Who the fuck is that?" Her eyes grow to the size of the lake.

The boy sprints down to the lobby in blue jeans and a bulky red sweater, holding a stuffed frog. "You swore," he says to her.

He kisses the frog's head and holds him up to me. "He needs juice."

"That's not how you ask." A voice tumbles over the balcony. We look up, and Joss drops to her knees.

"Dear Lord, what's happening?" she says.

"Told you." My smugness flattens her skepticism.

"Can he have juice, please?" The boy asks, twisting back and forth. "He likes orange and apple. No pineapple. It makes him fart." He looks up for approval and gets two thumbs up from the man on the balcony.

I smile. "Orange. I have orange juice."

"Yes, please."

"What gives?" Jim says. "I thought this was a lodge. Since when do you give out anything besides cold tea and weak coffee? What do I have to do to get some juice around here?"

"Time for *you* put a sock in it," Nate says. He gets up and tells me to stay in the lobby, says he'll get the juice.

"Thanks," I say softly.

Joss greets the truth with desperate questions. "What's your name? How old are you? Where'd you come from?"

"Don't scare him," I whisper.

"I'm three," he says.

"And very cute," I add.

"Is Nana here?"

"Yes, but I'm not sure where."

"If you find her, she'll give you a present. She gave me jelly beans last week."

"Finn, strangers don't play Nana's games with us." The boy looks up at his dad, swinging his frog in rapid motion like a windmill.

Strangers. Games. Finn. The maddening in my mind won't allow me to fill in the blank spaces. The man walking down the stairs *has* to be Eli. He can't be another Whitfield. The possibility of my dad or granddad sleeping with Virginia seems slim. They'd never … it's not another Whitfield, not Eli's age, not with his face.

This *is* Eli.

"Morning," he says.

He checked in as Ethan Pullman, age twenty-five, from Burlington, Vermont.

"Good morning," I say, because what else can I say? *I'm your sister. Someone abducted you the summer you turned four. Welcome home!*

"This is Finn," he says. The little boy blushes and hides his face behind his stuffed frog. "Trust me, he's not shy."

"Hi!" Finn says with a contagious smile, his arms thrown high.

Joss stands and slowly twists to face me. "Do something," she says through her teeth.

"Sure. It's time to make the morning coffee."

"What? That's it?"

I open the doors to the sitting room and turn on the lights. "You tell me the best thing to do. I'm too broken to function."

"Scream," she says.

"Nope. Too broken."

"Here you go." Nate hands Finn a glass of juice.

"What do say?" Eli looks down at his son.

"Merci."

"We're not in Quebec, Finn. This is New York. Here, bring the juice over here and don't spill it on the floor."

Nate grins and follows them into the sitting room. "You travel a lot?"

"Too much," Eli says.

"We went to Disney and I hugged Mickey," Finn says. He sits at one of the tables, feet swinging under the chair. The frog takes a pretend drink of juice before Finn takes a sip. "Nana sends us on scavenger hunts and we find her. We went to the ocean and up in the sky on an airplane. Then we find her and she cries."

"She cries?" I question.

"Yes. She's sad. But she said I don't have to cry. Then she gives me candy and we go home."

Eli puts his hands in the back pockets of his jeans and looks out the window. This is not an easy silence. I wear a cheerful smile, stay optimistic, but the fact that he doesn't recognize me fractures what should be a joyous moment. He moves closer to the window to observe the snow-covered tangle of dead weeds encasing the backyard.

"Did you have a tornado recently?" he asks.

"No," I say, embarrassed.

He taps the glass. "That hippo on its side ... it looks familiar. And the pool ... I bet we stayed here when I was a kid. When did this place open?"

"In the sixties," Joss says.

Nate waves a hand for her to shoo. He removes the coffee pot and bumps my hip to get the coffee grounds ready.

"This is crazy. I don't know how long I'll be able to hold it together," I whisper.

"It's him. Right?" Nate whispers back.

"He remembers Annabelle. I'm positive it's him."

Nate checks him out again. "You couldn't ask for anything better than this."

"I know, but I'm dying to say something. And Virginia ... I'm going to strangle that woman. Nate, *she* did this. She took him from us."

"I know. Play it cool, beautiful."

"Easier said than done." I scoop the grounds into the filter and wait for Nate to take care of the rest.

Eli studies the room, his hand on his clean-shaven chin, index finger pointed upward. His eyes lock on the octagon window near the ceiling. Finn cranes his neck to see what's up there, noticing the mica sparrow centered on the pane.

"A bird, Daddy." He points.

The mole on Finn's chin is identical to the one on the boy in the photos, the photos I thought were of Eli.

"I see it." Eli frowns as he stares at it.

"It's fat," Finn says.

"Yep, must've had too many worms for breakfast."

I have a pile of photographs of Eli, and now of Finn, but Eli has none of me, of our family, of the lodge. He grew up without an image to connect me to his past. Like Nate said after my nightmare, without a photo, the faces of the people we once knew are often a blur. No details.

Nate can't picture his dad without a photo, and yet other images surface. I can remember a doll I once had, as Eli remembers Annabelle, as Finn might remember his stuffed frog one day, but chances are he'll forget this room, Nate, and me.

Nate comes in with a pot of water. After the coffee machine is set, he leafs through a box of sugar packets, pretending to count them as he lurks. Joss shadows him. She places a container of creamer next to the sugar packets and whispers, "I have every right to be in here, too."

"So you travel a lot?" I ask, moving closer.

"Yes." Finn kicks his legs. "To funeral homes."

"Finn, shh," Eli hushes.

"One time Nana was in a casket. She opened her eyes and laughed. She cried and laughed. She said her friends are dead."

"No more stories." Eli sits next to Finn. He takes out his cell and scrolls through his messages. "They wouldn't understand."

I shift my gaze between them, my words submerged, swimming with wild desperation to break the surface. "She had a funeral," I manage to say. "I do understand if you want to talk about it. I'd love to know what happened to her."

Eli looks up through thick eyelashes. "She already had the funeral? It's over?"

"It was a few days ago." I search the stack of old newspapers and pull out her obituary with the scheduled services, placing it in front of him. "Our funeral director said some people have living funerals. Except he didn't expect to ever see one in our small town."

Eli pushes the paper away and clamps his lips tight.

"Daddy, is Nana dead?"

"Not for real." He spins his cell on the tabletop.

"Are we going to see a casket?"

"Not this time."

Finn burps. "Can we see a casket next time?"

"This is the last time."

"Why?"

"It's the third town, the last one. Number three."

"Three." Finn holds up three fingers. "I'm three."

"Almost four."

Finn holds up another finger.

"That's right."

"She's done this before?" I ask.

"Unfortunately."

Nate sets a cup of coffee and the creamer in front of Eli. He passes on the cream, tastes the coffee, and gives his cell a second spin.

"My mom planned a funeral in every town she's lived in to see who'd show up. So far, no one has."

I sit across from him. "No one showed up here either." My voice is dry. "That's why she said her friends are dead?"

Finn lifts his hands in the air. "They are all dead. Then she cries."

"What about other family? A husband?" I ask.

"She never married." He squints at my face, flashes over my hair. "I was adopted after my family died in a fire."

"You were *not*—" Nate sticks a sugar packet in Joss's mouth before she can finish her sentence.

She spits the packet at him. "Screw you."

"Give her time to sugar the pill," Nate says.

"What does that mean?"

"Enough. Both of you, please, out." I point to the door. "I apologize," I say to Eli. "There's a little tension between friends this morning."

He nods, combing his fingers through Finn's hair, parting it to the side and off his forehead. My worst nightmare would be for them to walk out and disappear like Virginia.

"My mom's lonely," he continues. "I moved out last year once I felt that I could care for Finn on my own. His mom"—he kisses the top of Finn's head—"my girlfriend … she died of sepsis after her C-section. I needed all the help I could get when he was a baby."

Finn looks up. "I'm not a baby."

"Not anymore."

"I'm a big boy." He swings his legs under the chair.

Eli looks at the table. He splays his hand across the Tilford Lake map under the thick layer of epoxy. A slight smile appears. He lucked out. With no storm in his eyes or thunder passing through his lips, he doesn't suffer from the menacing Whitfield jitters—a nervousness Connor and I picked up from our parents. Eli's more relaxed. And Finn … he's the same. He imitates Eli's actions, putting his feet on his dad's legs, offering up a toothy smile. Adorable. If it weren't for Virginia's baffling game, one that I'm unwillingly at the center of, Eli and Finn might be here for a visit, for Easter, for *every* holiday, *every* birthday, *every* forever.

"I got a text from my mom yesterday morning to come to Tilford Lake. She said she was staying here, but she hasn't returned my calls. It's the same as the other two times she did this. When was the last time you saw her?" he asks.

"Two days ago. She just walked out. Left her car, even."

"I saw it when I came in. Sorry you had to deal with all this."

"I looked everywhere." I pause. "I told the cops." Another pause. "No one has seen her."

"That's typical."

"Is it?"

"She's been saying she's invisible now that she's old." He traces the rim of his cup. "I think she thought the funerals would help, but they only proved her right. This last one in her hometown was going to be the grand finale, and it failed like all the rest. She must be pretty upset."

"Maybe it didn't fail."

"Daddy, I'm done."

"Good." Eli sits up, puts his cell in his pocket. "The sun's coming up, go put on your boots and get our coats. We'll head out to get Nana."

Finn runs out of the room spinning his frog. My head spins with it. The possibility that they may leave and never come back constricts my throat to a pinhole.

"I can help you look." I stand.

"We're good, thanks. If the funeral is over and she's not in her room, I know where she'll be." He stands and pushes in the chairs.

"Where? I can take you ... I can drive..." I sound like a stupid kid. I falter and look around for something to help me find my bearings in this rabid dream, but I'm it. It's up to me to level out and stop freaking out. I can do this. "I offer free tours of Tilford Lake and free rides to town if you're interested." Nate leans alongside the doorjamb, smiling at my awesome recovery. "I can take you anywhere you'd like to go."

Eli gives me the once-over. I love it that he's looking at me, even if it's with suspicion.

"That's okay. Finn and I can handle it. I need to get him breakfast first, then—"

"I can make breakfast," I offer.

"No. No. Just no," Jim says from the lobby. "She *can't* make you breakfast. This is a lodge, not a hotel. She doesn't serve breakfast here."

"He's kidding," I say.

"Daddy, catch your coat."

"Hold on, Finn."

A coat drops from the balcony and lands in a clump. Keys jangle and sunglasses somersault onto the floor.

"You're supposed to catch it," Finn says.

"Did you lock the door?"

"Yes." He races down the stairs. "Will Nana give me jelly beans today?"

"You didn't finish the last bag she gave you."

"I don't like the white ones. You have to eat them."

"I don't like the white ones either."

"Your dad likes only black and purple jelly beans." I press my lips tightly together.

Eli gives me a sharp look. "How'd you know that?"

I shrug. "Lucky guess?"

He picks up his sunglasses and slips into his coat, one eye on Finn getting a bit too close to the fire. His head rises from hearth to ceiling of the fieldstone fireplace before he makes a sudden turn to face the private quarters. He blinks. Ollie barks to come out. He blinks repeatedly and touches his neck as if to feel for his missing key.

"Doggy!" Finn blurts. Eli looks around with suspicion. He takes Finn in his arms and carries him to the door.

"Nice place. We'll be back at four when you reopen for the night."

"Four," Finn says, four fingers sprouting up.

"You can come back anytime!" I shout at the closing door. "Any hour. Any minute. Any second of the day!" My emotional brain zaps, waiting for relief.

"No one ever sees me. Not even my own son," Virginia says from the chair behind the reception desk.

Joss jumps. "What the ... where did..."

"Where did she come from?" Jim finishes her sentence.

I lunge at her, but Nate grips my shoulder and holds me back.

"He walked right past me. Not a hello or a goodbye," Virginia says.

"He's *not* your son!" I blaze, ready for a fight. "I hate you, Virginia. I hate you!"

She buries her face in her hands and starts to cry. Her chest jerks with each breath. I'm sickened that my first thought is to comfort her, but I'd never.

"Stop it. You have no right to cry. No right!" I rage.

She lowers her hands. There's not a tear on her sunken cheeks. "I'm not sorry," she says in a smooth voice. "I'm not." She smiles.

"Were you laughing?" I step forward. "You weren't crying. You were laughing?"

"Salem"—Joss pushes past me—"call the cops. Tell them I killed Virginia Pullman."

TWENTY-SIX

Watching Virginia smile is bad enough, but what's worse are her words. She's *not* sorry. She has no soul. Not a smidgen of guilt shows in her eyes, no pity or shame, no sympathy for my family. It seems like a decade has passed since the morning in the sitting room when she mentioned a fog had rolled in. Little did I know she was referring to herself. Ghost-gray. Noiseless. Sauntering through Tilford Lake like a "mild" alcoholic.

She must be the devil.

It makes sense that the devil would take on the shape of a frail older woman who drives a Cadillac sedan and walks through town in a robe and bootie slippers. And it makes sense for the devil to taunt me with laughter, not tears.

I fell for it. I was drawn to her maternal ways. I thought she fit in with the rest of us at the lodge. But I was wrong.

Dead wrong.

I smack the desk with my palm. "How dare you laugh!"

My words sink beneath the turmoil in the room. Jim and Nate carry Joss kicking and screaming into my private quarters to keep her from pouncing on Virginia.

"My laughter is pure delight. There's nothing sinful about it," she says.

"You're a pathetic woman," I speak over Ollie's agitated barks. "You must really hate yourself. I should just let Joss kill you if she wants."

Virginia snatches up her purse from under the reception desk and places it in her lap. "I don't expect anyone will kill me today," she says, then touches her lips as if to suppress her words.

Joss's malice and Ollie's barks muffle when the door to my private quarters shuts. Virginia cups her ear and listens to Joss. Her eyes crinkle. "Drab brown birds," she says.

"You stole my brother," I hiss angrily. "You took him from us. You broke my parents' hearts, my grandparents' hearts." I squeeze the logo on my constricted chest. "You destroyed us!"

Her throat ripples as she swallows. "Be happy I brought him back to you."

"What?"

Nate's hands are on my shoulders, holding me back. I swing my arms to break free, but he locks me in a bear hug from behind. "I'm not gonna hit her, Nate. I just want to spit in her face."

"Drab brown birds," Virginia repeats.

"What the hell are you talking about?"

"Sparrows are like mice, one may escape notice"—she winks at me—"but a community of them can destroy a beautiful place."

"You better not be referring to my family or me." I look over my shoulder at Nate. "She's a horrid nightmare!"

She comes out from behind the desk, clutching her purse in both hands. Her yellow-gray hair flows down her back like breaking ocean waves. Years of secrets hide in her deep-set wrinkles. She continues past me and sits in one of the leather chairs, straining to straighten her back like the high pines. A crack. Her shoulders sag, discouraged by old age.

"I once sold lemonade in the downtown square. Men in suits would stop to chat. But yesterday a young man on the church steps asked me if I had any prescription drugs to sell him." She looks at us with despair. "The big ending I had always dreamed of never happened. It was supposed to be a reunion with exquisite flowers and longwinded stories lasting throughout the night. There should've been friends and foes at my funeral. How can I renew friendships or offer apologies when no one comes?" She hesitates, pressing a finger to her lips. "I've searched for people I once knew. I've visited my past. Three funerals. One in each town I'd lived. Not a soul remains." She lets out a long sigh. "Do I still exist if the people I shared my life with are gone?"

"You can't be serious." A burst of adrenaline makes my muscles twitch. "How can you be talking about this right now when you took Eli? He doesn't even know who I am!"

"He doesn't remember you because he's had a good life."

My legs tighten. "He *had* a good life with us!"

"Was it? I gave him so much more than this." She raises her hands. "Salem, Sparrow Lodge is pretty near the likes of a pig shed. Felix would be disappointed if he saw it today."

"How dare you. How dare you come here acting like a sweet, innocent old lady when all you are is an evil kidnapper." I roll my shoulders away from Nate's hold. "I should smack you for being so insensitive. Eli thinks we died in a fire. That's how my grandparents died." I walk up to her. "You're cruel. Your entire life has been a lie, and you turned his entire life into a lie. How is that better for him?"

"Ethan."

"Don't call him that. His name is Eli!" I bend in front of her and scream, "ELI!"

My gusty breath sends her hair upward. She leans back, her feet crossed, hands clasped. A minor tiff between Joss and Jim comes from the other room. Ollie barks louder, Nate asks if he should call the cops, and Virginia is unflappable through it all.

She unzips her purse and takes out a travel pack of crackers, tears open the cellophane package, and starts to nibble. After a short while, she swallows and says, "Ethan would've become lost in this family and this town. He would've ended up just like Felix. A nothing."

"Oh…" My blood pumps away. "Oh, my granddad wasn't a nothing. He was a beautiful person."

"Beautiful in an ordinary sense."

"You disrespectful wretch!"

"Give it to her, Salem!" Joss shouts from behind the door.

Virginia studies me from head to toe, her smile much larger now. "Salem, can we have a conversation like two grown women? If not, I'll call Ethan to bring Finn back, and he can show you the proper way to throw a tantrum."

My tongue twists. I—the drab brown bird that I am—want to peck at her face and shit on her head.

"Give me the word and I'll call the cops," Nate whispers in my ear, leading me to sit across from her.

"A wretch," I whisper back.

"Yes or no?"

"Nathan," she interrupts, "be a gentleman and get us some tea."

"You're not getting any tea. You're not entitled to a damn thing here." I lean forward and grip the seat cushion between my thighs. "Wayland Casper told me—"

"Oh, Wayland." She flashes a schoolgirl smile as if she has a crush. "He's a handsome fellow. Why didn't you marry him?"

I make a deep grunt, my insides burning up. "Stop it. Stop changing the subject."

"Loneliness is the subject. Wayland is lonely. So was I."

"That's a brutal way of putting it. Is that why you took my brother? So you could have a playmate?"

She nibbles on her cracker. "Yes." She nibbles again. "We needed each other."

"He was only four when you took him away. We loved him. We needed him. Not you. He wasn't yours to take!"

She closes her eyes and raises a shaky hand for me to relax. I take shallow breaths, focusing on the crumbs in her lap piling up like an anthill.

I shift in the chair and jiggle my feet madly. "Okay, I can try to speak calmly to a deranged woman … for one minute."

"What about Wayland?" she asks.

"He said you've been all over this town, why not have—"

"A child of my own?"

"Yeah."

"Too old. I was in my late fifties when I thought it was time."

"So adopt."

"I wasn't about to do that. What a hassle, the way those people want to intrude on a person's entire life. And that process can take years." Her voice is firm. She spies on Nate while finishing her cracker. After the wrapper is tucked away inside her purse, the crumbs swept off her robe, and her lips patted free of any remaining bits, she takes out her cell and finds an image of Finn. "Looks just like his daddy."

"Is that why you brought him back? Because Finn reminds you of Eli when you took him from us? Same age. Same face. That must bother you. Tell me it does. Tell me that guilt is eating you alive. Tell me it's so bad you think it might kill you. I want to know you're miserable."

"Ethan—"

"Eli!"

She blinks at me slowly, but it's not the slow blink of a cat wanting to profess its love, it's the slow blink of a woman wanting to display superiority. And impatience.

"If I can go on … Ethan left me alone in a lifeless, quiet house. Not a sound. Do you know what that can do to a person's frame of mind? Especially at my age." She sets her cell in her lap. "I am a live model, Salem. I stand in stores and listen to strangers tell their stories. However, I'm not invisible to them." She spreads her fingers in front of her face and turns her hand back and forth. "I'm not invisible. I'm ignored. Such a shame." Her hand drops. "Who'll be Ethan and Finn's family when I'm gone? That seems important to me now."

By the look on Nate's face, I can tell we're thinking the same thing. The wheels are turning. Pieces are starting to fit. I want to say you're *not* his family, but she's saying it in her own mazy way.

"One time, I pushed the mute button of the remote to the television Ethan had left behind, just to see if my home had been hushed by some device. But the sound didn't return. I wasn't on mute." She shakes her head. "Ten years ago I could always find a friend to meet for brunch or someone to chat with on the street, this or that, didn't matter who or what, as long as it was a familiar voice. Now I spend my days talking to produce in the grocery store."

"I don't need to listen to some sad story to make me feel sorry for you. I don't care. I want to know—"

"Yes, no one cares. That's evident. People are miserable nowadays, aren't they? You have that tone in your voice like the rest of them."

"This *tone* is because you abducted my brother."

"No, not exactly. Ethan was handed to me."

I squinch a bit. "What does that mean?"

"He was going to marry her, you know. His girlfriend was stunning. They met in a photography class at the university."

"Wait. What did you say?"

"Now, my Ethan won't talk to any woman who shows interest in him. Isn't that the saddest thing you've ever heard? Almost four years now, and still he refuses to date. I don't want him to end up as lonely as me."

"Go back. How did you get Eli? How did you get in here that day?"

"He's a photographer. Did he tell you?"

My head feels like flour sifting through a sieve, only the lumps and imperfections have obstructed the wire mesh. What is the truth? What are lies? We're on an indirect route—her route. I think how different she is from my mom, my grandma, from every woman I've ever known. Plotting her life like the saber-toothed blenny—a fish Connor said pretends to be your friend before it bites your face—that's her. That's totally her. My granddad was right to steer clear.

"Why him, Virginia? Why us?"

A pause. "I don't believe the choice was easy for anyone."

Nate's sudden movement distracts me. He steps back and crosses his arms, disquieted by something. "I'll be right back," he says, moving past us and up the stairs to his room.

Virginia skims a finger over her cell, a mere four, five feet from me. She sat in that spot the night she checked in, was at the lodge twenty years ago to abduct Eli, and was in this town sixty years ago flashing her chest at my granddad. Her sitting here feels like a punch, a kick in the teeth.

"I'll have to call him soon. He must be worried," she says, touching her cell. "I'm not at the church."

"That's where you've been?"

"They're always generous. It's a comforting place for the homeless or anyone stranded in a nasty snowstorm."

"Liar. You weren't stranded. You lie about everything." I sit up and lean closer to her. "Why tell me you were married to an alcoholic? Why tell Wayland you have a Mathematics degree and were a professor? What the hell is the point, Virginia? Why put people through days of worry when you went missing?" I nod at her cell. "Why do this to Eli? I bet he wouldn't give a damn about you if he knew what you've done."

She stands and hovers over me. Her broccoli-scented breath swathes my face, dull eyes inches from mine. "Salem, you have all the answers that you need."

"I have nothing."

She looks over the lobby, takes in the tired room, my worn clothing, my tangled hair.

"I'm not talking about this." I dismiss her thoughts with a flick of my wrist. "I'm talking about him."

"You have a lifetime, which is everything."

I glare furiously at her. She creeps toward the front door like she's walking underwater. "Eli's alive," I say, "but he's not coming back. I'm the one who died. I died in a fire. Isn't that ironic? I'm dead to him, Virginia … I'm dead."

"The time was right for all of us." She looks back. "I paid for what I received. Nothing comes free. Now it's your choice what you want to do with the information. The time may be right for the two of you, or it may not. That's a decision you'll have to make on your own." She continues to the door, taking a final look at the photograph of my family overhead before stepping outside. She stops on the porch with the same hesitation she had when she left with the box of photographs the other morning. "Thank you for shoveling out my car," she says.

"Get out," I whisper.

She waits for me to say more, but I'm reluctant. At this point, I'd rather she just leave.

"Don't lose your friends, Salem. Gather as many as you can. Women should have more friends than shoes." She steps forward. Her outline fades.

I wipe a tear from my cheek, the chime singing louder than it ever has. My granddad said it caroled like a sparrow, and that my cries matched their songs. He said my fight for breath when I cried—a sequence of high-pitched shrills—was too sweet to be from sadness. But my tears flow only in silence now.

How did she get Eli that morning? Where has he been? Was he good in school? Did he have birthday parties and go fishing when he was a kid? Did he ever talk about us?

My eyes clamp shut.

What's his favorite movie, favorite book, favorite food? Does he like sports?

I wipe my cheek.

Did he ever learn how to ride a bike? Has he gotten sick from gorging on an entire gallon of ice cream? Was he taught right from wrong? The difference between *needs* and *wants*?

I *want* to know these things. I *need* to know.

The door to my private quarters jerks open. Joss struts out with Ollie. He jogs to my side and instantly locates the best spot to rest his chin on my thigh.

"I held her for as long as I could," Jim says. "She knocked me flat on my back again."

"Did you let her go?" Joss darts to the window. She draws the curtains wide, utters a mountainous gasp. "You did! You're letting her get away!"

"She's not getting anywhere, Joss."

"Babe, I'm watching her back out right now. She's leaving."

"I can call the cops anytime. Today, tomorrow, it doesn't matter when."

"But you're not going to." She snaps the curtains shut. "What did she say to walk out of here scot-free?" She turns and lifts her chin at me. "Was it a threat? To Eli? To Finn? What happened, Salem?"

Jim whispers to her in secrecy, only not well, the lodge is too quiet not to overhear.

"*We have to call this in if she doesn't,*" he says. "*We know who took Eli. We're toast if we don't report it and someone finds out we knew.*"

"Not true," Nate cuts in on his way down the stairs. "You're not concealing it. You're just not reporting it. There's a difference. It's not a crime."

"How can you hear me?" Jim asks.

"Because even when you whisper your voice sounds like a foghorn." Nate sits across from me and places a pile of papers on the coffee table between us. I recognize them immediately. They're Gert's medical bills, the stack Nate had on his dresser, the stack I snooped through in his room.

He taps the top bill, his finger stopping on the amount owed. He flips to the next, and the next, pointing out the cost of Gert's cancer treatment: doctor's visits, tests, procedures, hospital stays, treatments, and medications. Bills dating back to when I was a kid, lasting years, stopping and starting when the cancer was in remission and then returned.

"These were in Grady's safe-deposit box with the two keys and Connor's stash. I wasn't sure why he saved her bills for so many years, or why he had them with that other stuff. I thought maybe he was holding on to the memory of what killed her. But I think it's clear now."

Joss and Jim gather next to us and skim through the bills.

"Grady was a janitor. He didn't have this kind of money," Jim says. He points to a bill. "That drug cost them five grand a month. Even with insurance this probably adds up to over a hundred grand."

"Easily," Joss says, a glum expression on her face, the one she has whenever she remembers what my mom went through.

She hasn't caught on to what it all means, why Nate's showing me the bills. She wasn't here when Virginia offered clues.

Ethan was handed to me.
The time was right for all of us.
I paid for what I received.

Nothing comes free.

Nate and I exchange knowing glances. He clasps his hands between his legs and lowers his head, hiding hurt feelings about his family.

"Those spare keys in the stash were mentioned in a letter," I say to Nate. "They were given to Grady by my granddad. Grady had a way inside the lodge."

He nods. "He needed money to try to save my grams."

"And Virginia wanted a child," I add.

"An exchange." Jim releases a bill, and it floats to the table.

"No way." Joss looks down at me, then at Nate, who looks like a shamed little boy.

"That hag only cares about herself," Jim says, stroking his beard. "She could've given them the money without taking Eli."

"How can you just sit there and let her go?" Joss asks. "I don't get it."

I slide off the chair and sprawl out on the floor. "Her world is small. She'll die alone. That's far worse than anything I could ever do to her."

"But think of your parents and all the years spent without Eli. All the pain everyone went through. It's not fair."

"Joss, I wish she were dead." I look up at her. "I do. But some punishments are too easy." Ollie settles next to me, belly down, stretching his rear legs out. I pet his back then hold his paw. "Her loneliness will kill her. I'm sure of it, and that's far worse than prison."

Nate curls up behind me. "I'm sorry," he whispers.

Joss and Jim lay on their backs next to us, eyes on the ceiling, hands joined.

"You know you've got Christmas garland up there?" Jim says.

Joss laughs. "Jim, that remark is completely irrelevant to what we're talking about."

Ollie lifts his head. His tongue rolls out as if he's smiling in agreement.

"Jim can't cope with difficult situations, so he deals by changing the subject," Nate says. He wipes a tear from my cheek and kisses my temple.

Jim points upward. "I'm just saying she's got garland on her beams."

"I know," I respond.

"But it's almost Easter."

"And Christmas will come again."

He looks toward the window, squinting at blinks of sunlight seeping through the sides of the curtains. He crosses his legs and tiny motes of dust lift into the light. "I like people who don't try to hide their flaws," he says.

I smile and inhale a long breath through my nose. "Me too." I exhale.

"I'm better at this than you guys think. At least I got her to smile."

"You're *getting* better," Nate says.

"Salem?"

"What is it, Joss?" I bite my nail.

"What about Eli? You gonna say something to him?"

My nail snaps between my teeth and a sliver sticks to my tongue. The room deadens as everyone waits for my answer. I work the sliver out, hold it between my front teeth, and keep it there as I think.

There's not much time before Eli comes back.

A small part of me wants to turn off all the lights and crawl under my bed, stay in the dark until he leaves. I'll hear him come and go then erase the older Eli from my memory like he was never here. Then I'll always remember him as my four-year-old baby brother, not a twenty-five-year-old stranger with a son. He's supposed to be a little boy whose cheeks I can pinch, cooing, "Woolly, woolly bear." He wasn't supposed to grow up.

But a bigger part of me wants to tell Eli everything.

"Salem?" Joss asks.

With the weight of the three sparrow keys around my neck and all the fear bottled in the pit of my stomach, I can't give her an answer.

Too many possibilities lie ahead.

TWENTY-SEVEN

Late afternoon. The lodge is still.

Nate sweeps my hair back and feathers his thumbs across my cheeks. An hour of passionate sex has left him with dilated pupils and ragged breaths.

His name has stayed with me after calling it out repeatedly while I came. I didn't say *Jesus* or *God* this time. It was *Nate*.

Nate.

"You're amazing," I whisper.

"You too." We share brief tremors when we kiss, sweat deep between our legs. "I think I'll keep you," he says.

"Really?" I laugh.

"Yep." He rolls off me and relaxes at my side, his warmth against mine.

"Well, since you're a master at comfort sex, I think *I'll* keep *you*."

The laughter between us survives only a few seconds before it transforms into silence. So much has happened that we can't see straight, and that's only partly from the sex. Our minds aimlessly wander from Virginia, to Grady, to Eli.

Nate has apologized multiple times, taking on the responsibility for Grady. I admit that I'm crushed, crushed by Grady's betrayal, and crushed for my granddad. He was kind to Grady, and he never learned the truth. Would it be easier if I hadn't found the letters? Having them increases the pain, but not having them would've left us in the dark about so many other things.

Nate slips out of bed and opens the window a crack. He takes off the condom and drops it in the wastebasket, then pulls the blanket over my goose-pimply skin to protect me from the cold. I hold it up for him to come back to me, but he returns to the window instead.

"Jim better not break any of the bone sculptures," he says, scraping the frosted glass with his fingernail. "I should've given him and Joss fifty bucks each to load them into my truck."

"Thirty is plenty, and Joss will make sure they're packed well. She's good at that."

He sighs. "I don't even want them anymore. I'd leave them all in that root cellar if my mom didn't ask to see them." He leans forward, his nose pressed against the glass.

My body tingles when I think of his touch, the smooth curve of his back, his broad shoulders, and firm ass. I wish his silhouette would remain bathed in the thin sunlight of my bedroom window forever. I could just lie here and stare all day.

"You need me to do anything?" he asks, his eyes falling on my breasts.

"There's nothing to do except wait like we've been waiting."

He nods and turns away.

Eli said he'd return at four, and he meant it. Even if Virginia called to meet him somewhere or to tell him she was leaving Tilford Lake, he's not coming back until I reopen for the night. He doesn't know he's welcome here anytime. And without a cell number, I can't call to tell him to come *home*.

I slip out of bed and nestle my head against Nate's shoulder, my fingers sneaking up the nape of his neck to play with his hair. He continues scratching the frost until a drawing of a lopsided cabin appears.

"Grady," he says, finger pressed to the etched cabin, "he never came to my dad's funeral. That bastard. How my mom could stand to be around him"—he sucks in a breath, lets it drift out—"I know he's the reason why she got out of Tilford Lake as fast as she could."

I lower my hand from his neck. "I'm sorry about your dad. I didn't have a chance to tell you that last night."

He strokes his cheek up and down with the back of his fingers, fixated on the frosted glass. "He suffered, Salem. Grady was depressed over my grams, and I'm guessing over Eli, too. That's why he kept everything together in the safe-deposit box." I have the same running conversation in my head. "He couldn't watch my grams die, but the weight of what he did ... I bet he got worse over the years until he cracked. He left everything and took to the streets. Then took his own life. Either the loss of my grams was too much or taking Eli or both. But the two of them, Virginia and Grady"—he pauses, rubs his chin—"I don't feel sorry for them, not after what they did. Grady had a hard life, but that doesn't justify the things that he did." He puts his arm around me. "You think it's awful not to care that he was lost and alone like Virginia is now?"

I peek through the cabin etching and see Annabelle dead on her side. It's the saddest she's ever looked. Coated with ice, two legs in the air, her mouth wide open and filled with snow.

"I don't know," I whisper.

"How come? What the hell's wrong with you, Salem?"

I look up and smile. "Funny. I believe I'm the one who said that first."

He steals a kiss. "Thanks for listening."

"Same. It's nice to be more than just a good lay."

He looks at me curiously. "Should I take back the money I left on your nightstand?"

I laugh. "I'm serious, Nate. Last night with you was telling. I was sure Eli was upstairs, and you stayed awake and hung out like a best friend. Men aren't like that."

"Some are."

"No, not supportive like that. The ones who pretend to be expect something in return."

"Goes both ways, beautiful. That's why I'm falling in love with you." He wraps a lock of hair behind my ear.

Falling in love?

The door chime goes off. Tiny feet run inside.

Ding-ding-ding.

"I'm back. I'm back!" Finn yells. "Where's the doggy?"

Ollie appears in the doorway of the spare bedroom, eyes aimed toward the door to the lobby. His tail wags to be let out.

"Upstairs, Finn. Let's get our things."

"Oh my God." I cover my mouth, scanning the room. My clothes are scattered everywhere. "What time is it?" I try to get dressed in a rush, my hair in disarray. "Where's my bra? Holy crap, I lost track of time."

"It's okay. He won't leave without checking out. Get dressed and go out there."

"Oh my God."

"I'll be in the hallway if you need me."

"I don't know what to say. What do I say?" I look at him, my underwear dangling in my hand. "I haven't figured out what to say!"

"Just go with the flow. It'll come to you."

I button my jeans, straighten my hoodie, and flip my head forward to fluff my hair.

"How do I look?" I flick it back and finger it into place.

"Gorgeous." He smiles.

I run up and kiss him. "Thank you."

Ollie and I dash down the hallway. We step through the door to an empty lobby, a room that appears larger than ever. I suck in a ginormous gulp of air, holding it for five long seconds.

Relax. Release. Repeat.

Relax. Release. Relief.

The water pipes leading from the boiler cough, a bed is bounced on, and giggles ignite the heavens. I grab the sparrow keys and lay them on top of the reception desk just as the last ember in the fireplace dies out.

A door opens and Finn runs across the balcony. He stops on the landing and sees Ollie sitting next to the bottom step.

"Doggy!" A buzz of excitement fills the room.

Ollie offers a happy bark as if Finn's been his best friend forever. Finn races down and gives him a toddler-sized hug. "Good doggy."

"Finn," Eli says from the balcony. They're dressed to leave, coats and hats, luggage in Eli's hands. "What did I say about that?"

Finn steps away from Ollie, clasps his hands and twists back and forth. "Some doggies don't like hugs," he says innocently.

"And?" Eli walks down the stairs.

Finn throws his head back to look at him. "Some doggies bite."

"That's right."

"He won't bite, he's friendly," I say.

"He's friendly, Daddy. Can I pet him?"

"Be gentle." Eli sets his luggage in front of the desk and places the room key next to the sparrow keys. I follow his every move, trying to sort out the best way to begin before it's too late. I open my mouth but feel choked. Open it and close it again. Open and close. I'm disappointed he doesn't react to the keys.

"Leaving so soon?" I say weakly.

He rubs his tired eyes like he did when he was a baby, the smell of the greasy diner on his clothes. "My mom left. Sorry again for the trouble she caused. At least this is the last time anyone has to deal with her."

I want to shake him and say, remember me? Remember me? Look, look at the lodge. How about the keys? Look at them. Look! Let's head out back to the playground and start where we left off. You're four and I'm six.

"I know what you're thinking," he says. He leans alongside the counter and touches each of the keys. He holds up the leather cord of the third one—*his*—and spins the sparrow on the desk. It flickers in the overhead lights, the cord twisting tighter and tighter until it stops. He lifts the key off the desk by the cord and watches it untwist between us, resembling a pendulum during hypnosis. "You think my mom is ill. But she's not. I'm not going to place her in a home." He lowers the key and spins it again. "A priest in the last town called for a senior welfare check. He said she wasn't in the right frame of mind." He tilts his head when the key stops, an attempt to decipher the upside down initials. "That's not true. She's as sharp as a tack." He straightens up, wipes his hand down his face. "I don't know what's next for her, but putting her in a home isn't the answer. After losing everyone in her life, and me and Finn moving hours away, she doesn't need to lose her home, too. Her house is her last comfort." He picks up the middle key—*my key*—and thumbs the initials. "What I'm trying to say is I hope you think twice about calling the cops over what happened here. She's okay."

"Wait…" I pause, unsure if he's talking about Virginia or if he's being cryptic about something else. Does he know?

He observes the shelf of Sparrow Lodge merchandise, the sweatshirts and hats, the logo over my heart. "She's done searching for lost souls at funeral homes and churches. She'll be okay now." He sets my key down and taps Connor's before picking up his luggage. "Ready, Finn? Let's hit the road."

"Let's hit the road!" Finn runs to the door. "Bye Doggy. Bye nice lady."

"Hold on." I take Eli's key and walk out from behind the desk. "You're not ... you're ..." My voice dies away.

Finn hugs Eli's leg and throws his head back, gazing upward at the photo above the door. "Me," he says, pointing at it. His knit hat slips over his eyes. He pushes it up and looks again.

"Do I owe more money?" Eli asks.

"No. I just..."

My mouth is full of sand. I start to tremble, my mind straining to force out the words. *Any* words. I won't relive my nightmare, not now. Eli will hear me this time.

"You're not a Pullman. You're not her son." For a second I don't dare breathe. But then it sounds so simple after I repeat it. "You're not Virginia's son."

Easy. This is not a complicated situation.

The news should be puzzling to him, but he's unfazed. He looks down at Finn and doubles the folded edge of his hat so he can see. "Not the first time I've heard that one. My friends growing up always said Virginia couldn't be my mom because of her age. I know I'm not her real son." He walks toward the door. "Like I said this morning, I was adopted."

Finn stares at the photo as Eli walks outside. "That's me, Daddy. Look." He points at the photograph.

"Let's go before it gets dark."

"Finn, wait." I stick Eli's key in his coat pocket. "A present."

"I like presents."

"Finn, you coming?"

"Let's go see Nana." He runs out the door. "Okay, Daddy? Let's go."

"Watch for ice," Eli cautions.

"Look," I say in too tiny of a voice for him to hear. "Come and look at the photo." I stand on the top step and watch him buckle Finn into his car seat, my heart hiccupping.

Was expecting a happy ending unrealistic?

"Daddy, I miss Nana. Can we go see her now?"

Eli kisses Finn's cheek and closes the door. After the luggage is in the trunk, he turns to face the lodge. I feel a serious pain in my chest. Have I failed? There's nothing in the front yard to jog his memory. When he was here the wood was lighter, now it's worn to black. The shutters were red, not green. The sign was brightly lit, trees were in bloom, and I was only a child, not the woman standing here, unrecognizable to him.

He gets in the driver's seat and starts the car. Children's music lights up the atmosphere like magic. Finn's spirited voice harmonizes with the birds, and he entertains himself with a sweet fingerplay of "The Itsy Bitsy Spider." Inch by inch his little hands ascend, descend, ascend way up into the air.

"You let him go?" Nate rubs my back. I give him a sad smile and place my head on his chest.

"Yes," I whisper.

"You know why?" he asks.

"Down came the rain and washed the spider out."

I do. I do know why.

"Out came the sun and dried up all the rain."

The answer is in what remains, what's left here versus what's out there.

"And the itsy bitsy spider climbed up the spout again."

And the answer is in the secret that Finn holds. Unlike the rest of us, he doesn't need any reason to be happy, and I don't want him to lose that, not at such a young age.

I train my eyes on the car disappearing in the distance, still questioning if Eli knows. He could be the one who wants to hold on to this secret. That's sad to think about, devastating actually, but possible. I may never know. But what's apparent is that Eli cares for Virginia. He wouldn't have come here if he didn't. And he loves his son. And his son loves his nana and his daddy. I can't do to them what was done to us. I can't have Virginia arrested and taken away from Eli and Finn. I can't break Eli and Finn's hearts and destroy their lives. I wouldn't wish that on anyone. But if I tell Eli what happened, there is no simple answer to what he'd do, no simple answer for him either.

"Yes, I know why I let him go." I look up at Nate. His peaceful blue eyes match the clear sky, eyes not seeking an explanation, but a confirmation that I know what I'm doing. "Come on," I say, "let's go inside."

TWENTY-EIGHT

Fresh air pours into the lodge from the escape hatch. The back door is open a crack for Ollie to come inside as soon as he's finished sniffing every tree on the property. This time I don't feel anxious inside the room, soothed by the familiar sounds of a morning chorus of birds.

With a swift tug, the deer-patterned curtain that hides the room is freed from its rod, settling on the floor in a mound. Curtain clips jingle and showers of dust ignite. I wipe my hands clean of it and pour a cup of coffee, joining Joss and Jim back in the lobby.

Late winter downtime is at its end. Sparrow Lodge will soon be bustling with hikers, bird-watchers, families in town for summer reunions, and a long season of weddings at Clayton Barn, usually booked through fall. For now, three women arrived last night for a weekend of snowshoeing, taking advantage of the recent snowfall before April's warmer temperatures roll in. Their feet pitter-patter above me. The coffee pot gurgles. Ollie wanders inside. And Joss and Jim kiss. But the quiet humming from Nate's room overrides the rest. That's the memory of this morning that I hope stays with me.

"It's awesome," Joss says, her helmet under one arm, ready to drive to the plant to grovel for her job back. Her gaze falls over the built-in shelves behind the reception desk.

"Connor's quirky collection of natural wonders," I say with a smile. "His Wunderkabinett."

Jim steps forward and studies the shelves. "Those wonder crap things are supposed to be full of oddities, stuff not yet classified, or nutty stuff like Grady's skeletons."

"Who says?" Joss asks.

"Nate. I saw him look it up last night on his cell. He sent a link to his mom."

I shrug. "Connor was fascinated by every one of these items. That's all that matters to me."

"But—"

"Stop." I throw a stern look. "If I want this display to be about the lodge, the property, and my family, that's my choice."

He raises his hands in surrender.

Connor's objects and my family mementos are right where they need to be. Last night, my eyes darted throughout the lobby for a good hour before lingering on the family photo above the door. That's when all this started. That's when I said, "Someone deserves to live," then added, "We *all* deserve to live and have our memories live on."

With Nate's help, we transformed the shelves into the Whitfield's very own cabinet of wonders. The Wunderkabinett that Connor had started collecting now takes the place of the Sparrow Lodge merchandise that never sells. Bird skulls, beaver teeth, trilobites, feathers, and turtle shells. Pinecones, pressed leaves, and Monarchs in glassine envelopes, a vintage map of Tilford Lake, a flyer for the treasure hunt, along with photographs of the family, the two remaining sparrow keys, and the cutest photo of little Finn.

"It's like a massive shadow box. I love it," Joss says.

"Yeah, I never said it wasn't cool," Jim adds. "Nate should turn Grady's cabin into something like this. You know, take

Grady's 'art' and create a museum." He finger quotes the word *art*. "It might bring more people out this way."

"I wish," I say under a breath.

I do wish Nate lived here, worked here, loved it here enough to stay longer.

"What's the space on the bottom shelf for?" Joss asks.

I set my coffee on the desk and pick up the stack of my granddad's letters. "For these. But I still have one to read." I flip through them and lay the last one on the desk, placing the others on the shelf. "Isn't it great? Everyone's here, my whole family. They're no longer shoved under beds, confined to boxes, or hidden in rafters. And for sure their energy is attached to these objects, I know the whole display will bring good vibes to the lodge."

"Everyone's here but one," Joss says. "You gotta call him, Salem." I look up, her arm linked with Jim's. "You have Eli's home phone number. You have his address from when he checked in. Call him or drive out there. He's only three hours away."

I shake my head. "He's alive and happy. That's the best news ever."

"You don't know if he's happy."

"Yes, I do. I saw him with Finn. They're happy."

"You're so friggin' weak."

"Joss, it's not fair to ruin what he has."

"Fair? Excuse me?" She folds her arms. "Call him."

I shake my head again, flattening my granddad's crumpled letter. "Nope." I put it in my hoodie pocket for later. "I'm not going to be selfish. It can't all be about what *I* want."

"Sure it can."

"Joss, no ... give me time to think about what might happen if I call. I need to sort it out in my head first."

She walks up to me, cups my chin. "Jesus, Salem. You know what I think?" A pause. She wants an answer. No answer. "I'll tell you what I think." She speaks with heat. "Eli knows. He knows, but he's too much of a sweetheart like you to say anything. It's like, what happens when two Whitfields walk into a room? Nothing!" She releases my chin. "I saw the way he looked at this place. He remembered Annabelle, the sparrow window, and the fireplace. And he looked right at the door to the private quarters." She points. "He knows what's back there. He touched his chest where the key used to be." She taps her chest. "I saw him. He knows."

My chin stings from being gripped. I rub it while grimacing. "If that's the case, then our decision was mutual. But that's not what happened. I waited and he didn't say anything."

She throws up her hands, outright, utterly peeved. "Babe, you make no sense."

"I'm broken."

"Quit it."

"Hey, maybe I messed up, okay? Or maybe he'll come back when he's ready. But I waited and nothing happened."

"Why would he speak up if you didn't? Dummy. And nothing happened? Really?" She's as hot-tempered and as sassy as ever. "I know you. You're not okay with this. You're trying to make everything work out for the best in your head, but it'll kill you." She raises a finger. "First you're gonna start a million projects to keep yourself busy so you don't have to think about him. Like this display." A second finger shoots up. "Then you'll crash and get depressed." A third. "Then I'm gonna get a call that you thought you saw Eli walking through the forest. You'll say he came back to spy on you. Right?" Her wild hair bounces. "I'm right. So before that happens, please, please, just call him." She puts her hands on her hips and stands on her tiptoes to try to appear taller than me. I love her more than ever. What a badass.

"Don't you smile at me." I smile even wider. "I'll say something to him if I ever see him again. I will. Or maybe I'll be the one who calls."

"No."

"Why?" She puts her feet flat.

"Because you should always wait for the right moment before jumping off the boat so you don't hit your head on a rock."

Jim laughs. "What? Salem, your head's full of muck. Jump off the boat and go for a swim, would ya?"

Joss flaps her hand. "I give up. Babe, do whatever you want, but you better know what it is that you're doing. Otherwise, you'll have more regrets than Virginia."

"I know what I'm doing." I scan the items on the shelves, my chest out, beaming from ear to ear.

"This wonder cabinet doesn't meticulously correct everything that's happened," she says. "It's great for the ones you've lost, but the situation with Eli is like apples and oranges compared to the rest of your family."

"Stop pushing this," I say.

Nate's door opens. I ignore Joss to stalk him on the balcony. He hauls his shoulder bag down the stairs to the front desk, dropping it at his feet.

"Hi." He slides his long fingers between mine.

I squeeze his hand, and my heart squeezes harder. "Leaving?"

"I have to get back to work."

I duck my chin into my chest. For obvious reasons, I hate goodbyes. I've never understood what's so good about them.

He sees the disappointment on my face and leans over the desk, pulling me closer to drop a greedy kiss. His mouth is as warm as when I woke up in the middle of the night to find his head between my legs, him asking if *it* was all right. *It*—his stroking tongue—was more than all right.

"It's not over," he says.

Our foreheads meet and my body locks all the way down. "I'm not ready."

"Me either." His cheek dimples. "That's why I'd like to make a reservation."

"Really?" I light up.

"Every other weekend until you get tired of me."

"Aww, that's super sweet," Joss chimes.

"You don't need a reservation. I've got space." With a sunny smile, I gesture toward my private quarters.

"Nope, him too." Nate thumbs Jim.

"Both of you?" Joss asks.

"Yep, Jim has a list of work he'd like to do here at the lodge. I saw him planning it out last night."

Jim fiddles with his beard. "Is that so?"

"If you're gonna tag along, which I know you will, then that's so."

Joss laughs at Jim's fake pout. She knows I need the help, so she won't suggest he stay at her place.

"He'll get your pool cleaned up, the playground fixed and painted, whatever you need in exchange for a bed ... or even better, a tent." Nate smirks.

"A tent?"

"Oh, I have a tent." I grin.

"No tent."

"I'll air it out and get it ready."

"No tent!"

We laugh, walking to the front door like our shoes are stuck in thick syrup, wanting to delay the departure for as long as we can.

"Are you doing any work or are you gonna just sit with a cold beer and watch me do everything?" Jim asks Nate.

"I'll be taking care of my property."

"Salem or the cabin?" He rolls his shoulders and lifts his travel bag.

"Both," I answer, shepherding him and Joss through the door. "Bye, Jim."

"Bye, Salem."

"Love you, Joss, even though you think I'll just be moping. Still love ya. Fill me in later about the job."

"Love you, too, babe. No moping allowed. We'll talk when I come back to get my things."

She snaps the chinstrap on her helmet and straightens her goggles while Jim runs his hand over the curve of her waist. They're like the pheasants in the dense shrubs along the property, taking forever to get airborne and move on out. It's cute, but stopping on each step to make out is impossible to bear for long.

I return to Nate's reach, my cheeks throbbing with heat, the blush embarrassing. "I've fallen pretty hard for you," I whisper. "I'll miss you."

He tilts his head, his emotions pouring into one powerful kiss, a kiss that curls low in my stomach and spills out to my limbs. "Same." His voice is low and hypnotic, his strong fingers slipping away. "See you soon, beautiful."

I lean against the porch post, legs crossed, Ollie dropping his rump next to my feet. He whines when the engines start, then barks when the two vehicles back out. It's not long before I'm staring at an empty road, chewing on a cuticle, my nails down to nubs from the erratic week.

"Coffee," I say to Olls, "more coffee."

He follows me inside to the sitting room where two guests are pointing out the window at Annabelle.

"That hippo used to be so pretty," one says.

"I remember," says the other. "Bright purple with a white scarf in the wintertime. Such a shame the property is in such poor shape."

Ollie startles them with a sneeze. I cringe at their comments, but can't object. No need when they're right. It *is* a shame.

The women stay in a stunned hush for a minute, but then slip away and take their coffees to their rooms. I don't move, allowing them a painless escape from their jab at the lodge.

Annabelle hasn't worn her white scarf in years. She hasn't had kids scurrying under her fat belly or riding on her back for over a decade. She hasn't had the weeds trimmed around her webbed feet or a friendly rub of her nose in forever. Bought from a neglected mini-golf course, my dad thought she'd be much better off with us. Now she lies on her side, screaming for help. The women are right, such a shame.

I slip on my boots and power walk out the escape hatch. My arms swing as my feet trudge through the snow. I'm about to cross the threshold and touch her head when my cell rings.

Brad is cutting into my rescue.

"What is it?"

"That was harsh," he says.

"Well, it's been a tough week." I don't feel like explaining to him why a thirty-year-old fiberglass hippo on its side has me upset. "Come on, Brad. Talk." He makes slurping noises with a straw while I kick snow and ice away from Annabelle's side.

"So … I have eerie news and bad news."

"Not good and bad news?"

"No, eerie and bad."

"Eerie how?"

"Which do you want first?"

"Eerie how?"

"Okay, I'll start with that."

"Whatever. Just spit it out. I'm in the middle of something." I tuck a strand of hair behind my ear, fingers cold against my skin.

"Salem, you're not going to believe this, but I … I think I saw Eli yesterday."

"Oh, yeah?" I smile a little, thinking I'll let a sarcastic comment fly. "Like the time I saw him at my wedding?"

"No, not at all like that. This was real."

I stop clearing the snow and hold on to Annabelle's leg. "Why, because it was *you* who saw him and not me? That makes it real?"

"Listen, he was walking out of the church with a guy who looked like Connor."

I laugh. "I really don't have time for this."

"Don't laugh. I drove past them, but they were gone after I circled the square and drove back."

"So why'd you wait so long to tell me? If you thought it was him, you should've called yesterday."

"Because … I just said Eli was with Connor, Salem … Eli was four. Connor was a man." He whimpers like Ollie. "Don't tell Chief about this, okay? He'll think I'm losing my mind."

I stare at a cardinal on a branch by the edge of the forest, and the three sparrows on the rusted metal fence next to the pool. It's past breakfast. Their feeders need replenishing.

"You there?" he asks.

"Yep."

"Am I crazy?"

My mouth twists, a debate over whether to let Brad in on all the secrets or let the secrets reside at the lodge.

"They spooked me out," he says. "Didn't Joss tell you?"

"What?" A slight breeze blows my bangs. The birds scatter with a trill. I tip my head back to track their path, taking more than a minute to grasp what Brad just said.

"I told her and Jim at the diner yesterday afternoon. Joss said they'd drive through town and look for them once they finished eating."

"Oh. No, she didn't say anything."

My breath tastes bitter. I suck the saliva from the inside of my cheeks and swallow it down, remembering the scent of grease on Eli's clothing. If he was at the diner after Brad left, and Joss was there ... Did Eli rush in and out of the lodge last night because something was said? Did she talk to him? Did she drop hints? A more significant clue than the key I put in Finn's pocket? What did she say?

"You don't believe me, that's fine," he complains.

"Feels shitty, doesn't it? How many times have you not taken me seriously?" I punt snow clumps away from Annabelle. The pointed pines feel like they're leaning in, the sky darkening, crowding down. Through the open back door comes the sound of the chime.

"Brad, I need to get back to my guests."

"Can I finish?"

"Make it quick. What's the bad news?"

"That woman. We found her."

"Virginia?" I gaze out over the yard, biting my bottom lip in trepidation. Same feeling I had when I thought Grady was in the forest. Someone's here, spying. "Ollie!" I call for his company. He sticks his head out the door. "Olls, come here." I whistle. He looks inside and wags his tail, turns to me, and back. "Ollie?"

"Salem, she—"

"Virginia was here yesterday to get her car. She left."

"She left but didn't go far. Matt Collins from Big Boy's Plowing & Towing called in tire tracks heading down the marina road. One set going in, none coming out. Chief had Logan check it out. He said she drove right through the wooden gate. He found her there."

"What do you mean by *found* her?"

"The tracks went down the boat ramp and into the lake."

"*Into* the lake?" My lip twitches.

"The car's roof was visible. Big Boy's was able to tow the car out late last night. Virginia was inside."

A vision of my mom settles in front of me, the smile on her face enough to keep me satisfied for the rest of my life.

"I see," I whisper.

"Chief wants to ask you some questions about her behavior before she left. Routine stuff. I gotta contact her family."

"Oh." I hesitate. "Um … Chief should talk to Wayland Casper. She had a funeral for herself, remember?"

"Yep. I already told him."

"Even with the funeral, do you think … you think she had a heart attack or something? Veered off the road and ended up down there?"

"Nah. The road's too long. She would've gone in a ditch before the lake. Besides, once she busted through the sign, the tracks are steady, straight down to the water. I'd say she planned it."

"Hmm." Pine branches rub and creak in the wind, surrounding me with hushed whispers.

"Well, I'll let you get back to your busy life, Salem."

I make a noise in my throat like I'm either weeping or elated. A noise I can't distinguish. "I'll call you later. We'll talk."

My fingers are frozen, but my mouth is hot and moist, somewhat surprised, somewhat pleased. After my cell is away, I squat alongside Annabelle and stroke her back. The poor girl, miserable for over a decade, left here after she tumbled over in a windstorm the year Connor and my dad died.

"Let's do this." I scoop my fingers under her, tighten my stomach, and lift with my legs. No-go. I try again, hear a *crack*, and get her dislodged from the hard snow. But I can't raise her more than an inch. "Phew, you're heavy. What have you been eating?"

I rest my head on her back, take a quick, hard breath, and heave a groan as I try again. She moved easily for my dad and Connor, as if she lived on wheels, but alone I can't get her up. I bet she weighs over a hundred pounds.

"Dammit, Annabelle." I drop her down. "Stand up for me."

Two hands sink in the snow next to mine. The wind tosses my hair across my face before I can see who it is.

"Lift," he instructs.

I suck in a giant lungful of wintry air, and a toothy smile explodes as Annabelle steadily comes back to life. "She's up!" I shout with delight, throwing my fists in the air. "Yes!"

The figure takes two steps backward and wrings his hands. One step forward and wrings them again. I whisk the hair from my face and stare for a minute. Stare at my likeness, the pale skin, the icy-gray eyes.

"Salem?" he questions.

I never told him my name. I *never* told him my name.

He scans the playground, the pool, and the area where our mom's flower garden used to be. *He remembers.*

"Salem," he says a second time with confidence.

I hug myself when he looks at me. The speculation is over.

He removes the sparrow key from his coat pocket and squeezes it over his head. "Say my name," he pleads as if he's unsure.

I step closer, clutching our granddad's letter in my hoodie pocket, willing myself not to cry.

"Eli?" he questions.

"Eli." I nod. "It's you."

He smiles as he rubs the EW initials, and I smile back.

Behind him, Finn pets Ollie in the doorway. He waves hello, and a family of tree sparrows sings a series of sweet twitters, a call that links to my heart, returning it to a steady, rhythmic beat.

TWENTY-NINE: THE LAST LETTER

Grady,

I'll be over on Sunday to pick you up for the pancake feed at the Post. But don't you dare laugh at my trim, you hear me? I'm counting on you to keep a straight face. It's Carol's fault. She said, "When a man's eyebrows meet, his heart is full of deceit." My wife thinks that of me. Me, Felix Whitfield, charged with dishonesty because I have caterpillar brows. Worse, now that I'm an old man. But they're gone. Carol clipped them. Took a razor and swiped them up the middle, looks like a mini lawn mower went through my forehead. Gotta love that woman!

Thought I'd write to tell you as a warning before our breakfast. Wouldn't want you to have a heart attack, seeing me looking like I went to a fancy beauty shop to get it done. Prepare yourself. I'm a sight. Elastic-waist pants and trimmed brows, that's what my life has become.

Heck, can you believe our age? Where has life gone? Carol and I even got our affairs in order last week, if that doesn't depress a person.

We don't have much. The lodge was already passed down to Tom, our mobile home isn't paid off, but we'd like the grandkids to have a little something. Hard to believe we're close to the end and have nothing to show, nothing apart from family. But that's a treasure, isn't it? Our kids and grandkids are gold. We'd all be better off if we measured wealth by flesh and blood, not by green. That's why we thought we'd give them the original keys to the front door of the lodge. The first set, Carol's and mine. Not about money, but about holding on to the heart of the sparrow that symbolizes our love. Our keys will be a confirmation that our home is their home forever. And if Sparrow Lodge is where our souls will rest, then someday theirs will too.

See now, Grady. It's after midnight, and this is what I do. I write. I write to quiet my head. Am I the only one, or do you have the same thoughts keeping you up late at night? Writing seems to help. You think about it like me? Is your bank account, your land, your bone art, or your love, going to be your fortune? Don't answer if I ever ask you that in person. I think I have you figured out. Your entire world revolves around Gert. You'd do anything for her.

We know you're going through a lot. These are tough times, but don't lose hope.

Gert said she's thinking about leaving the area. She said she doesn't want Carol coming over or anyone to see her so sick. We understand, but it still hurts. I guess all we can do is pray. The two who never pray are praying. You'd do the same for us ... you did with Eli.

My poor grandbaby, I miss him, Grady. I miss him every day. But like I always say, our littlest sparrow will come home. My gut tells me so. Believe me. Maybe I won't be alive to see it happen, but someone will. And even if I miss that day, the time without him has taught me not to lack the milk of human kindness. Compassion for others is everything. You get it. You know all about it.

Sunday, Grady. Pancakes. Fancy brows. Elastic-waist pants.

Maybe now I can get some sleep.

Felix

MEGAN MAGUIRE

Megan Maguire's hippie grandparents raised her in an Airstream Overlander. A homeschooled, free-range kid, she spent her childhood traveling the country in search of the strange and unfamiliar, and she survived her young adult years by not taking anything too seriously.

When Megan's midlife crisis hit, she resigned her position as a college professor and took to the open road in an RV of her own. She's spent the past five years crisscrossing the country with an affectionate cat, Miranda, and a slobbering dog that hitched a ride and goes by the name, Max. The three drifters enjoy setting up camp in beautiful forests across America. They live happily without social media, far away from the tragedies of society.

Writing, rolling in catnip, and fetching sticks are their top priorities. Manicures, hairdressers, going to bars, and watching reality TV, are not.

You can contact Megan by beeping your horn when you see her silver RV on the road. It's the one dotted with smiley face stickers, with a cat on the dash, and the windows crusted in dog drool. She also checks her email twice a month:

authormeganmaguire@gmail.com

As for her novels, Megan's characters are often loners, on a search to unearth life's great mysteries while looking to find true love—just like her.

THE RELEASE OF SECRETS

Littlest Sparrow Gone

Megan Maguire

85162354R00190

Made in the USA
San Bernardino, CA
16 August 2018